I0637553

Sirens

A Novel

By

Wig Nelson

© 2010 by Wig Nelson
All rights reserved.

ISBN-10 0983314403
ISBN-13 9780983314400

Printed in the United States of America

This is a work of fiction. Names, characters, places and incidents are either the product of the author's imagination or are used fictitiously. Any resemblance to actual persons, living or dead, events or locales is entirely coincidental.

Cover art designed by
WranglerRoy Images
Carrollton, VA

Also By Wig Nelson

The Psychic

The Conga Player's Dues

Jacks and Hands

Starry Night

Tall Tales Long & Short

Tall Tales Long & Short II

The Little Shop of Lyrics

A Feeling of Power
The Musical

XP

Xeries Press

Indialantic, Florida

C D's By Wig Nelson

Wigged Out

Fire and Life

Get There

Soundscapes

Fools You Bet On

A Feeling of Power

The Musical

Just beyond our close examination by the light of day exists a space between the lines of our lives. Therein resides a life force that escapes detection as it plants a seed within our consciousness. It steals our sleep in the night. It teases forth our dreams and vanishes without so much as a wisp of smoke or a tantalizing scent. Quickly now, catch it before it leaves behind the ghosts of long lost memories.

It's the summer peach that somehow never tastes as sweet as it once did. It's the way that first kiss made your heart beat faster. It's the illusive sweet musky smell of fleeting flesh that never seems to linger long enough. It is youth and success and the deed to the promises of manna. The more we take of it, the more it remains just beyond our reach.

Finally, we're not even sure it was ever really there.

This book is dedicated to the sirens.

They know who they are.

Acknowledgments

I'd like to thank my favorite siren Mary Kathryn.
As is the case with all sirens, the letter *h* appears in her name.

Love is our true destiny. We do not find the meaning of life by ourselves alone - we find it with another.

- *Thomas Merton*

Man must first find peace within himself.

- *Christos of Siren*

Sirens

Prologue

"What did I tell you about making up stories, Ben?"

"Mom, I swear it's true." Tears were beginning to well up in his eyes. "Why can't you just believe me?" he shouted just before slamming shut the door to his room as a loud exclamation point. Slamming doors was another taboo in the Farmer household, and Ben knew he was pushing the envelope. She stormed up the stairs to Ben's room and tried the door. It was locked. She banged on the door once and shouted, "Open this door, Ben."

"Go away," was his tearful reply.

"This instant," she demanded, rattling the door lock a second time. She could hear Ben's footsteps as they approached the door. There was a soft click as he disengaged the lock, and she then heard his footsteps retreating back to his bed. When she opened the door, she found him sobbing into his pillow, and her heart sank with the sight. Being a single mother was hard enough, but when the role of a disciplinarian reared its ugly head, there seemed to be no place to hide. She could feel a great weight on her chest, holding back tears of her own. Crossing the room and sitting on the bed, she asked, "Hey, buddy, what's all this crying about? What's got you so upset?"

"You," said the small voice muffled by his pillow.

"I didn't mean to upset you, honey, but I told you that it is important to always tell the truth, especially when your words can hurt. You know that words can hurt, we talked about that, didn't we?"

"Yes," said Ben raising his head, "but I was telling the truth. Mrs. Bloome just didn't believe me. That's when I told her to talk to Johnny Poole. He'll tell her, mom. I swear I wasn't making anything up."

"And the Poole boy said that Mrs. Bloome's daughter would be taken away? Is that what you're saying, Ben?"

"Not exactly that, Mom, but he said she wouldn't be riding on the bus tomorrow."

"Start at the beginning, Ben. Tell me exactly what you heard Johnny Poole say."

"Johnny went up to Cindy Bloome on the bus and said to her, *'I hope he doesn't hurt you, Cindy.'*"

"Go on."

"Then Cindy asked him, *'You hope who doesn't hurt me?'* and then Johnny said to her, *'the man who takes you from bus stop tomorrow.'*"

"You heard him say that, Ben? You heard Johnny Poole tell Cindy Bloome she wouldn't be riding on the bus?"

"Yes, Mom, and that's all that I said to Mrs. Bloome at the bus stop today. She was there when we got off, and there were two policemen and a reporter, too."

"Oh, dear God, the poor woman. I can't imagine what she's going through. Tell me what you told Mrs. Bloome about Johnny Poole."

"Well, they asked us if Cindy got on the bus in the morning, and we told them that she didn't. Then I just said that Johnny knew she wasn't going to be on the bus."

"Was Johnny on the bus with you, Ben?"

"Sure."

"Did Johnny admit to saying that Cindy wouldn't be there tomorrow?"

"He didn't want to talk about it," said Ben. "That's when they took him to the police station. Johnny will tell them the truth, and then Mrs. Bloome won't be mad at me anymore."

"How did John say that he knew what would happen tomorrow?" she asked as her brow creased with worry.

"Oh, Johnny always knows about tomorrow, and he's never wrong. He knows if it's going to be rainy or sunny – or who's going to have a cold. Even stuff like if someone's dog runs away," said Ben. "He always just knows."

"And how does Johnny say that he knows about tomorrow, Ben?"

"He says *he sees it*."

"What do you mean *he sees it?"* she asked.

"Johnny always says, *'I can see tomorrow when the Earth lines up.'*"

"Lines up? Lines up with what?" Confusion filled her voice.

"With Siren," said Ben.

~

Chapter One

VERO BEACH GOVERNMENT COMPLEX
DEPARTMENT OF CHILD SERVICES

Detective Cathy Ellis sat on a small couch opposite John Poole in a child conference room at 4:15 P.M. John was brought to the complex after an officer telephoned Senator Poole's wife Johanna and informed her that he was a material witness in the case of a missing child.

"Will you be bringing him home when you are through with him?" she asked in a casual tone.

"Yes, ma'am," said the officer, "unless you would like to come and get him yourself."

"Thank you, no," said Mrs. Poole, "I'm confident our tax dollars are at work, and I'm sure Vero Beach's finest is well up to the task." She ended the connection.

When the officer delivered John to Detective Ellis, he related their phone conversation with a sense of confusion.

"I swear, politicians are a whole different animal," said Officer Ted Brown.

"You think?" replied Cathy jokingly. "If it were my kid, I'd be breaking the speed limit getting down here."

"Tell me about it. We still on for dinner?"

"I don't know, Ted," she rubbed her tired eyes with her left hand, "this Bloome case is just breaking now and you know what they say about the first twenty-four." Cathy Ellis was referring to the statistic that showed 94 percent of all missing children recovered happened in the first twenty-four hours. After that, the chances fell exponentially.

"That's right," said Officer Brown, "what was I thinking. I guess you have a long night ahead of you."

"I'm coming off a double at the hospital, too. I worked a rape case last night."

"The fun never ends," he said darkly. "Want some company?"

"Not this time, Ted. I've got some road work ahead of me. There's the Bloome residence and the school St. Edwards, and who knows where else I'll end up tonight. Plus, I've got Bonnie to ride with me."

"How's she holdin' up?"

"She's fine, or will be anyway. He was a big guy, Ted. He could have disarmed a man just as well. You know it wasn't her fault."

"Yeah, I know. At least he never discharged the weapon. We really dodged a bullet on that one."

Cathy Ellis laughed in spite of the tense subject matter, perhaps to release something that was building up inside of her. Lately, she was rethinking her choice of occupation; thinking she could possibly make better use of her master's degree in child psychology. Perhaps she was longing to take up where her present job left off, with therapy. You can't buy the kind of practical experience that she gained in seven years working cases. She was only a couple semesters away from her doctorate at Florida Atlantic University's new medical school, but her case load was tragically steady because the average criminal knew no age boundaries. She lightly punched Ted on the arm and said, “Go home, Brown. I’ll call you tomorrow.”

She then entered the conference room to meet with John Poole. John was sitting with his back straight on the couch opposite Cathy Ellis. He made no attempt to handle the stuffed animals displayed around him or even look at the many colorful pictures on the wall. He was merely waiting. She had the impression that he was particularly unmoved by his present circumstances as though being held in a police station to answer questions was as familiar to him as shooting baskets in his driveway.

“Do you know why you are here, John?”

“Yes.” His eyes didn’t leave hers for an instant.

“And do you have anything you can tell us that would help find your friend Cindy?” Detective Ellis used the term “friend” in the hope that John would take more of an interest if not a sense of responsibility. *But why should he feel responsible,* she asked herself. *He probably doesn’t know a thing about the actual abduction particulars. Maybe it was only a lucky guess.* The incident report written by the responding officer stated that he briefly questioned the riders from the St. Andrews private school bus and was told that one child in particular spoke of her imminent disappearance a day before it happened. This child was John Poole, the son of Senator John Poole, Sr.

He now sat opposite Detective Ellis and displayed an icy coolness that she was unused to in a child of his age. Indeed, he almost demonstrated the profile of abuse, but she knew for a fact that was not the case. Although somewhat aloof and caught up in the drama and finery of John's Island, a very exclusive community of million dollar residences, Mrs. Poole was a very good mother. Cathy Ellis dealt with her in the past and enjoyed her good humor and the magnanimous generosity of her time as well as her money. She knew that her lack of concern for her son's present condition was born of her extreme confidence in him rather than anything neglectful.

John's demeanor spoke to the fact that her confidence was well placed. In fact, Detective Ellis was the more uncomfortable of the two; almost as though *he* was the trained professional and *she* was to be questioned by *him*. John was a handsome young boy, but there was also something about his appearance that was unsettling. His eyes appeared to have gold flecks in them that seemed to disappear whenever you looked close enough for a good look at them. It was almost as though he had control over their color, but she knew that was an impossibility. Rather than answer Detective Ellis' question right away, he seemed to be waiting for her to compose herself, as though he was aware of her being disquieted by his appearance. He raised his eyebrows as though to say, *'are you ready now?"*

"Nothing I have to say would be of any help."

"Are you sure," Ellis asked, "the Farmer boy, Ben, told a police officer that you knew Cindy was going to be taken away?"

"That's not entirely true," said the boy.

"Just tell me what is true, John. Let's start with that."

"I never said that she would be taken away, I merely said that I knew she was going to be absent."

"And how did you know that?"

"It's not something that I am at liberty to discuss."

"What? What did you say?" *My God!* She thought to herself. *This kid is nine years old, and he talks like Perry Mason. Kids just don't talk like that. What is he, a little machine or something?*

"It's just not something that I can talk about. I'm *not allowed* to talk about it."

"What do you mean you're not allowed? She asked knitting her brow and tilting her head slightly, "Not allowed by whom?"

"That, as well, is not something I wish to discuss."

"Well, your friend Cindy might be in some kind of danger. Aren't you a little bit concerned about that?"

"No, not really," he said, his gold flecked eyes holding hers in an icy grip.

"I can't believe that you don't care what happens to your friend, John." She thought she might be dealing with a child sociopath. It wouldn't be the first time.

"Naturally," he said. "That would make me a sociopath."

Ellis was taken aback by his calm straightforward statement of fact, almost as though he read her mind.

"Then you do care about Cindy Bloome."

"Yes, she's very nice. That was the reason I voiced my concern in the first place."

"Well, why aren't you concerned now?"

"Because the way I see it, the danger has passed."

"Cindy is still missing."

"That's true."

"Then how can you say the danger has passed?"

"Because Cindy will be back on the bus tomorrow."

"What did you say? How can you know that?"

"Again, it's not something I wish to discuss. Isn't it enough to know that the girl is safe? It's enough for me." His dark eyes again flickered with a suggestion of gold colored light where the outer edges of his cornea met the iris. The detective felt herself unable to break away from the intensity of his stare.

"Will there be anything else?" he asked, as though he were ready to dismiss *her*. *My Lord!* She thought. *This didn't go very well at all.*

She stood up and straightened her shirt – all of a sudden seeming very conscious of her appearance.

"Come on, John. I'll take you home now." Detective Ellis was clearly shaken by her interview with young John Poole. She had a sense of relief that there would be a happy ending to the case of Cindy Bloome's disappearance and although she knew that John had no Earthly way of knowing the things that he seemed to know, she didn't doubt him for a minute.

~

8:37 THE BELTWAY – WASHINGTON D.C.

"I wish Mom could have driven me. Then I wouldn't have to listen to Alexander's Ragtime Blab."

"Ha, that's really good, Billy, you made a joke. The point is that someone had to drive you at all. We're on our way to surrender your license; do you realize what that means?" Alex tried to glare at his son and negotiate the D.C. beltway traffic at the same time.

"Somehow I think you're going to tell me," said Billy.

"That's right, wise guy, I'll tell you. Obviously, you can't drive, you can't buy cigarettes, you can't get into "R" rated movies, you have no I.D., in fact, the only thing you can still do is report to selective services, which we just happened to have received a letter from yesterday."

"I'm in school, Dad."

"You still have to report, Billy."

"Seems like a waste of time to me."

"Just be glad they don't have the draft like they did in my time," said Alex.

"What was your draft number?"

"That's not the point. I could have been forced to go to war."

"But you weren't," said Billy.

"That's right, I was lucky. The point is you don't have to be lucky," said Alex doing his best to glare again between death defying defensive moves through the traffic, "all you have to do is not smoke marijuana."

"I wish Mom had driven me," said Billy.

~

The commonwealth of Virginia was good enough to sacrifice a small section of land to house the capital seat of the great nation of The United States of America. A territory in and of itself, like The Vatican, Washington D.C. is also the home of the two main governing bodies of that great nation, The House of Representatives and The Senate. The very air is electric with the power wielded by the politicians who shape the nation and the lobbyists who shape the politicians. One very minor player in the venue of all that immense power is a relatively benign, although necessary entity, known as traffic court. Traffic court is where misdemeanor convictions such as possession of marijuana and parking in a loading zone find a home in the criminal justice system. It is also where Billy Jansen and his father Alex had to appear to surrender Billy's driver's license.

The courtroom was full to the gunwales of optimistic humanity. Every seat was taken. On either side of the room were single file lines at which the lead person waited anxiously to take the next available seat surrendered by the next name uttered by the bailiff. Whether or not the person at the head of the line actually wanted a seat was not the issue. It was as though they were all involved in some kind of ancient ritual whereby failure to take advantage of your dutiful place in line resulted in the forfeiture of your inalienable right to your day in court.

After all, no one was ever called up from one of the lines, right? So it would seem to all the good lemmings that lined the sides of the venerable vault of retribution. All except one, as it turned out.

She tapped Alex on the shoulder and said, “Excuse me, what time do you have?”

Alex turned and saw a rather plain-looking, dark-haired woman standing behind him. He looked at his watch and said, “Uhh, it’s . . .”

“No,” she said, “I meant what time is your appointment?”

“Oh, I see,” said Alex. “We’re a nine-thirty, but I’m told that’s just a ballpark estimation. We could be standing here for some time.” He wore a smile he wasn’t feeling.

“Me, too,” said the woman. “I was wondering if perhaps you could do me a small favor,” she said – her eyes darting between Alex and his restless son.

“I’ll do it if I can,” said Alex. “But you realize I’m stuck in this line for the duration. I don’t plan on going through this twice.”

“That’s precisely the point, I don’t either.” The woman looked around her sheepishly and a quiet voice took hold of Alex’s attention, “I need to use the ladies’ room.”

He saw her blush slightly and gather her briefcase together, which was already entirely gathered together.

"You want me to listen for your name and fetch you if you're called?" said Alex. Billy shifted from one foot to the other clearly bored with the whole affair.

"Yes, that would be wonderful if you only could," said the woman. It was as though her persona took on another characteristic all of a sudden - like trying on a sweater. She now seemed helpless and innocent, the definitive damsel in distress that Alex could never resist reaching out to with a helping hand.

"No problem," he said, "what's your name?"

"Durbah," she said smiling. Her eyes were suddenly warmer as was the room in general, it seemed to Alex.

"And your last name?" asked Alex.

"You mean as opposed to all the other Durbahs in the room." Her laugh was musical and genuine.

Alex just laughed as well and said, "Go, we'll come get you if you're called."

The woman broke out of line and headed for the door. Billy said, "I'm going to miss class, Dad."

"Since when do you worry about missing classes?"

"Since Heather Connelly drop 'n added it."

"Do you still see Heather," asked Alex.

"I wish," said Billy. "She's an elite."

"What's an elite?" asked his father.

"Her shit doesn't stink, Dad."

"Oh, you'd be surprised," laughed Alex. "What if she had a big Mexican meal the night before?"

"Not even a whiff," said Billy seriously.

"Not a whiff, huh?" laughed Alex. "How about a big plate of clams?"

"Grow up, Dad."

"No, seriously, what's the big deal, Billy? You're both freshmen aren't you?"

"That's the point, Dad. An elite freshman would *never* date another freshman."

"I thought you left all that foolishness back in high school," said Alex.

"The whole process just continues on," said Billy. "In high school the senior girls dated college guys, and the senior guys dated underclassmen. Nothing ever changes except I never get any."

"Keep it in your pants, buster. You're an endangered species."

"That's easy for you to say. You're dead from the waste down."

"Ouch," said Alex as he suddenly had the picture of Durbah in his mind. *The picture was remarkably clear as though he had known her for some time. Now that he thought about it, he could recall even the smallest details of her facial features. He thought that he somehow knew her breast size as well although he never clearly got as much as a glance at them. And her scent . . . what was it about her scent that was familiar . . . ?*

"Hey buddy, you gonna' take that seat?" said the gruff voice behind him.

"What?" asked Alex coming out of his reverie.

“There’s a seat there that opened up on this side of the room. It’s your turn, take it.”

Alex thought of Durbah. Although he was next in line for one of the courtroom seats, he knew that he could not keep Durbah’s place in line if he took it. He turned to his son and said, “Go ahead, Billy. You take it.”

“I’ll take it,” said the man behind his son.

“Never mind,” said Alex. “Go, Billy, we might be here all day.” Billy went to the empty seat and sat down. He immediately started a conversation with the girl next to him who appeared to be about the same age. Soon they were giggling quietly and making the best of a bad situation. Alex looked at his watch, 10:15. Already they had waited more than 45 minutes and it seemed like the case-load was only about a dozen people smaller by the looks of it. The lines on the sides of the room still held more than a dozen people each. *What if they don’t get to us today,* thought Alex miserably. *Do I have to miss another day of work? I wonder where Durbah works.*

“Yo, dreamboat,” said the man behind him roughly, there’s another seat.” He motioned with his outstretched hand.

“Go, ahead,” said Alex, “you take it.”

“Oh, I wouldn’t dream of it. It’s *your turn,*” he said expansively. The man did everything but curtsy to top off his sarcasm.

“I’m saving a woman’s place in line.”

“Well, what do you know,” said the man, “chivalry ain’t dead.” He moved ahead of Alex and took the next empty seat.

A short while later Durbah returned from her trip to the ladies' room.

"I guess they didn't call me," she said easing back in line behind him.

"Not a single Durbah."

"Thanks for helping me out."

"It was my pleasure." And he meant it. He marveled at how he originally thought that Durbah was a plain-looking woman. Her looks were extraordinary. Her long straight nose accentuated her high cheekbones and full sensuous lips. Her coloring was a slight blush in the center of her cheeks that faded to a light tan porcelain finish of a flawless face. He found himself getting a little nervous standing so close to her. Again he caught just a suggestion of her scent. *'Why did I think her hair was dark?'* he wondered, *'it certainly isn't dark now.'* He needed to distance himself from her soon, or he very well might start coming apart at the seams.

Just then a seat opened up and as luck would have it the one beside it as well. A young girl rose at first and made her way to the front of the courtroom and then the girl's mother rose as well and followed her.

"There are our seats," said Durbah.

"After you," said Alex ever the gentleman, especially now.

They took their seats and made the cursory glances to either side of them to put a face on their fellow litigants. Having determined that there were no maniacal chain-saw murderers within easy reach, they turned to each other and made the commensurate attempts at court-room, time-killing, small talk.

"So what do you do here in Washington, Durbah?"

"I work for a senator. I'm an aide so I usually have to travel with him."

"So you don't live here?"

"Some of the time. I do a lot of traveling between here and Atlanta."

"You don't sound like you're from the South," said Alex.

Durbah just smiled and said, "I have a rather flat accent because I've moved around a lot."

Alex considered her statement and said, "So, what are ya' in for, kid," in his best Bogart.

Durbah giggled softly, "Speeding."

"Speeding?" questioned Alex. "Why didn't your senator just have that one fixed? Or why didn't you just mail in the ticket? You can take a test to erase the points. In fact, you can even do it online."

"Oh, I'm not guilty."

"Uh huh," was Alex's best attempt at being neutral.

"No, really," she continued, "I was in a school zone and the flashing light wasn't flashing. It may have been broken for all I know."

"And you expect to beat that? How fast were you going?"

"About forty," she said defensively. "Five miles-per-hour over the speed limit. I knew it was thirty-five."

"Yeah, but the school zone is the killer. I helped write the Forced Mandatory Referendum for School Zone Violations."

"That sounds terribly shortsighted."

"You may have a point, but the point is the judge's hand is forced. He has no choice but to impose the maximum penalty."

"I'm confident there will be no penalty," she said softly, "at least in my case."

"I'm glad you think so. Just don't be too sure."

"I told you that the light wasn't flashing, and there were no children in the area. I would have felt . . . I would have seen them," she said with an air of indifference.

"If you lose, you'll get the points; you know that don't you."

"I wouldn't concern yourself, Mr. . . . ?"

"I'm sorry, Jansen. Alex Jansen. Where are my manners?" he asked no one in particular.

"Well, Mr. Jansen . . ."

"Alex."

"Well, Alex, I wouldn't be concerned about my situation if I were you. The judge seems to be a reasonable man, and I'm sure he will see my side of the situation."

"What did you mean when you said you would have felt the children?" asked Alex.

"I didn't say any such thing."

"Oh, yes, you did. You just didn't finish it."

"I can feel children, Alex, can't you?"

"Well, sure, I suppose so, but no more than I can feel dogs or cats or adults or . . ."

"Children are different," she said, "they are uncast."

"What did you say? Un – what?"

"Durbah Purness," said the bailiff in a loud voice. Durbah rose from her seat and said, "It was nice to meet you, Alex. Good luck with your case." She made her way to the front of the courtroom and talked in a soft voice to the judge for less than five minutes before she picked up her briefcase again and started back down the center aisle striding purposely toward the doors to the lobby and out again into the heart of D.C. As she passed by, Alex detected a smile and the suggestion of a wink when she caught his brief eye contact. There wasn't a shadow of a doubt in his mind that she was not required to pay a fine.

~

Chapter Two

The sky was a dirty slate that was groping the smog on the horizon. There was no industry to speak of around D.C. but the sheer volume of hydrocarbon emissions had a strangle hold on any promise of a blue sky. Due to the parts per million of carbon atoms that continually hitch rides on oxygen and hydrogen atoms, the dry cleaning business in the D.C. area enjoys a steady flow of clientele second only to Los Angeles and New York City.

Senator Williams coughed as he slammed the door to the limo. Charles Donovan, his guy Friday of an aide, stood with his hand suspended in the air where the door to the limo had shortly been before.

"Are you going to stand there like an idiot, Mr. Donovan, or are you coming to the meeting?" barked Williams.

Someone has to be there to pay attention, he thought but had the good sense not to say.

"No, sir, there are plenty of idiots standing around the streets of D.C. I might as well come along with you in case any idiots are needed in the meeting."

"Have no fear," said the senator from Georgia in his thick southern drawl, "there will be plenty of them there as well."

"I brought the notes, Mr. Williams. Would you like me to brief you?"

"What's to know?" he asked rhetorically. "We all know who's in whose pocket around here. Blake was an officer in the company that owns that refinery . . . what?"

"Energix," said Donovan who always heard the senator's questions before they were asked. Sometimes it was a source of irritation for Williams. He decided not to scowl this time and said, "Just once I'd like to finish asking a question before you come across with the answer, Mr. Donovan."

"Just once I'd like you to call me Charles, Mr. Williams."

"Sorry, son, it's a habit I can't shake. It goes back to my time in the navy. I was a Chief Petty Officer, remember?"

"Well, I wasn't actually there to swear to it, but I've heard some stories," said Donovan cryptically. He was, of course, referring to the senator's celebrity status among all branches of the armed services for his heroic actions in the Gulf of Oman. CPO Williams single-handedly foiled a terrorist attack on a heavy cruiser by ramming a suicide zodiac with his transport vessel and diving into the enemy's craft. He knocked the terrorist out cold and piloted the zodiac harmlessly to a floating dock to await the arrival of the bomb squad. He was awarded the Navy Cross, which he proudly displays in a glass case hanging on the wall of his office.

"Don't believe everything you hear, son."

"I don't, sir. Especially when it comes to war stories."

"What branch of the service were you in ag . . .?

"Touché, sir. Point received loud and clear."

"God, I hope that Blake doesn't bring that split tail with him this time. What is it about that woma . . .?"

"Her name is Durbah, sir. She's quite good looking, isn't she?"

"I've seen good looking women before, Mr. Donovan. That's not what it is; she somehow has a hold on me."

"Sir?" asked Donovan. "In what way?"

"Oh, I don't know. It's like she's my daughter that I never had and I just want to take her and . . . and then I find myself not thinking of her as a daughter at all. It's like I think of her in a way that is not at all proper for a man in my positio . . . listen, Mr. Donovan; let's just drop the subject and forget that I ever brought it up, shall we?"

"Certainly, sir," said Donovan. He knew exactly what the senator was talking about although the charms of Durbah were not a factor where he was concerned. He could appreciate her beauty, but her alluring nature ended there. In fact, he appeared to be oblivious to animal attraction based on looks alone. His was a world of much more intense spirituality than emotionally charged reactions to pheromones.

There were more than a few congresswomen who had a similar conversation with their aids about Charles Donovan. He had an innate bond to Durbah that went far beyond attractions or sex. When they greeted each other it was with a mutual respect and understanding that has been forged by a thousand years of comfortable acquaintance; however, neither could remember actually being introduced.

Chapter Three

Alex Jansen couldn't remain on task. He had read the brief three times and all the words just kept circling around in his head like a Sunday afternoon holding pattern into Dulles Airport. There was a flaw in the logic, he was sure, but he just didn't get it. The issue before him was a case against a giant conglomerate of natural gas and pipeline distribution companies. At the head of the list was Energix Inc. out of New Orleans, Louisiana. They were using the collective weight of the natural gas syndicate to pressure the state of Georgia to drop the ban of a platform twelve nautical miles off her shoreline.

The proposed platform was to be constructed just outside international waters and, therefore, beyond the jurisdiction of the continental United States. But the ban was sticking, sticking in the craw of a senator named Samuel Blake. Blake proposed a moratorium of the ban with the contingency that the actual product from the platform must come ashore in the state of Georgia and be taxed accordingly.

The senior senator from Georgia, Harold Williams, made headline news as well as *The Daily Show* with John Stewart for calling Senator Blake the Heidi Fleiss of southern politics. They since have buried the hatchet and more than a few members of the Domestic Energy Commission were curious how they would receive each other at the upcoming conference. A logistics meeting was scheduled for this very morning to discuss the order of presentations.

Alex poured over the compendium and it might as well have been *The Book of Kells*. He couldn't seem to read the relevant issues facing the legality of the ban. If the platform was in international waters, it may as well have been the Japanese who broke ground, or sea floor, as it were.

But the Japanese had no opportunity to harvest a resource so far from her shores. Each gallon of natural gas would cost more than it was worth to transport. The only viable answers were either a way station to fill pressurized tanks for transport or a pipeline. A pipeline had yet to be discussed among the parties involved in the conflict, but the writing was on the wall that if a Georgia port was utilized for delivery of the gas, the pipeline was just a matter of time.

Alex put in a call to Senator Williams' office and Charles Donovan answered on the second ring, "Senator Williams' office."

"This is Alex Jansen. I was asked to review a brief for the senator regarding the legality of a ban in effect to block an offshore construction project."

"I'm familiar with the brief," said Donovan. "I work for Senator Williams. My name is Charles Donovan and I am the senator's secretary slash whipping boy."

Alex laughed and said, "Aren't we all, Charles. Listen, you can tell the senator that I'm well aware that you guys make the laws in this country, but as far as I can tell, you're breaking them now."

This was exactly what Charles Donovan was hoping to hear, although he wasn't exactly sure why. It just felt right. He said to Alex, "So the ban has no teeth to it, is that what I'm hearing?"

"You got it," said Alex. "I'd say you were skating on the thin ice of an obstruction suit, harassment at the very least. My advice is to pull it. The way I see it is all of your strength lies in the delivery aspects of the issue. Once hazardous materials approach U.S. waters, the state of Georgia has every right to oversee the safe delivery of the cargo. Your pilots will, of course, be used to approach any ports, and the resource is subject to a hydrocarbon emissions tax."

"Even if the gas passes right through Georgia to another destination?" asked Charles.

"As far as I know, yes. There is a state tax and a federal tax also. My advice is to tread lightly until the avenue of delivery is well established."

"Oh, why is that," asked Donovan.

"Well, you wouldn't want to get into a bidding war with South Carolina, would you?"

"Point well taken," said Donovan. "Is that all you have for now?"

"That's it," said Alex. "You took a good shot, but as of now, you are out of business."

"Gotcha," said Donovan. "I'll let the senator know."

"Thanks, Charles. See you around."

"Thank you, Alex." Donovan hung up the phone.

Alex was definitively smiling, but he wasn't sure why. It just seemed like the right thing to do. He had a sneaking suspicion that it had something to do with an encounter he recently had in traffic court, of all places. He buzzed his secretary, "Julie, could you do a search for me when you get a chance. Female aide to a southern senator, early to mid-twenties, name of Durbah Purness."

"Sure thing, Mr. Jansen. I'll get right on it."

~

Chapter Four

Sarah Poole reflected on her choice of careers for the fourth time in as many years. Library science was an early love and always held the promise that she could be free to do what she loved the most, and that was to read. Since she was a small child her every waking hour was either devoted to or somehow facilitating the circumstance where she could be left alone with her *keys to the universe,* as she called them, her beloved books.

But library science had one downfall: its stationary nature. It wasn't that she didn't enjoy the sleepy little community of Bar Harbor, Maine, that enjoyed five months of off season and the solitude she loved. Sarah's curse was that she was irresistible to men, all men.

The Bar Harbor library gained sixty-seven card carrying members since Sarah took the job as librarian a short six months before. She had a hard time taking her trash to the curb without some eager young man begging for the chance to be of assistance. At first it amused her, but that was years earlier. She had fled Houston, Texas; Phoenix, Arizona; Sacramento, California and Gunnison, Colorado for the same reason. She was trying to outrun her attraction.

It made no sense to her. Flesh was flesh – a mind was a mind. Everyone was as valuable as the next by our God-given birthright. Sarah was personally never drawn to one person rather than another except by the actions of a life that fell harmoniously in line with her own.

Looks were never a consideration despite the fact that she was an extraordinarily beautiful woman. She had turned down many offers to work as a model and actress, as well as sponsors offering to enter her in beauty pageants. She didn't see the point. When Sarah looked at a soul, she saw precisely that. She could look straight into the essence of a person and know more about him than he knew of himself. Sarah could *see.*

A great source of comfort for her was the fact that other people could not. Very few people could actually see her, the real her. Yes, they reacted to her pretty face and cute figure, but thankfully that was all the attention she suffered – except for the animals. Their behavior was usually suspect around her. It was not uncommon for a seagull or pelican to land on the deck of her apartment house overlooking the lobster boats and clamming trawlers. That in and of itself would have been a normal occurrence was it not for the fact that three cats usually were lounging there as well. The cats never bothered with the birds; in fact, their purring at the arrivals of their feathered friends seemed to indicate that they were fast friends. Her landlady, Mrs. Eldridge, was always so surprised to see her dog, Winston, lying contently among the cats. The first time it happened she told Sarah, "You know, it's the strangest thing – Winston would never have done that until you arrived here, Sarah. He used to fight like the devil with cats. He used to fight with birds, too, but those seagulls don't seem to mind him and he doesn't seem to mind them either. I'm so glad they don't do their business on the deck, aren't you?"

"You can say that again," said Sarah. "That would be pretty awful."

"Your cats are very well behaved in that respect, also. I've never seen them make a mess up here."

"Oh, they're not my cats, Mrs. Eldridge. They just come here to visit from time to time."

"They always seem to be here when you're here; Winston, too, for that matter. You do have a way with animals, dear."

"I've always loved animals. My parents would only let me have a turtle. Guess I'm making up for lost time," said Sarah with a soft musical laugh.

After about six months at Mrs. Eldridge's apartment house, the animals were beginning to get out of hand. The cats had increased from three to five, and another dog was often visiting Winston as well. It was another male dog, and yet neither one of them showed any kind of aggression or territoriality. Sarah knew she would be moving on soon.

Mrs. Eldridge didn't mind the animals on her deck and was quite taken by Sarah as though she were a prodigal daughter that had finally come home to the roost. She looked forward to Sunday dinners with Sarah and whichever young man was trying to find the key to her heart.

But Sarah was not a frivolous young girl to fall head over heels for her young man. In fact, Mrs. Eldridge hardly ever saw the same young man coming to call for longer than a week. They always remained very friendly when she would see them saying hello at the market or on the docks; everyone loved Sarah, it seemed. They just seemed to have an understanding of when the proper time to call on her was and when she preferred to be alone. There was never any semblance of a rivalry or bad feelings among the young men. In fact, there were a few whose behavior had taken a remarkable turn for the better after dating Sarah.

One morning Mrs. Eldridge was just sitting down to breakfast when she rose again and said, "Oh, dear me, I almost forgot. Actually I did forget and just remembered now. Sometimes I think I'm getting senile," she said walking across the room and picking up a letter from a white wicker basket on the counter. "This letter came for you yesterday. I think it's from your sorority."

"My sorority?" asked Sarah.

"I could tell by the Greek letters on the envelope," said Mrs. Eldridge. "That's who it's from, isn't it, dear?"

Sarah looked at the envelope and just as a passing cloud blocked the sun coming through the kitchen window her world became a little darker as well.

"That's right," she said, "It's from the Alpha Omegas."

"Strange," said Mrs. Eldridge. "I'm not familiar with that particular sorority. Are they new?" she asked Sarah.

"No, they've been around for a while," said Sarah. *About four thousand years*, she thought to herself, *give or take a few.* Sarah had liked Bar Harbor and would miss Mrs. Eldridge very much. The animals would miss Sarah as well.

~

Chapter Five

Mesopotamia 1774 B.C.

"Wake up Helen – it is your special day."

"I'm tired, Mother, can't I lie here a little longer this morning?"

"No, dear, you can't. The Sensor is here with your gift; all the way from the edge of the sea. Today you will receive your power. This is the day that Siren has exchanged places with this planet for the sixteenth time since your birth. This is your birthday, Helen, and today you shall receive the look in your eye. It is called electrum. It is a look that is fleeting when gazed upon for more than a moment, but the memory lives on. There will be the suggestion of silver and gold in your eye."

"Will it hurt, Mother?" asked Helen.

"You won't even know the gift has been given, but others will know. A siren will be able to sense you are one of them, as you also will be able to sense them. But you won't see the change in your own eye in the reflecting pool. And those who are not sirens will not be able to see it unless you want them to. But they will feel your power. You may shape their will.

However, you must understand that it is a very grave responsibility that you now have. It is a power that can never be used lightly or for your own gain."

"But what is it for, Mother? What if I refuse my charge for this thing you would have me do?" asked Helen.

"It is for the protection of our home, Siren. The men of this world are a fearful lot. They make war for no better reason than to hold the higher ground."

"But that makes no sense, Mother. Why would they do such a thing?" asked the young girl.

"Long ago this world passed through a wave from a sister of Sol. A wave that our beloved world of Siren was spared. It shaped the nature of all the creatures of this world, and none more so than the humans themselves. There will always be a darkness of human nature carried forth from father to son, and that is why they are a danger to our world."

"But Father says that Siren is on the other side of Sol. They can't even see our world, Mother."

"Not yet, Dear, but one day they will have the power to see what is beyond Sol. The Sensors speak of a great shield that will one day disguise the whole of Siren, Dear."

"Disguise it as what, Mother?" asked the girl.

"As nothing," said her mother. "Now quickly, rise and go to the baths. Your friend Ulysses has come to call on you. After you meet with the Sensor, you will find that he finds you even more beautiful than before."

"Can I tell you something, Mother?" she asked.

"Always, Dear."

"Ulysses has talked about the ceremony where the two of us may be bound together in the eyes of The Creator," said the girl.

"Oh? And how do you feel about such a ceremony, Helen?"

"I'm not really sure," said the girl wiping the sleep from her eyes. "Do you think that is what The Creator wants for us?"

"Let me ask you something, child: When the two of you are together - alone – does your flesh become a fire and does your heart beat faster?"

"No, Mother, I'm afraid that neither of those things are true."

"Then no amount of ceremonies will bind you in the eyes of The Creator, Helen. Soon you will learn to give him nothing of your heart and make him believe that he possesses every ounce of it."

"But isn't that a lie, Mother?"

"Only by him and only to himself."

Giza Plateau, Egypt 1373 B.C.E.

"Cleopatrah, wake up! This is your great day," said the girl's mother.

"But I am tired, Mother. Can't I lie here just a little while longer?" asked the girl.

"No, you may not." said her mother. Mark Antony has come to call and he has the mark of Siren in his eye."

"What is the mark of Siren, Mother? I don't understand," said the young beauty.

"You will, dear. You are sixteen years old today. Soon you shall be uncast like your father and me.

"What does it mean to be uncast, Mother?"

"Sixteen years ago your spirit joined with the flesh that now carries you. Even though your spirit is passive, you were cast among the humans to walk among them. You were at the caprice of fortunes both good and bad for all of those years. Now you shall be uncast and your future belongs to you."

"But shall I be happy like you and father?"

"That decision is finally up to you."

Washington D. C. The Present

Charles Donovan held the door for Senator Harold Williams as he noted all the major players of the Domestic Energy Commission who were in attendance at the logistics meeting. Senator Samuel Blake was already seated with his aide Durbah Purness, and Congresswoman Alyssa Grant was seated as well with her aide Shelly Simon.

Congresswoman Grant was unflatteringly known in Washington circles as the *Global Warming Queen.* She was genuinely concerned about global warming, but failed to realize that there is a time and place for everything. On the floor of the House of Representatives one would expect a congresswoman to rant about one of her pet causes and attach it by way of the pork barrel to every issue she promised to vote for. But there were other venues where her championing her cause was clearly out of place. One such venue was her daughter's high school graduation.

When asked to speak at the commencement ceremony for the class of '06 she couldn't pass up the opportunity to once again climb up on her high horse to beat a dead one. After experiencing the coldest winter in more than a decade, her persistent warnings about the seriousness of global warming were falling on deaf ears. Her aide Shelly warned her that it might not be received very well by all the other parents of the graduating seniors. That indeed proved to be the case.

What Congresswoman Grant failed to take into consideration was that many of the influential people of Washington were also in attendance, and she wasn't helping her chances of being reelected. Word travels fast in the nation's capital and lobbyists were quick to share her growing ignominious reputation with her constituency.

One might go as far as to say she was fast becoming an embarrassment to her political party. Not a small feat, by any means, considering the vast array of Barnum and Bailey players that were already dancing around the halls of congress with their red noses and big shoes.

Charles Donovan knew Shelly Simon as he also knew Durbah Purness. They were never really introduced, but it was always assumed that political aides had an innate sense of who their contemporaries were. It was their job to be interested and informed if not always respected.

Many of the movers and shakers were short with their "help" as they called them to each other when referring to their pages and aides. It was as though they were on the lower tier of their caste system even though if the truth were known – it was usually the aides who bore the lion's share of the actual workload.

They would be working with the speechwriters when their employers were off trying to land some kind of billfish or make a birdie. But they entered the arena with their eyes open and usually had an agenda of their own of which they were attending.

In the case of Durbah Purness, she was interested in Senator Blake getting his moratorium on the platform ban by the state of Georgia, but for her own reasons.

In the case of Charles Donovan, he was interested in Senator Harold Williams getting a steady deployment of troops in the Iraqi war, but for his own reasons.

In the case of Shelly Simon, she was interested in her congresswoman Alyssa Grant falling on her face and making a laughing stock of herself about her precious global warming, but for her own reasons.

Purness, Donovan and Simon were all unknowingly on the same team. They had an atavistic imperative to perpetuate the hostilities and warlike nature of man. The fight for economic incentives had fueled human conflict for eons. The Spanish Inquisition was never really about religion, and neither were The Crusades. The Spanish Inquisition was more an instrument of *social survival* than strict adherence to the doctrine of the Catholic Church. There was a fear of anarchy amid the dark nature of the middle ages and for civilization's sake, people were required to answer to some sort of authority. Purness, Donovan and Simon would have been decidedly against anything as potentially settling as the Spanish Inquisition. They would have been against The Crusades as well, but for a different reason.

The Crusades had less to do with the Moslems, as is typically thought, than with Roman-Byzantine rivalry. The Byzantine model had always been that each bishop, or patriarch, was independent and equal. The Roman model was that the bishop of Rome, the Pope, was supreme. An uneasy alliance kept the Church together until 1064, when the eastern Churches flatly refused to submit to the Pope. This split is called the Great Schism. This was painstakingly fueled by the sirens of the time, but they lacked sufficient numbers to make any real difference. Any reason to throw a monkey wrench into the prospect of man's eventual evolution was a boon to the planet Siren. Mankind would *sense* the presence of Siren in time despite the success of *The Great Shield.* From there it was a short leap to actually discovering her location.

The three congressional aides operated with an iron will on a subconscious level to keep mankind fighting over the possession of fossil fuels that were the false symbol of wealth as well as the undoing of the environment. If asked why, they honestly couldn't tell you. It was just a behavior that seemed beyond questions and clearly seemed the best way to serve the nature of man.

Mankind wants to fight. They also want to covet wealth and power for the sake of wealth and power. If fossil fuels could accomplish that end, then they were certainly worth going to war over. Obviously, the oil rich fields of the Middle East were the only logical reason why the United States took any interest. African nations were slaughtering each other in mind boggling numbers with machetes and any number of choreographed atrocities. America continuously turned a blind eye during all of them. The reason why was simple: they have no fossil fuels that can be bartered for symbols of wealth and power. Rest assured that if they did, the United States would be only too quick to come to their *rescue*.

The logistics meeting was chaired by the senior Senator from Texas named Jackson Cooke. Senator Cooke was hardly a sideline player in the heated debate over the burning of fossil fuels although he was nominated as chairman for just that reason. It was determined that he could do the least damage from the position of moderator as opposed to litigant or representative of big oil from the great state of Texas. He began, "This meeting shall come to order. The chair recognizes Senator Blake from the state of Georgia, you have the floor."

"Thank you, Senator Cooke," said the junior senator from Georgia. "I make a motion that the brief Blake vs. The State of Georgia shall be the first order of business when the commission conference begins," said Senator Blake.

Senator Cooke then said, "The floor is open for discussion of the motion by Senator Blake."

Congresswoman Grant raised her hand. Senator Cooke then said, "The chair recognizes Congresswoman Grant from the state of Rhode Island."

"Thank you, Senator," said Grant. "All of the members of this meeting are well acquainted with your pipe dreams Senator Blake," Grant paused for the laughter that she anticipated from her remark. There was none. She continued. "I'm sure I don't have to tell you that the burning of natural gas, although a cleaner source of energy than coal or oil contributes to the devastating effects of global warming. It is for this reason that I reject the notion that the senator's litigation with his constituency be given priority over other more pressing issues."

Senator Harold Williams raised his hand. Senator Cooke then said, "The chair recognizes Senator Williams from the state of Georgia."

"Thank you, Senator," said the senior senator from Georgia. "As you all know, I was instrumental in establishing the ban against the construction of the offshore platform until the issue could be effectively studied by the environmental factions of our great state of Georgia. However, Senator Blake and his company will probably get their gas pipeline eventually so . . ."

"Objection," shouted Senator Blake. "I am no longer an officer in the company known as Energix, and I resent the implication that I have any ulterior . . ."

"You can't object, Samuel. This is not a courtroom" said Williams. "The Senator from Texas is not a judge, and if I remember correctly, you're not even a lawyer." There were a few muffled laughs around the room as Samuel Blake sat back down at the suggestion of his aide Durbah Purness. Williams continued, "In response to the statement by the good Congresswoman from Rhode Island my reaction is as follows: I consider the whole issue of a natural gas platform outside the twelve mile limit small potatoes in the big scheme of things. I haven't found a way to effectively enforce the ban, and it seems to be a foregone conclusion that the platform will indeed come to fruition. Therefore, I would just as soon let Senator Blake go first and get his little barrel of pork out of the way."

There were more laughs at the expense of Senator Blake and Durbah held on to his arm gently to prevent him from rising from his chair and to the defense of his pride.

The three congressional aides were clearly bored by the logistics meeting. It seemed like a great waste of time. But there was another issue before them that they could reflect upon. It just so happened that Durbah Purness, Charles Donovan and Shelly Simon were all thinking of precisely the same thing: A letter that each of them had just received with the symbols alpha and omega prominently displayed on the outside of the envelope.

Chapter Six

Matthew Winter was a graduate student at The University of Arizona at Phoenix. He was enrolled in a fellowship program with the school of archeological studies under a rather famous professor named Joanne Riley. Dr. Riley had recently made the discovery of the decade in the Giza Plateau in Egypt.

A dig she and Matthew had been working for over four months finally produced a once in a lifetime find. Three ceramic vases held scrolls of parchment that were thought to be over 3600 years old. The parchments were made of lambskin and could be carbon dated to substantiate their age, and the hieroglyphics were in the process of being ciphered by a team of archeologists from around the world.

So far all that could be restored of the first scroll was a reference to Cleopatra where her name was spelled with an "h" at the end. It stated that Cleopatrah was to rule until she could be replaced by a representative from Sire . . . and then the parchment was torn and reduced to powder. The entire world was reflecting on the word Sire. Who was Sire? What was Sire? Was it the title of respect that one shows a monarch of a much later time period such as England during the 16th century? The scroll was an enigma, and there were two more that had yet to be examined. Many in the archeological community had hopes that some of the answers to the past were contained in the remaining two scrolls. Matthew Winter's hopes were that they weren't.

His mind was a veritable contradiction in that as a student of archeology he had a thirst for the knowledge that artifacts can share with us. At the same time he was sure that the scrolls would be a source of great sorrow for a great many people. He knew what his mission was. Never before had his purpose become so clear to him. He needed to expose the two remaining scrolls to oxygen and a small amount of yeast and water. They would be eaten in a matter of hours and reduced to a worthless pile of brown powder. It was a great risk that he knew he must take. It could be the ruin of his career and possibly even his freedom, but he knew in his heart there was simply no other choice.

The vases were placed in the center of the floor in Dr. Riley's tent. Around them were placed down pillows in the unlikely event that some seismological disaster might encourage them to fall over. It was an unnecessary precaution because the sides of the vases were at least an inch think. It would take a hefty swing with a hammer to deliberately break them. No earthquake was in the cards to damage the scrolls. That task was left to two small Ziploc bags of water and yeast in the pockets of Matthew Winter.

He went to Dr. Riley's tent shortly after the whole compound had turned in and was bedding down for the night. The two armed Egyptian guards knew him well and greeted him warmly as he approached them. He handed them a gift of fine Armenian wine in a camel skin sack and said. "We have much to celebrate, my friends. We will all be famous soon, no?" The guards laughed and accepted his gift. They exchanged knowing glances as Matthew pulled back the mosquito netting and stepped into Dr. Riley's tent. Joanne Riley was intoxicated with her new found fame and just a little too much wine for her own good. She turned as he entered and said, "Matthew, I was hoping you would come to me tonight."

"Shhhh," was Matthew's reply. "There will be time for talk later. Now we have only time for this," he took her in his arms and kissed her nearly squeezing the very breath from her delicate ribs. He would hold her tonight. He would make love to her for the first time. He needed her to tire. He needed her to sleep.

~

Chapter Seven

It was a tearful occasion when Sarah Poole tendered her resignation from the Bar Harbor Library. She assured her superior, "I promise, Mr. Seymour, if there's any way I can return back here I will. You have been very good to me and I appreciate everything you've done, especially the kind letter of recommendation."

"I feel you're like a daughter to me, Sarah. Whether you return or not, promise me you'll keep in touch, okay?"

"I will, Mr. Seymour, I promise," said Sarah.

"And if there's anything you need - money - anything - you'll . . ."

"Yes, Mr. Seymour. Please, I have to go. I love you," said Sarah as she broke the old man's heart and walked out of his life forever.

She knew the place of the alpha omega meetings well. This would be the fifteenth time she traveled to the abandoned coal mine in the hills of West Virginia. There were numerous signs surrounding the mine which proclaimed: Danger! This area is subject to cave-ins and collapsing mine shafts! No trespassing under penalty of law! Keep out! Extreme Danger! When the truth of the matter was the only danger was that the sirens might be detected by some wayward hunter or lost campers. In that case, there were ways to effectively handle the situation without bringing harm to anyone involved. The hunter or campers would merely suffer a slight headache and some small sense of delirium, similar to having just slept off one hell of a bachelor's party.

Sarah turned down the old mining trail wondering whether her life would have been better had she never been found by her *sensor* and uncast. She supposed it was inevitable since her parents were located by their *sensors* and uncast and directed nearly a quarter century earlier.

The direction was never a conscious effort on the part of the sirens as though when an imperative was implanted in their psyche, they were distracted from dwelling on it in their conscious mind.

Thousands of years of experience by the *sensors* led to the conclusion that the most effective way a siren could accomplish a task was by being directed from the subconscious only. The conscious mind was easily relieved of the knowledge of the task by direct contact with one of the Siren crystals while floating in the baths. There were many such baths around the world.

Under the mountain in West Virginia were a series of waterways and baths that the *sensors* would use to purge the conscious sense of a mission in their sirens. What was left was a gentle though insistent imperative that could not be ignored.

A typical conversation with a siren would go something like: "Why do you work for the senator when you know he represents big oil?"

"It just seems like the right thing to do," would be the answer.

"But aren't you concerned with emissions from fossil fuels or global warming?" you might ask them.

"Not in the least. I have meditated long and thoroughly and I am comfortable with my position on this. Many people die from the cold in winter. Without fossil fuels, there would be that many more."

Sarah wondered as she usually did if she would be better off being conscious of her task, but she knew she couldn't avoid the baths and the crystals. Plus, she welcomed the euphoria that accompanied her emersion. The only thing she didn't look forward to was surrendering her senses. And she never quite got used to her nakedness. It wasn't as though she was particularly shy; it was as though she felt exceptionally vulnerable being immersed naked in the bath with neither her sight nor hearing. The air through her breathing device had no taste or smell, and the only touch was the gentle pressure of the water on all sides of her. She never even physically felt the crystal, although she never had any doubt that it was there – mere inches from her forehead and reverberating with a silent frequency that she was sure to take with her until the next meeting.

As her Volvo came to a stop just inside of the huge entrance door of the old abandoned mine, she noticed a familiar car parked in the row of recently parked cars. It was a green Ford Mustang that she knew belonged to a handsome young man named Matthew Winter. She hadn't seen him since the last meeting when he was kind enough to sit with her in the baths.

They never made any attempt to contact each other after they left the meeting. That was one of the things that Sarah regretted losing as a result of the baths. She regretted losing the sense of comfort that she felt from close contact with another of her own kind.

When she entered the doorway that had been installed a short distance down the entrance to the mine, Matthew was there waiting for her, "Sarah, my good friend. I realize only now how I have missed seeing you."

"Yes, and somehow I feel that you will miss me again the day after tomorrow."

"Ours is a worthy cause, Sarah, if nothing else, of that I am sure."

"I wish I was as sure, Matthew. I was just called upon to leave a home that I had grown to love."

"I have a sense that our true home is very far from here. Don't you feel it, too? Can you honestly turn on the news at night and feel that you belong here?"

"You know I can't, Matthew, why do you tease me?"

"I only wish to remind you that there is a better place to call home and with any luck at all we may do precisely that."

"You're a dreamer, Matthew."

"Guilty as charged, Sarah, guilty as charged."

Matthew led Sarah deeper into the mine where they came upon a large meeting hall. There were soft lights suspended from the ceiling and nine very large tables, which were shaped like the letter "C" with the opening of each facing a stage and a large projection screen. A *sensor* named Jonah was adjusting the focus of a multimedia apparatus that he was to soon use in a presentation to the sirens. When he noticed Sarah and

Matthew enter the room he said, "Welcome, Matthew and Sarah. Come and be seated. Durbah and Charles are already here as you can see. Soon there will be refreshments before the presentation.

"Presentation?" asked Sarah. "What about the baths? Do you know what's going on, Matthew?"

"I'm afraid not. Sarah. Your guess is as good as mine."

"Durbah, do you know what's going on?" asked Sarah.

"No, Sarah. I got my letter the same time that Shelly and Charles did so we just assumed that we were due for a purge. I was kind of looking forward to getting rid of a lot of negative feelings," she said.

"Oh, Durbah," said Sarah. "We all know better than that. You've never had a negative feeling in your life."

"No, Sarah, you don't understand. It's not about other people; it's about me and my life. For the first time I've been questioning my role in all of this. It's something I have never done before."

"I've felt the same way, lately," said Charles.

"Me, too," said Matthew. "I recently had to resort to deception to accomplish my objective. That's a first."

"Well, I'm sure we'll find out soon enough what this is all about," said Durbah. "I can tell you one thing – I wasn't looking forward to moving this time."

"We must have drawn attention to ourselves or we wouldn't be here," said Sarah, "so we have only ourselves to blame."

"I recently met someone who I think may be coming into the transformation," said Durbah.

"Someone cast?" asked Matthew.

"Yes, I'm sure he was at birth, but now I'm not so sure. There was a gentle nature to him that I've come across a few times before. Something is happening to the people on this planet, and I get the feeling that it's about to spiral out of control."

"What, you think peace will break out?" offered Charles. This got a laugh out of all the sirens. Although they didn't exactly know the truth of whom they were or where they came from, each of them was aware that they were very different from the majority of the people around them. And there was a physical difference as well. They could see a suggestion of the color violet in each other's eyes, but somehow sensed that they were the only ones who could see it. There were also flecks of gold and silver on the edges of their irises. When they tried to see them for more than a few seconds, the flecks of metal faded away, but they were sure that most people never saw them to begin with. Jonah stepped up to the podium on the stage just as the lights went down.

~

Chapter Eight

The Awakening

Forty-eight people were seated in the great hall under the mountain. They came from all corners of the country and represented every age group as well; however, there was no one under sixteen except one nine-year-old boy, the son of a United States senator. The old abandoned coal mine was no longer a mountain in the traditional sense. It had been transformed into a vast underground complex with apartments, restaurants, clothing shops and even entertainment venues.

The mountain, known to the *U.S. Sensor Network* as, E.C. - 2 was completely self sustaining. E.C.–2 was the designation for the second meeting hall of two constructed in the East Central United States. Six meeting halls were in the continental United States. One was in Hawaii and one was in Alaska; all of them under mountains. They each had their own generators and stockpiles of food and water. Clothing and other goods were continuously manufactured within the halls for the attendees to use at will. No money ever changed hands within the halls, and there was never any incidence of hording or selfish behavior.

For all intents and purposed the meeting halls were a utopian society with every race and walk of life represented, although there were very few sirens from the service industries. This became evident to the attendees of E.C.–2 when Jonah asked for a show of hands from the people who were elected officials. Half the people raised their hand. Then he asked who in the room worked for an elected official. Half of the remaining members raised their hand. When he asked for plumbers, electricians and carpenters, no one raised their hand. He was at the beginning of his presentation.

"Kind members of this assembly," he began, "may I have your attention please." The members settled down from their conversations and Jonah immediately took in a sea of violet eyes with gold and silver flecks from the center point of the huge crescent-shaped tables. His voice was amplified through a sound system although no microphone was evident on his clothing. He continued, "This is a great day for the people of Siren," he said.

The members began a collective rolling, mumbled voice throughout the room as they questioned what they had just heard.

"Did he say Siren?" asked Sarah. "What or who is Siren?" she posed to the people with whom she was seated.

"That's what was mentioned in the scroll from the dig in Egypt," said Charles. "It wasn't sire, it was Siren."

"I've seen the scroll, as you know," said Matthew Winter. "It could have said Siren, but that was over 3700 years ago."

"Please, please, settle down people," said Jonah. "Let me explain a few things. All your questions will become clear and be answered in due time. Let me begin with a slide show of a series of beautiful paintings. Please direct your attention to the screen behind me."

The first slide appeared on the screen. Jonah continued, "These paintings were done by an artist who I am sure is familiar to all of you because she is quite famous. Her name is Leishia." There was a wave of applause reverberating off the walls and ceiling of the great room.

"Leishia was commissioned to do the paintings specifically for this presentation, and this work has never been seen outside of these walls. What I am about to explain to all of you has been told to Leishia some time ago, and she was anxious to help her people, your people - our people, understand their origins and the meaning of their life on this planet."

The screen showed a beautiful blue planet with large oceans and the suggestion of white wispy cirrus cloud cover over most of the land masses.

"This is your home," said Jonah.

"Earth," stated many of the people in the hall. "Why is he showing a picture of Earth?" they were quick to ask.

"No, not Earth," said Jonah. "Your home is very similar to Earth, but it is not Earth."

"That's absurd," said a man seated at the first and smallest circular table near the front of the room. "I know where I was born and what planet I'm from."

"Yes, you were born here and have always lived here, but this is not your home. Your home is called Siren."

There were more mutterings throughout the room. Jonah clicked to the next slide. The painting was of the sun with Earth on one side and Siren directly opposite on the other.

"This is the position of Siren in the solar system of Sol, or the star you have learned to call, the sun. Siren is a sister planet of the Earth with one major difference. Long ago Earth passed through a wave of intense gamma radiation. This gamma wave came from a nearby solar system whose star had just collapsed from a red giant to a white dwarf. It was very early in the chain of evolution for man, but he was indeed homo-erectus at the time. Bipedal hunter gatherers were just beginning to cultivate crops and keep domestic animals. Then everything changed. The gamma wave actually changed the nature of many Earth creatures and man most of all. This was the time of Cain and Abel. This was the birth of hostility from one humanoid to another. Let me see with a show of hands, who in this room considers hostility something that they have to deal with in their everyday life?" No one raised their hand.

"Okay, now with a show of hands, who in this room has committed a hostile act on another human being?" Again - no one raised their hand.

"No one," considered Jonah out loud, "that's pretty amazing in a gathering of this size, wouldn't you say?" he asked rhetorically.

"Raise your hand if you have ever harbored any ill will toward anyone in your whole life." No one raised their hand.

"If you have ever been in a fight, even just to defend yourself, raise your hand." No one did.

"Now, why is that?" asked Jonah to a silent room. "Why do you suppose that in a room of nearly fifty people, we can't find even one incidence where there has been any hostility, violence or feelings of ill will? After all, we're all human right?" The room was silent. Jonah continued, "Wrong! We are not human; we are Siren." He let his statement hang in the air for a full fifteen seconds before continuing.

The next slide appeared on the screen. It was the planet Siren with a crystal clear backdrop of stars behind it, but the planet itself was somewhat opaque. When you looked closer you could see that it was sitting exactly in the center of a perfect cube of gossamer like gauze or fine netting. This was Leishia's depiction of the reason Siren has escaped detection throughout the modern age. It was the six photo-reflective planes that concealed the planet Siren known as *The Great Shield*.

"This marvel of engineering is called, *The Great Shield*. It is an interconnection of six planes that form a perfect cube that is one hundred fifty thousand square miles on each side. This renders the planet Siren virtually invisible.

If you look at any one of the planes from any angle, you will see an exact projection of what is seen looking out into the cosmos on the opposite side. In a sense it is six giant view screens that show precisely what you would see if the planet had never existed at all." Jonah paused in his delivery to give the concept a chance to sink in. The members in the room were talking excitedly and a few were visibly shaking as the truth of their origin and nature was becoming clear to them. Jonah then continued, "Remember my reference to Cain and Abel? That, of course, was from the Bible, specifically The Old Testament. Now, while the Bible may be a very good book in its intentions, it has gotten most of the historical facts of this planet entirely wrong.

As metaphors and allegories they come wonderfully close; however, the only real truth of Earth history was sent to Siren. Siren had no need to suppress the facts or use them to her advantage; she merely received them and recorded them for future reference.

But Earth history is not the reason we are gathered here today. Today is a day for celebration. Today is judgment day." Voices whirled around the room in forceful whispers.

"But God is not who stands in judgment over you today. The judgment is yours and yours alone. You are the judge of your actions and are in complete control of your lives as you have been since the age of sixteen. When you first turned sixteen, your mother sent you to a person known as a *sensor*. The *sensor* who first brought you to a meeting like this one has been your guide and guardian for your whole life until this day. Now you will no longer have a *sensor*. Your tasks or *directives* have all been accomplished, and now it is time to reap the rewards.

When I said that today is judgment day, I meant precisely this: you will have the next three weeks to decide whether you would like to remain on this planet for the rest of your life or return home to the planet Siren. Before I continue, please take a minute and reflect upon this moment in time. There will come a time when you choose to recall exactly what you are feeling now."

Jonah walked to the side of the room and took a large sip from a glass of water. He replaced what he had drunk from a nearby pitcher and set the glass back down. He bent over and touched his toes stretching his back and trying to loosen tight muscles. He was reacting to some tension in the room as many of the sirens were emitting anxious thoughts and questions. His receptive nature was acting like a receiver and there were just too many channels broadcasting at the same time. When he returned back to the center of the room, he addressed this issue as he continued the presentation.

"Ladies and gentlemen, if I could have your attention once again, please," he paused and waited for the room to settle down. "I know that many of you have a lot of questions, and it is my hope to address them all by the time this meeting concludes the day after tomorrow. I would like you to please meditate on the words *peace* and *Siren* briefly, as I am receiving an overload of cerebral dialogue. I am a *sensor* and as the name implies I can sense many of your thoughts and questions. Naturally they are too great in number for me to deal with at one time. You are blowing my mind, to coin a phrase," he chuckled briefly. There was still a little electricity in the air, but Jonah could sense that they were concerned for his well being and trying to calm their thoughts. Jonah continued, "Another reference to the Bible would be helpful by talking briefly about The Rapture.

The Rapture may very well have been written by one of your ancestors or some other siren's ancestor in anticipation of this very day. The Bible tells us that upon judgment day certain people will be brought into heaven from the Earth and others will be left behind. Well, the truth of the matter is they got it pretty darned close. About four hundred and eighty-six people living on Earth are descended from a little over a dozen Sirens who came to Earth thousands of years ago.

Another civilization more advanced than their own transported the sirens to Earth almost five thousand years ago. They landed, as you would expect, on the Giza Plateau where the three pharaohs' pyramids are situated in an alignment, which is exactly that of the constellation of Orion.

Just what do you suppose the odds are of that happening by chance? Here is another statistic that might surprise you although I'm not sure why it would by now: Let me see by a show of hands, how many people have loved another person in their lifetime?" Every person in the room raised their hand. He continued, "How many people can honestly say that they love someone very much right at this moment?" Again – everyone raised their hand. "Now, for the kicker, how many people in this room have ever had an argument with their spouse or significant other?" No one raised their hand. Jonah scrutinized the room for a few seconds looking for a raised hand. He finally said, "What are the odds?"

After letting his last statement sink in, Jonah said, "Over the next three weeks by the grace of some very careful coordination and spectacular innovation, the descendants of earthbound sirens will be transported back to Siren. This action is not compulsory by any means. It will be your choice, your judgment, whether or not you stay here on Earth or return to Siren. No one will try to convince you to decide one way or another, and by the same token, there will be no one to dissuade you as well. The choice is entirely yours, and the members of this sector, E.C.–2, will have about two weeks until the first *exchange* is accomplished. Your journey will be facilitated by a *space/time exchange* with an identical *space* on Siren. You can't be transported to a particular *space* on Siren because something already occupies that *space.* No two things can exist in the same *space* at one *time.* But a particular *space* can be exchanged with another *space* with the use of a beam of light that has been slowed to a sub-light speed. Normally a beam of light would take roughly sixteen minutes to reach Siren from Earth. Your journey, however, will in fact take just under an hour because the *exchange* is done at sub light speed. *Time* is only *relative* in relation to *space.* From your point of view, the *exchange* will only seem like a few minutes. Although the exchange only takes about fifty-five minutes, the power utilized is so great that it takes about seventy hours to store enough energy cells to do the job again. Therefore the turnaround time between trips is approximately three days. Roughly twelve people can fit comfortably in the *space/time exchange* chamber and the departure schedule will be done by lottery. The entire exodus should be able to be accomplished in about one month. If you choose to go, you will have about a week to tie up loose ends so to speak.

I'd like to address a few issues that might play a part in your decision to stay on Earth or to go to Siren. Let me try to answer a few obvious questions. Number 1: Can any Earth natives return to Siren with you? Possibly: Earth natives may undergo a very meticulous psychological screening to detect any undesirable nature or hostility. I seriously doubt that many would hold up to the scrutiny. Number 2: Should you be reluctant to surrender the wealth that you have accumulated here on Earth, although I seriously doubt that that is a strong consideration for a descendant of Siren, let me state this. Your ancestors have been well provided for on Siren, and as their descendants, you will find that on Siren you are quite wealthy. You will want for nothing, I assure you.

If you are wondering whether anyone in this room will have the opportunity to disclose the existence of Siren or the exodus operation to the public in general, rest assured, no one will retain the memory of the specifics of this meeting. The baths will purge the memory from your mind, but we will leave you with just enough knowledge to carefully consider your decision to leave.

We will meet again in one week, and the crystals in the baths will restore the complete picture once again. Now I'd like to continue with the presentation if I may." He clicked to the next slide. This time it was an actual photograph and not a painting by Leishia. The photo was taken by Matthew Winter although he had no idea at the time that the scrolls were not depictions of the planet Earth. He now understood why the *sensors* had them destroyed. They were buying time for the exodus.

"Here we have a photograph of one of the scrolls recently unearthed in the Giza Plateau in Egypt. In it you can clearly see that the scroll depicts the position of the planet Siren in relation to that of Earth." Jonah then clicked to the next slide. "And here we see the third scroll depicting *The Great Shield*, which is presently cloaking Siren along with the specifications for the eight satellites which remain at a geosynchronous orbit at the corners of the cube. This scroll is merely a blueprint of sorts as the actual shield was not finished until twenty-six hundred years later, roughly about the same time when humans had the capacity for space travel. Many tasks were necessary in a chain of events to bring about *The Great Shield*, and many of those tasks were accomplished by sirens here on Earth.

Those eight satellites are what tie together the corners of the photo-reflective fields that facilitate the shield. They are powered by nuclear fuel, and Cassini, the recently launched space probe from Earth to map Saturn's moons, supplies the remaining fuel needed to power the shield for the next hundred years. The reason Siren needed fuel manufactured on Earth is that the half-life of radioactive elements on Siren is infinitely small. They just seem to naturally stabilize into inert matter.

There is, however, a project under consideration to construct a nuclear manufacturing facility on the dark side of Earth's moon. Siren has no moon and therefore no tides. She is tilted on a twenty-one degree axis similar to Earth, which regulates the temperature with the changing of the seasons. Siren has everything that Earth has and more. The reason is - Siren has everything Earth has and less. It has less hostility, (actually none at all) and therefore less discomfort. There is no poverty on Siren, no crime, no hatred, nor any jealousy or envy.

What you can expect to find on Siren is millions of people who are all very different, and yet at the same time, they are all precisely like you."

~

Chapter Nine

Matthew Winter was sitting with Sarah when Jonah surrendered the stage to a well known performer. He was a guitarist in the style of Leo Kottke who played with such flair and abandon that the sirens couldn't understand how he was so unaffected by Jonah's presentation.

"How can he do that?" asked Sarah. "He acts as if nothing has happened, and he has just been given the biggest surprise of his life."

"He's on automatic," said Matthew. "He's played that piece so many times before he could do it in his sleep."

"What do you think about the exodus?" she asked.

"It's fantastic, wouldn't you say?"

"Yes, I suppose it is," said Sarah.

"You suppose?" asked Matthew with some confusion. "You've just been given the most fantastic news anyone could ever get. Now you have the answer to the nagging question that has plagued you for your whole life."

"What question?" asked Sarah.

"Why don't I fit in?" said Matthew knowingly.

"I don't know, Matthew, it's all a bit too much to take in."

"Your parents are here, aren't they?" He instantly recognized Senator Poole from his pictures in the newspaper and television commercials. The reason he took notice of the senator in the first place was that he and his wife were accompanied by their young son John. John Poole was the only member of the gathering under the age of sixteen. John was a *"seer"* and in time would grow into a *"sensor"* like Jonah if he were to remain on Earth. A midterm election was nearing, and the senator's ads were a topical subject because they avoided the typical mudslinging.

"Yes, they're here," she said.

"They'll go, of course, won't they?"

"I'm not really sure," said Sarah.

"I just assumed that at their age . . . I mean retirement is just around the corner. What better way to retire than to take a fantastic journey to a new home."

"My father is pretty committed to his constituency. He represents a lot of older people who depend on him. And then there is John," said Sarah, worry filling her voice.

"How old is your brother?"

"He's nine, going on ninety," she said.

Matthew laughed, "He is a rather remarkable guy. Does he understand what's going on here?"

"Oh, yeah," she said rolling her eyes, "he understands a lot more than I do. On an instinctual level, no doubt."

"How do you suppose they keep him under the radar?"

"What? You mean his gift?"

"Well, yeah," he said. "How many genuine psychics do you know, Sarah?"

"Only one. And that's only here at the retreat. I suppose on Monday, I won't remember anything about his gift at all. If his abilities can be hidden from his own sister, then I don't think we have to worry about the general public."

"You mean the crystals, don't you?"

"That's right, the crystals," concern filling her brow.

"Maybe that's all for the best."

"And losing you again? That's for the best, also?"

"This whole thing is bigger than us, Sarah."

"I suppose there are quite a few sirens who'll still decide not to go," her wrinkled brow reflected a distant hope in her eyes as though she could convince Matthew to somehow change his mind.

"You're not serious, Sarah?" asked Matthew.

"Oh, yes, I am," she said.

"You'd consider staying here on Earth?"

"I just mean that I haven't decided yet."

"I'm going," he said. "There's nothing to think about."

"Do you remember the last meeting, Matthew, when we were together at the baths?"

"Yes, I do now," he said.

"That's the point," she said. "You didn't yesterday, did you?"

"No, Sarah, I didn't"

"What else did the baths and the crystals take from you?"

"You're sounding like one of those conspiracy theory figures," said Matthew.

"Think about it. Why do we have to surrender any part of our minds? Jonah said that our directives and deep-seeded imperatives are finished."

"There's a lot at stake, Sarah. They have to protect the exodus from those who would feel threatened by it."

"I don't intend to tell anyone about it."

"You won't have that choice, Sarah."

"That's precisely my point. The choice will be taken from me, and who knows what else," she said miserably.

"I can't believe what I'm hearing," said Matthew.

"What do you feel about me, Matthew?" asked Sarah.

Matthew took a few seconds to consider if Sarah was seriously asking him for an honest declaration. It was something that wouldn't normally occur in the everyday world where they came from. People normally build walls around their hearts for protection against the callous nature of human interaction. Only after many months together would someone normally let down their guard and trust another person with their feelings.

"I love you, Sarah," he said.

"You see? What does that mean?" she asked.

"It means that I love you."

"You've only seen me two or three days before. And even then the memory of what we meant to each other was taken from you."

"All I know is what I feel, Sarah," said Matthew.

"I love you, too, Matthew, and I'm frightened."

"What do you mean?" he asked her. Matthew's instinct to protect Sarah was coming into play.

"When I leave here tomorrow, will I love you then?"

"Of course, you will, Sarah."

"But the crystals, Matthew," she said visibly shaking. "They've taken you from me before. I'm not sure I can let that happen again."

"Sarah, please," said Matthew reaching out to hold her trembling body against his. "You have to have faith. You have to trust me that our hearts will always hold each other. But we may have to surrender our minds for just a short while."

"Listen to what you're saying, Matthew. I'm not sure you can even have a heart without your mind."

"There's no other way, Sarah. There's too much at stake to risk detection by humanity. Thousands of years and thousands of lives have been protecting the existence of our home from exposure to the people of this planet. I have faith that when we get to Siren, I will find you and love you just as much as I do now."

"I hope you're right, Matthew."

"I have to be right, Sarah. It's the only thing that makes sense."

~

Chapter Ten

Durbah and Charles were sitting in the baths. The temperature of the water was 85 degrees, and the air was a comfortable 72. They decided to spend a few minutes with the crystals before considering their decision to travel to Siren. They had the opportunity to discuss it briefly before putting on the eye patches and activating a breathing device.

"Which way are you leaning, Durbah?"

"There's really no question for me," she said. "I'm going to Siren. It's where I belong, Charles."

"I suppose it's where we all belong," he said.

"That's right," she said. "It's a wonderful opportunity. I'm just glad that they would welcome us."

"Why wouldn't they?"

"I don't know, overcrowding maybe. Their numbers are about to increase by four-hundred and eighty-six people."

"Apparently they are anxious for us to come. We will enjoy celebrity status there if I'm reading this right."

"I'm not sure I'm comfortable with that. I've never really wanted to be a celebrity."

"Don't worry, Durbah. According to Andy Warhol it'll only be for about fifteen minutes," said Charles with a chuckle.

"I'm pretty sure Andy Warhol wasn't a siren," said Durbah.

"You're probably right," said Charles. "So, who is this guy you've met?"

"His name is Alex," she said. "I met him in traffic court of all places."

"So, what did you mean about man evolving? Were you serious?"

"Of course, I was serious. Man has to evolve, doesn't he?" she asked rhetorically. "I think he may be on the brink of a new plateau."

"You're getting all this just from just one man you've met in traffic court, is that it?" he asked doubtfully.

"Oh, don't be ridiculous, Charles. You've seen it, too, haven't you?"

Charles chuckled and said, "Yes, Durbah, I've seen it coming for some time. I knew it was inevitable."

"So maybe there's hope that mankind won't always be a threat to Siren."

"Mankind *will* always be a threat. You heard Jonah talk about the gamma wave. That influence will never entirely go away. There may just be some individuals of humanity who have outgrown its influence."

"I'm certain that Alex is one such individual."

"What does he do?" asked Charles.

"He's a lawyer, I think. He said he wrote a bill for someone regarding speeding in school zones."

"Well, it's a small world, indeed."

"What? You know him?"

"I know of him, but we've never met."

"He reviewed the legality of our ban against your boy Blake."

"You're kidding?" asked Durbah wrinkling her brow and smiling.

"Why would I kid about that?"

"What's his last name, then?" she asked still thinking that Charles was pulling her leg.

"Jansen," said Charles smiling. "I told you I know who he is. I've even talked to him on the phone."

"What was your impression of him?" asked Durbah.

"My impression? You mean over the phone?" he asked laughing at her transparent infatuation regarding Alex Jansen.

"That's right," said Durbah pretending to be mad at him for making fun of her feelings.

"He seems like a really nice guy," said Charles truthfully. "Who knows, he might be one of the next tier."

"I'm sure of it. You would be, too, if you met him in person. I never get that kind of feeling from ordinary humans."

"What about Senator Blake?" he asked facetiously. "Do you think he might be going back to Siren?"

"Oh, sure, Charles," she laughed. "He'll be in the same chamber with Alyssa Grant and Senator Williams." Then they both started laughing at that one.

~

Chapter Eleven

When Sarah Poole woke up on the day after the meeting, she was confused as to where she intended to go. Apparently, she had checked in to a Day's Inn on I-95 for the night, but for the life of her, couldn't remember doing so. She remembered having the urgent feeling that she needed to relocate for her own safety, but couldn't remember any of the details. The apartment house in Bar Harbor was a safe place to live as far as she could recall, and she remembered having many friends there. *Why would I want to move?* she was wondering. *I love my job working with Mr. Seymour at the library, and I miss Mrs. Eldridge terribly.*

As soon as she climbed into her Volvo in the motel parking lot, she placed a call to Mrs. Eldridge on her cell phone.

"Sarah," said Mrs. Eldridge excitedly, "I'm so glad you called. Is everything all right?"

"Yes, Mrs. Eldridge, everything's fine."

"Are your parents well?"

"My parents?" asked Sarah.

"Yes, I assumed that's what you meant when you said you had to travel to the South. I thought perhaps that the senator or your mother might be ill."

"No, as far as I know they're both fine. I've been at a retreat with the alpha omegas," she said truthfully.

"Oh, how nice," said Mrs. Eldridge. "Have you spoiled yourself with a massage and mud bath?" she said jokingly.

“Something like that,” said Sarah. “I’ve definitely recharged my batteries, but now it’s time to go home.”

“Are you going to Florida, Sarah?” asked Mrs. Eldridge.

“No, Mrs. Eldridge, my home is in Bar Harbor.”

“You’re coming back here to me?” she asked hopefully.

“Unless you’ve rented the room already,” said Sarah.

“How does beef Stroganoff sound?”

“What?” asked Sarah. “What about beef Stroganoff?”

“For dinner, Dear. Will you be home for dinner?” asked Mrs. Eldridge.

“I sure will,” said Sarah. All of a sudden she had the feeling that she couldn’t wait to get home to Bar Harbor. She couldn’t think of anywhere else she would rather be. Somehow that seemed important to her for some reason, but she wasn’t sure why. She was so grateful to the alpha omega society for giving her the opportunity to unwind and clear her mind. She remembered her trepidation upon receiving the last invitation and it puzzled her. It somehow triggered an impulse to be on the move, but Sarah hated moving.

She remembered moving four times in the past four years and was determined to finally establish some roots for a change. Bar Harbor had always been good to her, and she was grateful to have a place she could call home. Her last treatment with the crystals in the baths drove the point home to her. The baths were always so helpful to rejuvenate her and crystallize her thoughts.

The crystals and baths had an entirely different effect on Charles Donovan. His last treatment left him with the feeling that he needed to leave the state of Georgia and Senator Williams far behind him. He wasn't sure how, but he had a very strong feeling that his life was about to change in a very big way. He felt out of place all of a sudden. It was as though he had been denying his true nature and purpose in life and was finally determined to straighten things out before it was too late.

When he returned to Atlanta, the first thing he did was have a long serious discussion with Sylvia Porter, his housemate of the last seven months. At first their relationship was merely one of convenience. Sylvia answered his ad for a roommate in the Atlanta Constitution. He traveled with the senator often enough to question the expense of keeping an Atlanta townhouse by himself. Sylvia sharing the rent and feeding his fish was the perfect answer to the situation. Then she began to express the desire to sleep with him. That's when everything started going downhill. He was uncomfortable with his relationship with Sylvia before he went to the alpha omega retreat. The crystals and baths just clarified the issue before him. *I don't belong in Atlanta,* he thought. *In fact, I'm not sure where I belong, but I know it's not Atlanta. And I'm not sure what my purpose in life is anymore, but it certainly isn't working for Senator Williams.*

Matthew Winter's reaction to the crystals in the baths was quite different. His reaction was a lot like Sarah Poole's. *I miss Joanne terribly*, he thought. *I think I'm in love with her. I feel so dirty for what I've done to her. How can I have destroyed such important artifacts? What was I thinking? I must have been insane. Temporary insanity – is there really such a thing? One thing is for sure, Joanne must never find out what I've done. She'd never forgive me. I'm not sure I can ever forgive myself,* he thought miserably.

~

Chapter Twelve

Shelly Simon was the first to arrive at Alyssa Grant's Washington office at 9:00 A.M. on the Monday following the alpha omega meeting. She usually felt refreshed and recharged, but this Monday was a different story. She felt agitated. She didn't know how she was going to handle the Congresswoman's usual gruff disposition that began each workweek. She just wasn't in the mood for it this time and didn't care who knew about it.

Actually it was quite liberating feeling in control of her destiny for the first time in a long time. *What was I thinking,* she asked herself when she thought of how Alyssa Grant had pushed her around and abused her over the past six years. *If you let someone push you around, they will,* she had always believed. *Just let Grant say anything short to me today, she was almost hoping. I can't wait to tell her to stick this job up her . . .*

"Good morning, Shelly." said Congresswoman Grant. "You're here bright and early. You know I don't usually come in until ten o'clock."

"I'm here every Monday at nine, Mrs. Grant."

"Yes, I suppose you are, Dear."

Dear? That's a first.

"I suppose I have been unappreciative of you, Shelly. Please don't let me get away with it any longer," she laughed softly.

My God, she's gotten laid! Shelly thought. *Or maybe I should check the basement for pods! I remember Invasion of the Body Snatchers.*

"I've been so consumed with what I think is the most important issue facing us," said Grant, "and I just have the feeling that no one takes me seriously. It's because I'm a woman, I'm sure. When Al Gore talks . . ."

"People ignore him," said Shelly.

"What?" asked Grant. "Did I hear you correctly, Shelly? Did you say people ignore Al Gore?"

"That's what I said. Don't take it personally if people seem to be ignoring you about global warming. The president has us all trained like a bunch of seals. He ignored the Kyoto Accord's efforts to demonstrate some responsibility. The president has always represented big oil just like his daddy. But even his daddy had the sense to ratify the accord. Junior decided he could deliver an uninhabitable world to our grandchildren and sleep like a log."

"Why, I've never heard you talk like this, Shelly," said Grant.

"Well, maybe it's something I should have done a long time ago," said Shelly.

"Maybe it is," agreed Grant. "Maybe we should be talking about the next step in your career, dear. How does the title of Councilwoman Simon sound to you, Shelly?"

"I'm not kissing any babies or asses," said Shelly.

"Bravo," said the congresswoman. "I'll organize a luncheon to announce your candidacy." She thought for a minute and then said, "Oh, you know what I mean. You do it." Shelly smiled and thought to herself, *I'm definitely checking the basement for pods.*

~

Chapter Thirteen

Matthew Winter slept soundly on the flight to Cairo. He could barely get himself out of the chair at Gate 40 in Dulles Airport to board the plane. The last three days were very draining in more ways than one. His strength was drained from his lean, powerful body, and his mind was stuck in first gear. He often looked forward to the retreat in West Virginia as a source of rejuvenation and inspiration. He usually bounded into Dulles with a sense of purpose and a fresh new outlook with his batteries charged. Not today.

He thought he might be coming down with a cold or flu. He didn't want to bring any debilitating illness back to Joanne Riley. Her work was very important to her, and being under the weather would certainly slow her down.

Too bad, he thought to himself. *It's always about Joanne and her fast track to stardom. When she publishes, I never seem to see the name Matthew Winter mentioned anywhere. I've spent as much time at that damned dig as she has. And for what? Cleopatra was once spelled with an h at the end, big freakin' deal. Now there's even some question as to whether or not it is the famed queen of Egypt at all because the name was somewhat common in the Nile valley at the time. I've got to move on soon. I can't spend my life patting someone else on the back. I've always kept a low profile; held back for reasons I'm not really sure of. But all that is about to change. Watch out world, Matthew Winter is about to get his. And God help anyone who stands in his way.*

"Can I get you something to drink?" asked the pretty, young flight attendant. *Coffee, tea or me?* she thought playfully as she tried to coax a smile from the handsome man she had just awakened.

"I don't usually drink when I'm sleeping," said Matthew irritably.

"I'm sorry, Sir, I shouldn't have disturbed you."

"That's all right," he said, "You staying over in Cairo tonight?" he asked.

The flight attendant's first thought was, *It's none of your business, buster.*

"As a matter of fact I am," she heard herself saying.

"Well, I'm not a big fan of coffee or tea, but I might try a little of the *me*," he said.

A nervous giggle escaped her as she made her way down the aisle to the next passenger. She thought to herself, *my God, did I say that out loud? What was I thinking?*

~

Chapter Fourteen

Senator Williams' patience was going the way of the dodo and the saber-toothed tiger. Charles Donovan was not returning his calls, and he was anxious to review the notes on the offshore platform ban. Charles had downloaded them from an email he received from Alex Jansen over three days ago. He cursed himself for not knowing Charles's password to his computer files. He was dialing Charles's cell phone for the third time just as he entered the senator's office.

"Well, I hope I'm not taking you from anything important, Mr. Donovan. I wouldn't want to interrupt your day."

"I'm sorry, Mr. Williams. It was the beltway again. I was jammed in for about an hour on the way here. It's the damned bottleneck. Why can't they get that thing fixed?" he asked showing his irritation at the D.C. roadways.

"And your cell phone wasn't working, is that it?" asked Williams facetiously.

"As a matter of fact it wasn't," lied Charles. The truth was he just didn't feel like talking to the senator until he absolutely had to.

"You got those notes on the platform ban on Friday. I've yet to see them, Mr. Donovan."

"Friday you were on the links, Sir."

"Well, I'm in my office this morning, and I don't have access to a file that I paid good money for, son," said the senator angrily.

"I should have printed it out on Friday and left it on your desk," said Charles.

"Is that supposed to be an apology, Mr. Donovan?" asked the senator.

"Yes, Sir," said Charles. *Fuck you, Sir*, he thought.

"I'd like to have the password to your files."

I'll bet you would, you asshole, thought Charles. *You'll get it, but only until I change it this afternoon.*

"It's Zorba, Sir."

"Like Zorba the Greek?" he asked.

"That's right," said Charles. *Man, I am so out of here, thought Charles. How long have I been stuck in this shithole of a job,* he thought. *I'm goin' nowhere. Well, that was then and this is now. But first, I think it might be time to play a few hole cards. Paybacks are hell, Williams,* he thought.

~

Chapter Fifteen

Durbah Purness was thinking of traffic court. She recalled her court appearance on the Thursday before her weekend at the mountain retreat. She was having trouble focusing her mind around those two foggy days. She wondered if the vitamin supplements that she received there had kind of a reverse Ginkgo Baloba effect or something. All she could remember was the wonderful massages and the baths. She knew she wasn't alone in the baths, but couldn't actually remember who the other members were.

Oh well, she thought. *A few cobwebs are a small price to pay for such a relaxing and selfish extravagance.* The retreat was really the only way she had spoiled herself since the age of sixteen. Her parents had given her a weekend of lavish attention for her birthday. Then the gift was just an ongoing expression of love. She looked forward to her bi-annual invitation that she received in the mail.

But usually her mind was much clearer when she returned from the weekend under the mountain. In fact that was when her mind had been most clear. She usually came away from the mountain with some new energy and resolve that pointed her in an exciting new direction and redefined her life. She began working for Senator Blake shortly after one of her mountain weekends. The job just seemed to fall into her lap as did most of her positions of privilege. She always thought she was just lucky.

If she needed a new car, one was provided for her. She would win a contest, or her parents knew someone who was getting a new one because the ashtrays were dirty or some other ridiculous excuse. Her parents always spoiled her and made sure she had the best of everything. She supposed it was one of the benefits of being an only child.

Now it seemed to Durbah that there was only one thing that she was ever interested in that hadn't fallen into her lap – Alex Jansen. She couldn't stop thinking about him. She couldn't remember feeling the same way about any man she had ever met before. Men were interesting for a short while and then she often tired of them. They threw themselves at her even at the most inappropriate times. It was not uncommon for Durbah to be "hit on" at someone's funeral or in church. It was troublesome for her at times, and she would seek the comfort of isolation.

This feeling she was having was somehow different. She imagined herself in various walks of life at Alex Jansen's side. Dinner and a show or a concert by the Atlanta Symphony Orchestra . . . *but Alex lived in Washington, didn't he? He was in traffic court there, but then again, so was I,* she thought hopefully. He didn't actually say he lived in Washington. Durbah decided to do a little bit of detective work.

~

Chapter Sixteen

When Sarah Poole arrived in Bar Harbor she wasn't in the mood for Mrs. Eldridge's beef Stroganoff just yet. She went to one of the local bars called Barnacle Bill's. To call it a tourist trap / meat market was being kind. Sarah had never been in the bar during the entire time she lived in Bar Harbor.

The cup was running over with shallow conversations and fictitious names. Barnacle Bill's was known as the area's penultimate pick-up joint. Sarah didn't have long to wait. She no sooner sat down on a barstool when a tall young man eased his way beside her and said, "May I buy you a drink." He was clean shaven with light brown hair and a nice smile.

"That was quick," she said.

"Why waste time?" said the young man casually.

"Okay, what comes next?" she asked sarcastically, *"What's your sign?* or *Do you come here often?"*

He had a nice laugh as well, "This place is kind of obvious, isn't it?" he laughed again.

"I guess everyone here has his eyes wide open," said Sarah. "We're all consenting adults here."

"You're pretty direct," said the young man. "I like that; it's refreshing to meet someone who cuts through all the small talk."

"Oh, I'm not completely out of small talk, first the drink. I don't want you to think I'm a cheap date."

The man just laughed again and shook his head slightly. He motioned for the bartender and sat down on the stool next to Sarah. "You know you're beautiful, don't you?" asked the young man.

"I've been told I'm beautiful, so have you," she said.

"You know, I don't think I've ever met anyone like you. What's your name?" he asked.

"What's the difference," said Sarah.

"You're the difference," he said. "I'm suddenly very interested in you. That's something new for me."

"Yeah, well this is kind of new for me, too," said Sarah. "Sarah Poole, and you are?"

"Brad Early," he said.

"I believe you," said Sarah.

"Excuse me?" asked Brad.

"No one would make up that name," she said.

He just laughed and said, "I guess you're right. I like you Sarah Poole."

"I like you, too, Brad Early. Buy me a Long Island iced tea."

"Coming right up," said Brad. *Things are suddenly looking brighter for Brad Early's love life,* he thought to himself.

~

Chapter Seventeen

Associated Press

Cerro Pachon, Chile:

Two very sensitive mirrors were severely damaged by two strong gamma wave pulses over the last 48 hours. The scientists at Mauna Kea, Hawaii, and Cerro Pachon, Chile, have declared that the very expensive mirrors used in the 8-meter telescopes may not be able to be repaired sufficiently to carry on with Project Gemini – an international partnership to explore the cosmos.

The gamma wave pulses are believed to be relatively harmless to plants and animals on the surface of the Earth due to the protection afforded by its atmosphere; however, the astronauts aboard the International Space Station are scheduled for an early departure from their latest mission. Scientists fear their exposure to the intense radiation presents a serious health risk. The mood of the astronauts is described as somewhat dark, and they are exhibiting signs of hostile behavior.

Gamma waves have bombarded the Earth many times in the past and her fauna and flora have evolved over time to be resistant to their effects.

The Gemini telescopes, one on Mauna Kea, Hawaii, (elevation 13,822 ft.) and one in Cerro Pachon (elevation 8,895 ft.) near Cerro Tololo in central Chile, provide complete sky coverage, making key astronomical objects (e.g. Magellanic Clouds, M31, M32 and M33) accessible regardless of location on the celestial sphere. Both sites offer high percentages of clear weather and excellent atmospheric stability.

The telescopes are designed to exploit the best image quality allowed by the Earth's atmosphere at these sites. The combination of large aperture, excellent imaging, and low IR background give the Gemini Telescopes an order of magnitude sensitivity increase over existing 4-meter class telescopes for many applications.

Durbah Purness was the first of the sirens to have a reaction to the gamma wave that had sent pulses toward the Earth for the last forty-eight hours. Immediately she could see her future as clearly as she saw the crystals in the baths. She was hoping she could be in the first group to enter the *space/time exchange chamber* to Siren. She was committed and knew she would retain the knowledge of Siren and the importance of protecting the exodus. She would do anything in her power to help the cause for Siren. And if there was any way in the world she could make it happen, she was determined to take Alex Jansen with her.

Chapter Eighteen

Alex Jansen was sitting in his office, gazing out the window at the setting sun trying to break through the afternoon haze of our nation's capital. He was thinking of taking some time off knowing that his ex-wife, and present law partner, Brianna, was well up to the task of taking over his case load. He didn't begrudge her the fact that he was billing fifty percent more hours than she was, but it helped him justify in his own mind that he was entitled to abandon ship. He found himself smiling for a reason he couldn't quite put his finger on when the intercom light began pulsing a green light on his desk. He reached over and pressed the button, "Yes, Julie."

"I have that profile you were asking for, Mr. Jansen."

"Do you have it on hard copy?" he asked knowing he would want to take the information with him when he left within the hour.

"It's a simple matter to print it out," her voice told him that she was poised with her finger on the left click button of her computer's touch pad. "Would you like it before you leave?" she asked knowingly.

"Please." Alex broke the connection and rocked back in his soft leather chair. A few minutes later, his secretary came into his office and placed the single piece of paper on his desk.

"Thanks, Julie," was all he said. He made no attempt to pick it up and read it in front of her, so he rose from his chair and put on his jacket waiting for her to ask him if that's all he needed for the day. She was hoping to be let off early as it was Friday afternoon, and she had plans to join her friends at Beech Mountain Lodge near Banner Elk, North Carolina, for some time on the slopes.

"Will there be anything else, Mr. Jansen?"

"No, Julie. If you are current with all the briefs, why don't we knock off a little early this week." He didn't have to twist her arm.

Julie, glanced at her wristwatch knowing full well it was exactly 3:18 P.M. "Thanks," she said adding, "I'll see you early Monday morning."

"Have a nice weekend, Julie. Unless you need a lift to your apartment."

"No, thanks, I drove to the office this morning. I'm all packed for my trip down South."

"Then go. I'll lock up and get the lights."

"Thanks again, Mr. Jansen." Julie had her jacket, and grabbing her purse off her desk, she was out the door in less than a minute. Alex paused and sat on her desk before following her out to the elevator. He knew she wouldn't wait and would take the elevator car down to the lobby by herself. He looked at the piece of paper in his hand.

Name : Durbah Purness
Age: 26
DOB: 01/01/84. *A New Year's Baby* he noticed

Education: BS in Political Science from Georgetown University 2005'

Honorary MBA from George Washington University. 2006'

Honorary?

Occupation: Aide to Samuel Blake - United States Junior Senator from Georgia

Hobbies and Interests: None listed - *Hmm, I love a mystery*

Address: 1450 D Street NW Apt. P – 2 *A Penthouse?* He wondered

Washington, DC 20057

Telephone: Samuel Blake (202) 993-4529

Home: (202) 997-2666

Cell Phone: ?

Parents: Walter G. and Edith J. Purness

Parent's Occupations: (Walter) Lobbyist for The Virginia Coal Collective, Inc. (Edith) Homemaker

Siblings: None

Julie was her usual efficient self, which came as no surprise to Alex. He had to remember not to allude to too much information when he next met Durbah so as not to appear that he was investigating her. But then again there was a part of him that didn't want to play any games of deception with this woman. He knew somewhere in the back of his mind that he would immediately admit to checking up on her the moment that their eyes met once again. There was something about her that he couldn't quite see clearly, but he knew that it was an extremely endearing quality. He felt that he would be grateful for any kind of further contact that he might have with her. It was remarkable the hold that she had on him almost as though they shared some intimate bond that went well beyond romance or sexuality. All he knew for sure was that he was having a hard time crystallizing his thoughts ever since a short episode in traffic court where he conversed with Durbah Purness three short days before. He dialed her home number as he was getting in the elevator car. She answered on the first ring and said, "I thought we might get together for a cocktail this evening."

"That's curious," said Alex, "I thought I called you."

"Yes, I know," she said smokily. Alex could hear her slow and even breaths through the phone.

"No, seriously, you know who this is, don't you?"

"Alex Jansen. Traffic court litigant at large," she said.

Alex laughed and said, "It's just that I thought I had the idea to ring you up. I thought this phone conversation was my idea."

"Of course, you did."

"You're saying it was yours," he stated rather than asked.

"What have you been thinking about lately," she posed.

"Excuse me?"

"Something has been on your mind that is stealing your attention. You're having trouble concentrating on your work." She said it as a declaration rather than there was any question about it.

"Well, I suppose you're right."

"And what have you been thinking about, Alex?"

He liked the sound of his name falling from her lips. He imagined her face as she spoke it and it excited him.

"You."

"And why do you suppose that is?" she pressed with a downward pitch of a velvet voice.

"I have a feeling that you're going to tell me."

"It's because I planted a seed."

"A seed?"

"In your mind. Remember the last moment we saw each other? I was leaving the courtroom and our eyes met briefly."

"Indeed, I do."

"I planted a suggestion that perhaps you might like to get in touch with me again."

"And do you always get what you want?" asked Alex playfully.

"Every time."

"Where would you like to meet?"

"Actually, I was thinking of a road trip."

"Oh, really?"

"There is a bed and breakfast with a wonderful view. It's on Grandfather Mountain in North Carolina near the Tennessee border. I'd love to get away from the city and I was thinking Banner Elk or Beech Mountain for a day or so."

"A bed and breakfast?" asked Alex, his mind trying to match the speed of the conversation and falling considerably short of the mark.

"That's right."

"You're saying we should stay over? In North Carolina?"

"Oh, yes."

"Separate rooms?" he asked sensing he already knew the answer.

"Not on your life." She broke the connection. *Three weeks,* she thought. *Not an awful lot of time to make my case to the sensor, Jonah. He said that no Earth dwellers could accompany the exodus without a meticulous screening. Would Alex pass their examination?* She felt it was strange how she could have forgotten about it for a short while. The news of Siren and the exodus is the most astounding thing that had ever happened in her life, and yet . . . she had forgotten. *Something's changed,* she thought. *I've change. I've changed for the better.*

Alex reached the ground floor of his office building and stood in the elevator until the doors closed again, the elevator car remaining there waiting for someone to come along and push the up button. He shook his head to clear what cobwebs he could and pushed the door open button. When the door opened, he made his way out to the parking garage and walked over to his car. He pushed the auto-lock button on his key ring, opened the door and climbed inside. The first thing he did was enter Durbah's address into his Garvin GPS on the center console and start the car. The engine sang with an expected whine being the high performance BMW that she was. He would put her through her paces on the way to Durbah's apartment. North Carolina was a three hour drive, and he was hoping that there would actually be a dinner engagement before he fell into the arms of a woman whom he had only briefly met once before. If he weren't weaving through the hectic downtown traffic of Washington, D.C., he might have occasion to glance in the rearview mirror and see two dilated pupils, the definite result of a dopamine high.

That was the strangest phone conversation I've ever had in my life, he reflected. *I called her, didn't I? She answered on the first ring and knew who had called her. This was not the result of caller ID. She had no idea of my phone number, yet there was no mistaking the surety and confidence that she emitted knowing exactly who had called her and why. Here was a woman who knew what she wanted and made no bones about going after it. It should be unsettling, but somehow it wasn't. It merely seemed very natural and straight forward almost as though the world would be a much better place if people could act on their feelings as honestly and clearly as this remarkable woman.*

~

Chapter Nineteen

Charles Donovan woke the next day and realized that he came away from the mountain retreat with something he hadn't quite bargained for, that being the complete recollection of the weekend under the mountain. For the first time, he saw Durbah Purness as the beautiful creature that she was. He remembered her from the baths. He remembered how the water glistened on her skin and how the vapors of steam rose from her lovely form when she emerged and reached for a towel. Durbah Purness was as beautiful as any goddess throughout time. *How could I have missed that until this very morning?* he wondered. On a number of occasions, he had worked side by side with Durbah and never gave the slightest thought to how she looked. *I must have been blind,* he reasoned. Blinded by her was all he could come up with. It was as though she could turn her beauty on and off, but that didn't make any sense at all. Something was different this time. Somehow *he* was different.

Now, at last, he could recall his whole experience at the alpha omega conference under the mountain. He also knew that on the occasions when he left the retreat without being able to recall the weekend, he was leaving with an agenda that was not his own. He was a tool of a society of people from a distant world. Now, he was no longer infused with an imperative to perpetuate the hostile nature of mankind for power through possession of fossil fuels. *What a ridiculous concept,* he thought. Blood for oil. Human history is littered with countless examples of war for the sake of war. It was power for the sake of power, and never with respect to the judicious use thereof.

Charles reflected on his position with Senator Williams. He thought that the senator was a kind man and somewhat of a war hero; however, he wasn't sure he was in any kind of agreement with his mission. Senator Williams, though resigned from his commission, was a soldier's soldier. He believed in the deployment of armed forces in the interest of expansionist government. He would like nothing more than for The United States government to annex a country in the Middle East.

He was outspoken during the Gulf War of the early nineties about how Kuwait should become one of the United States territories like Puerto Rico. Funny how people like the senator never suggest the same for places like Somalia. Now that Charles retained his memory of the alpha omega weekend, he could see clearly how out of place his life had been. He always felt that he didn't quite fit in and now he had the answer why. He hated that he had to endure this miserable planet for at least another three weeks. But sometime in the next month he would be off to his home planet of Siren. He would be leaving with Durbah Purness, who he truly saw for the first time. She was such a beautiful person that he was amazed his mind could be clouded not to notice for so long. But now his destiny was taking shape. Their destiny was coming together in a bond much stronger than any Earthly agendas. *But what about her new friend, Alex Jansen?* He wasn't sure why, but suddenly he felt something akin to ill-will directed toward a mere human. It was a sensation that he had never experienced before. It was always a simple matter to manipulate people to do *his* will and make them think that it was *their* idea. But now he would be rid of that nonsense. He had some loose ends to tie up before the exodus.

For some reason he wasn't quite sure of, he was able to circumvent the bath with the descending crystal that obscured his true identity. Jonah and the other *sensors* instructed all the sirens to be immersed in the baths prior to their return to the society of mankind. They didn't want the sirens to remember who they were or where they were going during human contact. *Was this new feeling of ill will part of what they were worried about?* Charles would never want harm to come to Alex Jansen; however, he was very sure of one thing: *Alex was not suitable company for Durbah Purness. She actually had the mistaken impression that he was somehow evolving to the level of the sirens. She would learn the error of her ways when she was exposed to his dark nature, which all mankind is plagued with.* But there was one thing that he had to admit to admiring in humans. It was their passion. Sirens were logical and peaceful but also decidedly lacked passion. For the most part, it was a fair trade off. Passion often leads to heartache and distress as well as bliss. To be spared the throes of passion was to have contentment. Somehow that wasn't enough for the person he was quickly changing into. Indeed Charles was changing and he liked the new blood that flowed through his veins. He liked longing for the company of Durbah. He liked recalling his time with her in the baths and longing for it to happen again soon. He wondered when they would be called into the mountain again. The first *space/time exchange* to Siren was due to happen in three weeks. Could he wait that long to see her again? He didn't think so.

~

Chapter Twenty

Sarah Poole left Brad Early at Barnacle Bill's after two drinks. She enjoyed his company and accepted his invitation to dinner and a movie on Friday night. *That's a first,* she thought. *I purposely charmed that poor young man, which isn't at all like me. And I liked it. Why did I fight it for so long? I know I can get very used to this feeling, and I'm glad that it's finally happening to me. But why? What has changed?* Then it dawned on her. The thin layers of her memory's veil obscuring the mountain retreat were lifted from her mind. *The planet Siren,* she thought contentedly. *That has such a pleasant sound to it.* There was also something else that had a pleasant sound just now filling her mind. It was the sound of the name Matthew Winter. *Was it someone to love? Someone I loved in a past life perhaps? Could it have been on Siren?* She wondered.

Mrs. Eldridge was expecting her for dinner, and she was looking forward to the beef Stroganoff. There were quite a few animals who would celebrate Sarah's return as well as Mrs. Eldridge. Brad Early was clearly taken aback by the feelings he was having for Sarah. He prided himself on being a ladies' man and was usually quite successful in his approach to meeting new women. But his experience with Sarah was something entirely new to him. He surrendered himself to her caprice as he never had with another woman. Being with Sarah was its own reward. Whatever excuse he had to spend time with her was fine with him. He was looking forward to dinner and a movie, but if she had asked him to trim the bushes on her landlady's property, he would have been equally excited just to have the opportunity to please her. Magic was a word that came to mind regarding Sarah. He had gone to Barnacle Bill's to hook up with a date; however, when Sarah left him for the evening, that prospect suddenly became the last thing on his mind. He felt that anyone he might meet would pale in comparison to the enchanting goddess he had happened upon. He made a mental note to be on his best behavior when he was around her. Surprisingly, prayer was even considered to be a part of his near future activities. Although he was never an avid reader, he would be the first in line to get a library card in the morning at the Bar Harbor Public Library.

Sarah was tickled to find that news travels fast in the animal world. When she and Mrs. Eldridge took their dinners out to the deck overlooking the harbor, the animals started arriving like a choreographed production number of a Hollywood musical. They all filed in as peaceful as could be and sidled up to Sarah to get any attention she might afford them. Mrs. Eldridge was bursting with pleasure as she served her beloved Sarah saying, "I'm so glad you came back to me, dear."

Sarah felt the beginning of a tear coming to her eye as she said, "There just didn't seem to be any place else where I belong."

"That's odd," said Mrs. Eldridge, "is that a snake?" I didn't know they could climb stairs," she added with a confused chuckle. Sarah was torn by her connection to her home in Bar Harbor and her soon to be home on the other side of the sun. The realization was so incredible that she was having a hard time digesting it. She had to call her parents. She was sure that they came away from the mountain with the same vision that she had. They, too, could now see their true origins and knew the fantastic future that was before them. Surely they would choose to go. *Wouldn't they?* She felt sorrow for her friend and landlady. She felt sorrow for Brad Early, too, and all of those she might have to leave behind.

What Mrs. Eldridge couldn't know was that Sarah would be leaving again in three weeks, and that this time it would be for good. Sarah had a future nearly one hundred and eighty million miles away. She would try to be on the first *space/time exchange* to Siren beginning the great exodus of four hundred eighty-some people finally going to their home planet. But something had changed in her recently. She was normally very cool, calm and collected and carried herself accordingly. She found herself excited in ways that she was not accustomed to. Brad Early had excited an ember in her that could easily grow to a flame with the slightest encouragement. It seemed that he was in a position to fill a void that she didn't know even existed until a short 24 hours ago.

Sarah was definitely a different girl than the one who entered the retreat under the mountain in West Virginia. And then there was the experience of waking up in a hotel along I-95 and having no recollection of ever checking in. That was definitely a first. But one thing stood out in her mind above all other considerations, and that was that she had only so much time to enjoy all the pleasures of life that she had been denying herself. Perhaps a lover was one of those things. Perhaps Brad Early was a likely candidate. But there was also a feeling she couldn't quite let go of that he was to be merely a surrogate replacement of someone who she truly belonged with, although she couldn't get her conscious mind around the identity of whom she was missing. Somehow it was just a name. All of her experience with the person connected to the name had been under the mountain in West Virginia. She had never known him outside the retreat. *Is that why my mind can't give him substance?*

Life was changing for Sarah Poole and she was ready to embrace it with all her sensibilities. She was becoming someone new and for the first time in her life she had the feeling of embracing a passionate self that she had been editing out of existence. She had a sense of mourning for what her life had not given her and was determined to let herself freely feel this new persona and have the courage to explore every new feeling she could.

When she went to the library the following morning, Mr. Seymour broke into tears upon seeing her and asked, "Tell me you have come back to us, Sarah."

"Unless you've replaced me."

"Impossible," he said wiping his eyes with the back of his hands, "there is only one of you, my dear, and I'm thrilled to say that you're all ours." A large seagull landed on the window sill of an open window and was considering the risk reward aspects of actually entering the building.

~

Chapter Twenty-one

Alex Jansen had just turned down the fourteen hundred block of Georgetown's D Street NW, when he spotted Durbah just stepping through the door of the 1450 brownstone apartment. She was carrying a small suitcase and a large purse hung from her shoulder on a long strap. Alex noted that a pair of snow skis stood beside her leaning up against the building. She walked to the curb and leaned over as Alex was just pulling up.

"I don't see a rack, Alex. Do you usually rent your skis?"

It then dawned on Alex why Durbah wanted to travel all the way to North Carolina to stay in a bed and breakfast. *Of course*, he thought. *Beech Mountain and Banner Elk. This is a ski weekend. What did you think you were going to spend the weekend in bed?*

"Usually," he said trying to recover. "My stuff isn't tuned," referring to sharpened edges if it's icy, and waxed bottoms if it's soft snow. "It's old technology. My skis aren't parabolic and I broke a binding during my last fall, a real *yard sale*," he said referring to the disastrous condition where after a healthy *face plant*, your skis go one way, your poles go another and your body decides to go off on its own.

Durbah laughed and said, "Well, I hope you have a first aid kit."

"I have a flask."

"Close enough," she said moving to the trunk of the car and putting her bag and purse inside. "You'll have to put the back seat down or else my skis will be in our face for a hundred and eighty miles."

Alex got out of the driver's seat and opened the back door to put the back seat down, "I'm on it," he said realizing that Durbah knew he wasn't expecting her to be bringing skis.

As she got in the passenger's seat, she said, "You thought we were going to spend the weekend in bed, didn't you?"

Alex wasn't sure what to say so he didn't.

"Well, you were half right." She held him with her eyes to speak what words can never say. Alex was taken by the gold and silver flecks on the irises of her beautiful blue-green eyes. He just stared at her for a full thirty seconds until Durbah released him and turned to look forward through the windshield. She felt a little guilty and at the same time elated that she could have such an effect on him. *Would it be the same on Siren?* she wondered. *What effect will that world have on him? And what will I feel for him?* Her woolgathering wasn't getting them to North Carolina, so she made a conscious effort to mute her charms for the time being.

"Earth to Alex, time to blast off," she said chuckling.

"I'm sorry," he said, "I just couldn't tear my eyes away from something beautiful."

"Now who's the charmer? Drive." She smiled and tucked a strand of her silky blond hair behind her left ear. "I hope there's snow," was all she said for the next ten minutes. Alex didn't need any distractions getting out of the hustle of the

Washington's poor excuse for roadways. The beltway was kind for once, and they found themselves on I-95 South in less than half an hour.

~

Chapter Twenty-two

Shelly Simon was seeing the wheels of progress moving rather quickly after Alyssa Grant had her organize a luncheon in her honor to announce her candidacy for the 21st District City Counsel of Washington, D.C. She would be effectively running unopposed due to the fact that the incumbent councilman was nearly ninety years old and would soon go the way of the dinosaur. His constituency was leery of being in the position of a mid- term election in order to replace him, so he had received their last endorsement for re-election. Alyssa Grant had only one bit of advice for Shelly, "Just be yourself, Dear. Give them a chance to like you." What Congresswoman Grant failed to understand was that Shelly possessed a magnetism that would all but obscure any attention she would hope to gain for herself. Both the men *and the women* at the luncheon were enamored by Shelly to the point of the ridiculous.

Two waiters jockeyed with a busboy who was constantly trying to keep her water glass full. Even the head chef decided to make a rare appearance at her table and deliver the current specials of the day. When Shelly rose to go to the ladies' room and powder her nose, all the men in the room stood instantly by their chairs, looking on intently with their napkins in their hands. They seemed to have a pained expression on their faces, which mirrored their worst fear that perhaps Shelly was leaving.

"Oh, my God," was all Alyssa Grant could manage, and she didn't suffer any great pains to keep her voice down. "Relax, boys," she said shaking her head, "she just has to do wee wee." There was a scattering of laughter around the room when the men again seated themselves. Congresswoman Grant leaned over to the woman seated next to her and said quietly, "If they stand up when she comes back, I'm gonna' puke." She had created a monster. Little did she realize that the monster would be entering a *space/time exchange chamber* and be out of her bottle-colored hair in a short twenty-some days. But Shelly suddenly knew. She knew she would soon be receiving another alpha omega letter and be returning to the mountain. She knew that at that time she would receive the timetable necessary to realize the fruition of her exodus back to Siren. If she committed to the exodus, she would be assigned a date of departure. She knew that sometime in the next month she would be going home. She didn't expect to be one of the first to leave in only a week. It would give her plenty of opportunity to say good-bye to good friends, old friends and perhaps even Congresswoman Alyssa Grant.

The men didn't rise again when Shelly came back into the room, but all eyes were upon her. They watched her every move and didn't bother to hide the fact that they would treasure any eye contact she might afford them. Most of the women were very relaxed and understanding regarding the behavior of their husbands and significant others. They, too, were enchanted by her and let their minds wander off to places where there was a certainty that the world would seem like a better place just to be with her. Her enchantment went well beyond any semblance of sex or lustful behavior. What everyone in the room was feeling could be described as an urgency regarding her good will. Everyone wanted Shelly to succeed in her political aspirations and was hopeful that she might one day represent them. At that very moment, even Alyssa Grant would have surrendered her seat in Congress to her if there were any way in the world to make it happen.

Matthew Winter arrived at (CAI), the international airport in Cairo, Egypt at 6:10 P.M. on Tuesday evening after a layover in Frankfurt, Germany, of two and a half hours. Upon deplaning, he made eye contact with the pretty young flight attendant who apologized for waking him during the flight. She seemed to blush slightly as she said, "Thank you for flying Egypt Air. Have a nice stay in Cairo."

He said knowingly, "Thanks, I will." He noticed her turning away briefly from the next passenger deplaning and looking back at him as he walked up the ramp. He couldn't help smiling. *Is it Joanne I'm smiling about?* He wondered. *I thought so, but now I'm not so sure.* Yes, he missed her; however, he wasn't sure he wanted to ride out to the dig on that particular evening. Instead, he took a cab into downtown Cairo and told the cabbie to drop him off at the Hilton Hotel. He paid the fare and went into the lobby and walked to the front desk.

A pretty young Egyptian woman was talking on a small headset that had a microphone traveling across her left cheek from her ear half way to her lips. When Matthew held her eyes with his, she seemed to lose focus on her conversation and then caught herself. “Yes, that’s right,” she said into the mic, “the hotel is booked full, but if they have any cancellations, they’ll be sure to call.” She looked at Matthew and seemed a bit lost in his eyes. He knew from the conference under the mountain the effect that he was having on her and that she was concentrating on the little gold and silver flecks on the irises at the edge of his corneas. He decided not to make them fade away just yet and held her gaze musing that were he not careful, he might bore a hole in the back of her head.

“Full,” she managed sleepily. She shook her head briefly.

“Excuse me,” said Matthew clearing his eyes and letting her off the hook.

“The woman cleared her throat and seemed to straighten the tie she was not wearing, “The hotel is fully booked,” her woolgathering turning to wit gathering.

“But they might have a cancellation, correct?”

“You can be put on a list, Sir, but they can’t guaran . . .”

“They might have *two* cancellations, isn’t that correct?”

“Yes, that is possi . . .”

“Or three or four. Here’s what I propose you do. Just give me a room, and I won’t check in until 11:00 tonight. I’ll leave my bag in your lost and found. If they get a cancellation, I check in, and you’ve booked a room that otherwise would have been a vacancy.”

The woman seemed to be trying to shake cobwebs from her mind as she said, “And what if they do not have any cancellations?”

“Why, then I’ll just have to spend the night with you.”

“Room 314,” she said sliding a card key across the desk.

~

Chapter Twenty-three

Brad Early was early to pick up Sarah Poole at Mrs. Eldridge's house on Friday evening. She was dressed in close fitting designer jeans, a thin white turtleneck sweater and a light brown leather coat with ermine trim. Her silky dark hair fell across her shoulders and her soft pink lip gloss highlighted the blush of her high cheekbones.

"You look fabulous," he offered.

"You're not so bad yourself," she took in the total package and liked what she saw. He was in light brown slacks with a fresh crease, speaking to the fact that he owned an iron, and a dark blue sports coat over a light blue oxford button down shirt. His longish brown hair was swept back at the temples and showed the slightest hint of gray. She was pleased that he had no facial hair because why cover up something pleasing to look at.

"Where are you taking me?"

"Tired of lobster, yet?"

"Are you kidding? I work at the library."

"Don't tell me no one's ever asked you out," he said knowingly.

"On occasion, but it's usually something like all-you-can-eat crabs. I'm not a big fan of crabs. Too much work."

"You took the words right out of my mouth," he told her. "How do you feel about lobster Newburg."

"You know the way to a girl's heart."

"I'm just following the signs."

Alex and Durbah drove the first hour trading stories about high school and college. He had gone to Penn State and she to Georgetown so there was no semblance of a rivalry as if that foolishness could ever rear its ugly head. *This woman is no nonsense,* he reasoned from her direct behavior toward him. It was a refreshing change to cut through all the games of the dating scene. *Is that what this is, a date?* It seemed that they had skipped the dating ritual and had somehow evolved into something more . . . existential for lack of a better term.

"So your father works for the coal collective," he stated rather than a question.

"Very good."

"My secretary, Julie, is very good."

"And what else did she have to report?"

"Well, you haven't done any hard time as far as she could tell."

Alex loved the sound of her laugh and she said, "It's really not fair. All I know about you is that you are a lawyer and a skier."

"And how did you find out that I ski?"

"You said she was very good," she chuckled.

"What? Not Julie, the traitor," he said with false anger.

"She played a little trick on you. The first thing she did was call me. We've known each other for about a year now. How else do you think she found out all the things on her report?"

"Women are devious, you know that?" He shook his head.

"Someone has to be." Her grin was contagious.

At precisely 11:00 P.M., Matthew Winter walked out of the cocktail lounge of the Cairo Hilton and approached the front desk. The beautiful woman named Alankha seemed to be ending her shift and handing the responsibilities of the desk over to a dark young Egyptian boy with a very thin mustache. When she saw Matthew sidle up to get her attention, she said, "Well, I'm sorry sir, but we haven't gotten any cancellations, and we're still booked full."

The young Egyptian boy raised his eyebrows excitedly and said, "But Miss Alankha, there were . . ."

The woman's raised palm stopped his comment in its tracks. If looks could kill, the young man would have been dead before he hit the floor. Matthew slid the card key for Room 314 over to the boy and said, "I won't be needing this."

~

Alex Jansen was curious why a woman like Durbah Purness chose to work for a man like Samuel Blake. He tried to nail the subject down, "So why Blake?" He asked out of nowhere.

"Why anyone?" she answered cryptically.

"I mean why Blake's politics. You know he's a rape-the-resources kind of guy."

"You mean he's human."

"Well, yes, he's only human, but not all humans share his agenda."

"No?"

"Not everybody is a money-hungry officer of a company like Energix."

"Ex-officer."

"OK, ex-officer. You don't side with his politics, do you?"

"And here I thought you were going to get laid tonight," she said with feigned seriousness and then broke out laughing, "You should have seen your face when I said that. It was priceless."

"OK, have your little fun," said Alex, "at my expense."

She laughed again, and it was music to his ears. God, how he loved being with her.

"Seriously, why Blake?" he asked her again pointedly.

"To pour fuel on the fire."

"What do you mean?"

"Blake only thought I worked for him. Actually, I was working for people much farther away than Georgia. By about one hundred eighty million miles."

"So you're a spy, is that it?"

"Was a spy. I don't work for Blake any longer."

"Wow, that was quick. When did you quit?"

"Monday morning."

"Any particular reason?" He glanced at her with the question in his eyes.

"It was time to move on," was all she offered.

"So where to now?"

"Oh, a nice little planet on the other side of the sun."

"Wouldn't that be nice," he said honestly.

"Be careful what you wish for."

When they reached Blowing Rock Highway in Linville, North Carolina, Durbah told Alex how to make his way up the mountain.

"I think you're really going to like it here, Alex."

"I like it already." *Being with you.*

"Grandfather Mountain is nearly 6,000 feet high and features a swinging bridge we can walk out on for an incredible view of the valley. The only thing better is coming here in October," she said.

"Because of the leaves," he declared.

"You wouldn't believe it."

They made their way up through the fog on a road winding around the mountain and came upon a charming bed and breakfast that looked every bit like a Swiss Chalet. The sign in front of the main building proudly displayed the name Missy Kathryn's Hideaway – A Bed & Breakfast. Cable TV – Viking Saunas. After three hours of highway driving, this seemed to be just the place where Alex could relax and unwind and hopefully get in a good day on Beech Mountain, sixteen miles away. There was a fresh three inches of snow on the ground, and Alex was enjoying the reddish chill on Durbah's otherwise ivory complexion. The cold seemed to agree with her, and he was thankful that he was so easily talked into the weekend diversion from business-as-usual around the nation's capital. He was quickly realizing just how close he was to retirement, at least from his everyday practice. His present circumstance spoke volumes about just what he had been missing in life. He had been missing the company of a good woman, not that Brianna was not a good woman. She was a good law partner and the mother of his child, but ex-wives don't tend to be very affectionate company for one reason or another. Still, he would miss her and from his present state of mind, a little sooner than he had originally planned.

Alex was disappointed to see a No-Vacancy sign hanging from a yardarm just outside the front entrance to Missy Kathryn's. Durbah opened the car door and said, "Go ahead and stretch your legs, Alex. I'll check us in." *That's funny,* he thought. *Didn't she notice the sign?* A few minutes later Durbah emerged with an attractive young woman in tow who sported a name tag, which read Alice Reed – Manager. She walked up to the car and reached out her hand, "I'm Alice, Mr. Jansen. My mother is Kathryn who owns the place. I'm her whipping girl." The woman laughed giving Durbah a warm hug. "We're so glad that you're staying with us. Please let us know it there's anything you need. Anything, OK? Lift tickets, or a late night snack, just name it."

"Well, thank you very much, Alice. You certainly make a person feel welcome."

"We want you to feel at home, Mr. Jansen. In fact, we wish we could see more of Durbah. We feel that this *is* her home." Alice smiled and waved as she retreated to the office of Missy Kathryn's Hideaway. Alex was a bit confused and said, "What is it about you that puts everybody in the palm of your hand?"

"I try to be nice to people."

"Oh, it's more than that," he ventured. "You seem to have people wrapped around your little finger. All of your fingers, for that matter."

"Oh?" she asked innocently, "was there anyplace else you wanted to be."

"No, I guess not," was all he could say.

Matthew Winter followed the beautiful Alankha to the bank of elevators off the lobby of the Cairo Hilton Hotel. She pressed the up button and when the car opened, she led Matthew inside and took his suitcase and placed it beside them on the floor. She then reached up to him with her full sensuous lips and took hold of his, wrapping her arms tightly around him. He could feel her hips pressing into him, and when she broke away from the kiss, her breath was a hot wind of passion against his neck. She was clearly a startling beauty, and Matthew was silently applauding his decision to put off his trek to the dig until the next morning. He placed his hands on her ribs just below her breasts and held her out in front of him to take in her beautiful coffee-and-cream complexion, "So you live here," he asked. "In the hotel?"

"Just for tonight," she said as she pressed the highest button.

~

Chapter Twenty-four

Charles Donovan couldn't get his mind off of Durbah Purness. Something changed in him – something snapped. He knew it was not only the retreat under the mountain. He was being directed by and soon to be acting on urges that were altogether new to him. He was never preoccupied with matters of the heart in the past. He always thought that relationships were for losers. *You get what you want and then you get out,* was his usual state of mind. *What kind of future was there in building a web of strings that tie you down and hamper your every move. Better to be free to do whatever you choose.* This had always been his hard and fast rule . . . until. Charles imagined a future with Durbah on a new and exciting world. They could have fresh experiences together and learn all the secrets of the home world that they never knew existed until a short time ago. *A future with someone to love, finally. Someone worthy of my love,* he thought. But would he maintain the passion he felt for Durbah on Siren? Something deep inside him knew the answer. *There is peace on Siren. There is harmony on Siren. There is contentment on Siren. But . . . is there also passion?* He wondered. Is eternal vanilla the price you have to pay to live in a world full of ice cream? Somehow he knew in his heart he would miss his Rocky Road. And so would Durbah. She didn't realize what she was bargaining for. There was no question in her mind or her words that she would be going to Siren. She would soon be taking that awareness away from the mountain retreat due to an accident of the heavens. She would have an awareness of her true home and her true nature. She would carry that with her knowing full well that she will soon leave this planet and all of the conflict well behind her. *But what else will she leave behind?*

Charles felt that he now had a mission in life much more important than any directive he was given by his *sensor*. The strings he had pulled and the influence he exerted on Senator Williams' potential opponents were small potatoes compared with saving a beautiful creature like Durbah Purness from making a horrible mistake. He had to save her. He placed a call to Senator Blake's office as soon as he reached his home.

"Senator Blake's office," came the cheerful voice of the receptionist.

"This is Charles Donovan. I'm trying to get in touch with Durbah Purness, the senator's aide."

"Oh, I'm sorry, Mr. Donovan. She terminated her employment with the senator."

"You mean, she quit? Just like that?" he asked perplexed.

"All I can tell you is that Ms. Purness doesn't work for Senator Blake anymore."

"Can you tell me how to get in touch with her?" he asked knowing the answer.

"She didn't give us any notice of a further position, but I'm sure I'm not even supposed to be talking about this. Can I give you the senator's new aide?"

"Forget it," said Donovan. He was afraid he would run into a dead end and that's exactly what happened. He thought he might be able to use some of his leverage in his own office where he worked for Senator Williams. He dialed the number from his cell. For reasons he wasn't quite sure of he was leery of having the record of the call on the phone company's records.

"Senator Williams' office," came the receptionist's reply.

"Jill, it's Charles. Is the senator in?"

"No, Charles, I'm afraid he's not. He won't be in until Monday morning, and he's incommunicado. Sport fishing off the Cape."

"Come on, Jill, it's me. I know he gave you the boat's emergency cell number."

"Is this an emergency, Charles?" she taunted.

He thought for a few seconds too long before saying, "Yes."

"Sorry, Charles. You know the drill."

Donovan pressed the off button on his phone in disgust. *That little twelve dollar-an-hour bitch,* he thought. *Screw em,'* he decided. He had enough money saved until the exodus if he decided to actually go. And if he decided to stay on this miserable planet, his new knowledge of who he was and his potential influence over people would make living here like shooting fish in a barrel. He might even become President if it suited his fancy, but he knew in his heart what he really wanted. *Who* he really wanted. It was a sobering thought that he actually *wanted anything* for the first time in his whole life. *They say we always want what we can't have. Only on Earth,* he mused. *On Siren I'm not sure I'll really want anything or anyone as much as I do on this miserable rock in space.* He had some thinking to do.

~

When the elevator reached the twenty-fourth floor of the Cairo Hilton, the doors opened onto a landing that had only two doors. The hotel had four presidential suites on the top floor and Alankha had taken Matthew Winter up to 24-A. The Eastern vista of the Giza Plateau from the top floor of the Cairo Hilton was so spectacular that Matthew gained a new respect for the beauty and wonder that he had only seen from ground level at the dig. The sun had set hours before, although the night sky to the east was filled with stars so bright that he felt he could almost reach out and touch them. Instead, he touched Alankha. A fire rose in her that was so intense he was almost pulled from his feet as she all but dragged him into the large bedroom. In seconds she was standing naked before him with her eyes glassed over and the lids half closed. She seemed to be in some kind of sensual trance that was at first unsettling to Matthew. He wasn't a prude, and hardly a virgin, although he hadn't ever had an encounter that equaled this one's sense of urgency and selfless abandon. She was, for lack of a gentler term, an animal. She fiercely tore at his clothes, nearly pulling the buttons off his shirt, and dropped to her knees frantically loosening his belt and freeing him from the confines of his slacks and undershorts. Matthew had the urge to say, "*slow down,*" but he couldn't bring the words to his lips. Instead, he brought Alankha. They made furious, if not passionate, love for more than an hour. They then lay spent on the bed, she straddling him trying to catch her breath as their bodies cooled with the evaporation of the sheen on their glistening forms. Her panting was warm against his chest and punctuated with short phrases, which seemed almost apologetic, as though she alone were to blame for their wanton expression of lust. Between gasps, the words escaped her lips, "I'm sorry, Matthew," she struggled for another breath, "there was no way we could have avoided this." She paused for more air to fill her oxygen- starved lungs.

"What are you talking about?" he asked trying to fill his own lungs with sorely needed air.

"We had to have this," she breathed, "this night together."

Matthew was confused as to what the beautiful Alankha was alluding to as though there was some otherworldly purpose to their chance encounter.

"Why do you say that?" he asked her.

"We had to have this night together to hold each other in a firestorm of need." She took three more breaths before she continued. "To douse the fire that would otherwise haunt us if we denied ourselves the pleasure."

"I hear what you're saying, Alankha," speaking her name for the first time that he learned from the boy addressing her at the desk in the lobby, "and I have thoroughly enjoyed every minute we have had together, but I don't understand why you say we had to have this."

"It is because," she raised herself on her forearms away from his chest and looked at him with a blazing intensity that belied the spent energy they both were feeling. At that moment, Matthew could see the suggestion of gold and silver flecks in the corners of her beautiful eyes and she continued, "It is because we may not have this on Siren."

The full realization hit Matthew all at once, and he knew that Alankha, although breathtaking, was no ordinary person. He knew at once that she was a siren as well and that she would be leaving Earth to travel to the other side of the sun. It made perfect sense once he thought about it. The sirens originated from Egypt in the first place. He had learned that they first came to the Giza plateau, which was only a twenty minute cab ride from where they now lay atop the Cairo Hilton Hotel.

The *sensor*, Jonah, had told them at the retreat that a mere twelve sirens were placed on Earth nearly five thousand years ago. Through the centuries their number only grew to four-hundred-eighty-six, which spoke to the fact that they reproduced very sparingly and judiciously. In addition, there was another reason for their sparse numbers over so long a period of proliferation. The siren lineage is passed along by the females alone. They rarely mated with their fellow sirens, although Matthew knew from his own parents that there were indeed exceptions. He was the progeny of one such conception. He also had an atavistic awareness of another siren that he was linked with somehow. It was someone who also is the child of a man and a woman who are both sirens. There wasn't an image that he could bring forth in his mind, but it was someone whom he was sure that he had had direct contact with. There was not an image, but a name. It was a very beautiful name. Much more beautiful than the name Alankha with whom he now had the pleasure to embrace. For reasons he was not quite sure of, he felt that the most beautiful name in the world was Sarah.

Matthew looked around the room at the sumptuous furnishings of silk pillows and satin sheets. He noticed that a wet bar on the side of the room had an ice bucket and full bottles of liquor and wine instead of the traditional hospitality bar one would expect in a hotel room. Indeed, the *Presidential Suites* were not for everybody. He realized that only the very rich or the very privileged would ever see the inside of one these rooms. He said to Alankha as he gazed around appreciatively, "I guess working here definitely has its strong points."

She looked at him slyly and said, "Whatever gave you the idea that I work here?"

~

Chapter Twenty-five

Alex Jansen and Durbah Purness were seated at a small table in the corner of the dining hall at Missy Kathryn's Hideaway. There was a linen tablecloth underneath fine china and Alex noticed that the tableware was solid sterling silver. *Very trusting,* he thought at first, and then he realized that theirs was the only table where that was the case. All the other tables had plain silverware setups, and their candle holders were old wine bottles whereas theirs was undoubtedly Lenox china.

"They seem to take very good care of you here."

"They're very nice people," Durbah took a sip of her wine.

"Obviously you've stayed here many times before."

"That would seem obvious, I suppose," she said cryptically.

"How do you know Kathryn? A friend of the family?"

"Oh, you mean the owner? We've never met."

Alex was a little confused by that statement, but decided to let it go. He figured that she was probably a good friend of Alice who met them when they checked in. There was something still bothering him about their earlier conversation so he said, "Durbah, do you mind if I ask you a question?"

"Not at all."

"I'm not trying to talk shop, but something is puzzling me."

"Ex-shop," she said. "I told you that I don't work in Washington anymore."

"All right then, ex-shop."

"Go ahead and ask your question."

"It's really nothing, but I was wondering what you meant when you said that your job was *pouring fuel on the fire*."

"Oh, that's something that I'm not proud of, but perhaps I should explain myself since you seem like such a straightforward man. I have been an unwitting accomplice of a rather large master plan. Or, I should say, almost unwitting."

"Well now, that's as clear as mud," he said mockingly.

"I suppose I should offer more than that. Let me try to explain. Senator Blake is involved in an offshore project, which hopes to bring ashore millions of metric tons of natural gas in the state of Georgia. They could pressurize the gas offshore at the drilling platform and ship it into port; however, his company Energix has determined that a pipeline would be much more efficient due to the fact that shipping burns nearly as much fuel as they hope to bring ashore."

"I'm familiar with the proposal, Durbah. I even worked on the brief of Senator Williams' ban and the subsequent moratorium to lift it. In fact it was my advice to the senator that there was no legal precedent for the ban."

"Then you did my planet a great service," she said simply.

"Hmm," he said lightly, "your planet, huh. You take this stuff kind of seriously, don't you?"

"Not anymore." She took another sip of her wine. Part of her wanted to derail his line of questioning and part of her wanted to get it out in the open. She then added, "I think that now my people will stop interfering."

"Your people?"

"The people of Siren."

"You are one mysterious lady."

"And do you like mysteries?" she asked and allowed herself to startle him with her eyes.

Alex again noticed the suggestion of gold and silver in her eyes being reflected by the candle in front of them. He then said, "I seem to be losing my appetite for food, Durbah."

"Nonsense," she said and released him from her charms.

He shook his head briefly and said, "It must be the altitude, but I feel a little lightheaded here."

"Yes, it's the altitude. You get used to it."

"We're over a mile up, you said."

"That's right. We're soon to join *the mile high club*."

Alex laughed and said, "So that's why you dragged me down here. And here I thought it was for the skiing."

"There's always an ulterior motive. You should know that by now."

"Well, let's just say I let myself be bamboozled."

"You have no idea," she said. She planted the suggestion of food in his mind and asked, "How's your appetite now?"

"I'm famished. What's good here?"

"I'm not really sure."

~

Brad Early took Sarah Poole to a restaurant on the harbor called The Captain's Table. The walls were adorned with fishing nets and floats of all colors attached to the edges. There were lobster traps hung under criss-crossed harpoons and the paintings were all either seascapes or high seas adventure scenes. Moby Dick was seen sounding in one of them with the small boats rising out of the water in his tremendous wake. Another painting depicted Hemmingway's *The Old Man and the Sea* where an ancient Cuban stood next to a small boy on the shoreline looking down on the carcass of what once was a magnificent blue marlin. They ordered drinks at the bar while waiting for a table to open up. The wait was to be a little over half an hour.

No sooner had they settled themselves at the bar on the high swivel chairs and reached for the pretzels, when the hostess walked up behind Brad and tapped him on the shoulder.

"Your table is right this way, Sir," she said gesturing toward an adjoining room full of eager diners engaged in lively conversation, some of them sporting lobster bibs.

"I thought there was a wait," said Brad confused.

The hostess ignored his comment and said, "Your waitress will be with you soon. Would you like another drink from the bar?"

Brad and Sarah looked at each other and then to their nearly full glasses. Brad said, "No thanks, we're fine."

The hostess retreated and Brad and Sarah sat quietly for a moment taking in the atmosphere of the restaurant. Brad noticed a waitress standing next to a table about twenty feet away reciting the specials of the evening. When one of the diner's at her table asked a question, Brad heard her say, "I'm sorry, ma'am. We've just run out of Newburg."

"Bummer," said Brad sourly.

"What? What's the matter?" asked Sarah.

"I just heard the waitress say they were out of Newburg."

"Oh, that's all right," she said. "I think I'll have the scallops."

When the waitress came to their table she said, "Welcome to The Captain's Table. I'm Stephanie, and I'll be your server this evening."

"Hi, Stephanie. I hear you're out of Newberg," he said with disappointment in his voice.

"That's right," she said. "We saved the last two for you."

~

Chapter Twenty-six

Charles Donovan was not about to give up his quest to find the whereabouts of Durbah Purness. He found her number listed in the Washington area phone directory, but when he made the call, he got only her answering machine. Senator Williams' office was a dead end because Jill, the receptionist, had strict instructions not to contact the boat he was on unless it was an extreme emergency. Charles wasn't even sure why he was exploring that avenue anyway. Perhaps he thought that the senator might somehow have her cell phone number. The senator said that she had captivated him for one reason or another, and Charles was clinging to the small hope that perhaps he had acted on it. He checked the call memory of his own cell phone. At first he thought that would be a dead end as well and then he happened on the name Julie Collins.

Of course, Jansen's secretary," he remembered. *She had called our office on her lunch hour to tell us that Jansen was finished reviewing the brief. Maybe she knows where her boss is and if I'm not mistaken, Durbah is probably there as well.* He dialed the number.

"Hello," answered Julie. There was a high-pitched scratching sound across the miles into Charles's cell phone.

"Is this Julie Collins?" he asked.

"Yes, who's this?"

"My name is Charles Donovan. We spoke briefly before about some work your office was doing for Senator Williams."

"Oh, hi, Mr. Donovan. I remember. How can I help you?"

"Have I caught you at a bad time?"

"Not really. I have a few minutes, what's up?"

"I'm trying to locate your boss."

"I can't help you there, Mr. Donovan. I'm not even in Washington."

"I hear a lot of interference on the line. Our connection isn't very good."

"I'm surprised there is a connection at all," she said. "I'm a mile high on the top of a mountain."

"Oh, well, how's the snow?" he asked in an attempt to make small talk.

"They say it's a little softer than I like it, but it's better than nothing."

"What mountain are you on?"

"Beech. Near Banner Elk."

"I'd say break a leg, but I think that's for the theater."

"Shuud up?" she said with mock fury.

"I'm just kidding. Look, could you give me Mr. Jansen's cell number. I've got a question about the brief."

"I'm sorry, Mr. Donovan. That's against office policy. What I can do is take your number and try to get a message to him to call you."

"No, never mind. I guess it's nothing that can't wait till Monday. Have a good time on the mountain."

"Thanks, Mr. Donovan." Misty broke the connection. She dialed Alex Jansen's cell phone.

"Mr. Jansen, it's Julie."

Alex had just apologized to Durbah for not turning off his phone during dinner. "What's up, Julie?"

"Probably nothing, but I just got a call from Senator Williams' aide Charles Donovan."

That's odd, thought Alex. *What does he want with me? We closed our discussion of the pipeline ban days ago.* "And?" prompted Alex.

"He said he was trying to get in touch with you. Asked for your cell number."

"And what did you tell him?"

"I offered to get a message to you to call him instead of giving out your number."

"And what did he say then?"

"He told me to forget it. Did I do the right thing?" she asked hoping.

"Yes, Julie. That was exactly the right thing to do."

"Thanks, Mr. Jansen. I've gotta' go. We're having dinner at the lodge."

"The lodge?"

"Beech Mountain Lodge. I'm down here for some skiing."

It is indeed a small world, thought Alex Jansen. He told her, "Have a nice time, Julie." The then pressed the off button on his phone.

"Julie works on Friday night," Durbah declared rather than questioned. "That's dedication."

"She was just giving me a heads up. She's a good kid."

"I like her as well. What did she have to tell you, unless, of course, it's classified." She asked with mock seriousness.

"She said that a congressional aide was trying to reach me. Nothing important, I suppose."

"Why do you say that?"

"Well, Julie said she offered to get a message to me and he declined. Something doesn't smell right," he told her.

"What was the name of the aide?"

"Charles Donovan."

"Somehow I knew you were going to say that. He wasn't trying to get in touch with you. He was trying to find me," she said knowingly.

"What? How would he know about you and that you're with me?"

"I mentioned you to him."

"You know Charles Donovan?"

"Not well, but I've worked alongside him. We have something in common."

"You mean besides working for congressmen, right?"

"You catch on fast, but not fast enough," she said taking his hand in hers.

"Then I shouldn't be jealous?"

"We really need to talk."

~

When the waitress at The Captain's Table left Brad and Sarah with their order, he said to her, "That's pretty weird. I distinctly heard that other waitress say they were out of lobster Newburg, and yet we just ordered two of them."

"Happens to me all the time," she said mysteriously.

"What happens?"

"Good luck. Being in the right place at the right time. Maybe that's why I'm sitting here with you right now."

"Well that's a very nice thing to say. I hope I don't disappoint you," said Brad drinking in her beauty. He felt he could just sit and stare at her all night long except that that would definitely creep her out.

"No more than I will disappoint you," she said sadly.

"What does that mean? Do you turn into a frog at midnight?"

"I don't want to spoil the evening, Brad. Let's just forget it."

"What? You can't just drop a bomb like that and say forget it. How are you going to disappoint me?" he asked with a plaintive voice.

"I have to leave . . . the area. Maybe soon," she said.

"What? You're moving?" *Man do I have lousy timing*, he thought.

"Where are you going?"

"Someplace very far away, but not for a while, maybe even a month, but eventually I'll have to go."

"But we could write or something, right?"

"Sure," she said. She didn't care to tell him what he didn't need to know. She felt that it would be important not to get too close to any Earth person knowing that eventually he might be left behind. Actually, it would be business as usual for Sarah, but for entirely different reasons. Before she became irradiated with the gamma rays, she didn't have intense feelings for anything human. Now that she was imbued with the intensity to feel, she must exercise extreme caution in the interest of self preservation concerning her own heart and preservation of the sirens and their mission to complete the exodus from Earth.

"So how long have you lived in Bar Harbor?" Brad was trying to change to a lighter subject.

"About six months, but it seems like much longer. I've really grown to like it here."

"You don't mind the cold?"

"I hear it's worse inland. I think the ocean helps to keep the frost out."

"Yeah, I've heard that, too. Where did you come from?"

"Most recently it was Gunnison, Colorado. Beautiful state. Golden mountains. Big sky with a lot of stars at night."

"You ever been to Sand Beach?"

"No, where is it?" she asked him raising her brow.

"Oh, about a ten minute ride from here."

"Why did you bring that up?"

"You mentioned the stars."

"You mean Sand Beach is nice at night?"

"Have I got a treat for you."

~

"I should have sensed you were a siren," declared Matthew Winter.

Alankha looked down on him from her sitting position straddling his hips. Her long black hair all but obscuring her beautiful features as it fell forward almost reaching his chest. She tucked it back behind her small ears, and her eyes bore into him. He could clearly see the silver and gold in the moonlight reflected off the Great Pyramid a short distance away. Her irises were dark pools in the center which drew him in deeper and deeper the longer he looked at them.

"Yes, I am surprised that you did not," was all she said.

"And you recently learned that we are offered the chance to return to Siren," stated Matthew with certainty.

"Yes, very recently."

"Where is your meeting hall?"

"You have been looking at it all night long."

"What? I don't understand," said Matthew. "You don't mean the hotel, do you? Is your meeting hall beneath this building?"

Alankha laughed and shook her head. "Let me go about this another way. Give me your wallet."

"My wallet?"

"Just give it to me"

Matthew gathered his pants and took out the wallet and handed it to Alankha. She took out a dollar bill and handed it to Matthew.

"There," she said, "now what do you see?"

"George Washington"

Her laugh was beautiful as it echoed off the walls and seemed to surround them. "Turn it over."

As Matthew turned the bill over, Alankha swept her hand toward the window facing east and pointed to Khufu's Horizon as it is referred to in Egypt. The Greeks called it Cheops, but most of the world knows it as The Great Pyramid of Egypt.

"Our great place of meeting is somewhere I have traveled to twice a year since the age of sixteen. But only now do I retain the memory of it, and it astounds me as well."

"What are you talking about? Your retreat is *under* the pyramid?"

"You are a student of archeology, correct?"

"Yes, that's right?"

"I know this because we were told of the great service you did for Siren by destroying the two remaining scrolls that would have disclosed its existence."

"I have mixed feelings about what I did. Part of me thinks it was an atrocity."

"Well, I love you for it, and so does all of Siren. You bought us precious time and for that we are grateful."

"So tell me what it is that astounds you about your meeting hall? And what does it have to do with archeology?"

"It is a very secret place. The entrance is a very sacred secret among the sirens here in Egypt. It is in a very deep chamber within the great pyramid of Giza." Her eyes opened wide as she was still trying to digest the enormity of the existence of an unknown chamber within the most studied archeological artifact in the entire world.

"A chamber," said Matthew numbly. "Undiscovered within the pyramid at Giza," he continued. "And you can take me there . . . and show it to me." He felt he was in an otherworldly dream that that only had roots of reality in this world and then faded to a gossamer veil. He wasn't sure if he were hearing her correctly.

"That is right," she said. "I will take you there very soon. But right now we have something even more magnificent than the hidden chamber. Now we have love."

Shelly Simon's luncheon was a categorical success. Over twenty-three thousand dollars in campaign funds were raised for advertising and transportation expenses, and a headquarters was established for free on the ground floor of a well-known office complex just off the Washington Mall. From her desk, she would be able to see the great expanse of the reflection pool all the way to the Washington Monument. When they were seated in the back of Alyssa Grant's limousine, the congresswoman said, "Well, I guess you could say that went well."

"You think?" joked Shelly. "I have the business cards of over thirty of Washington's movers and shakers along with the understood promise that I am welcome to call on a favor at any time."

"You do have a way about you, dear. I'm surprised I haven't noticed it before."

"Well, maybe it's because I haven't noticed it myself until recently. Now I think I understand the power of the Washington woman."

"What makes you so sure?"

"All the support and all of the unsaid flirtation. Some of them were even single."

~

Chapter Twenty-seven

When Brad and Sarah had finished their meal, Brad paid the check and drove them to a national park called Mount Desert Island. The park was open at all hours of the day and night because it featured many campsites and the most interesting feature for night time viewing, namely Sand Beach. There were absolutely no lights for miles around and the stars were so bright and so numerous that you could actually read a newspaper at midnight during a new moon. Although there were absolutely no clouds in the sky, The Milky Way looked like a string of thick cirrus clouds stretching in either direction, North and South to the horizon.

"It's beautiful," said Sarah.

"It sure is," agreed Brad. "And you're beautiful, Sarah." He walked up behind her and wrapped his arms around her, his hands cradling her ribs. He rested his head on her shoulder and placed his cheek against hers. Their warmth comforted each other in the crisp night air. The vapor of their breath intertwined and rose before them obscuring the magnificent night sky for moments at a time. Brad asked her, "Do you ever look up there and wonder who's looking back down at us? Whether or not we are alone in the universe or just one of many inhabited worlds? Do you ever wonder that?"

"No, not really," she said.

The Planet Siren

The grand council had only five members. It was a lifetime appointment unless for some reason a council member chose to step down. Each member, called Regents, represented a specific land mass and their collective group of inhabitants. There was little to discuss when they were in session as most of the motivation for change was non-existent on Siren. Every person on the planet was well cared for both financially and spiritually. The religious order was made up of regional prayer *connectors* who guided the populous in recognizing the creator and giving thanks for all of their blessings. When someone felt that they were not with the creator in spirit, it was called a *sickness of being one,* and a connector was soon to assist the poor soul in a journey to clarity. These were rarely necessary because the state of mind on Siren was largely static. That is not to suggest that they had no growth, quite the opposite. It was through growth spiritually that the Sirens became closer to the creator on a daily basis and could even call on the forces of the universe to solve problems and supply the needs of the masses. A collective prayer often bore the fruits of enlightenment and answers to stumbling blocks that the society faced as a whole.

What was fortunate was that Siren was spared the concept of bigotry or jealousy as well as simple greed or extreme avarice. When one has everything in life to fulfill the needs of the physical and the spiritual nature of mankind, the pursuit of power for the sake of power is considered in bad taste. A close examination of their sad sister planet Earth would serve to demonstrate this phenomenon in many ways. Their monitors showed how the power mongers of Wall Street reduced the general populace to near poverty level by enticing them into a sense of security with the promise of financial gain. Whole fortunes of the masses were lost to the gain of a select few, who had no possible way to utilize their vast fortunes. Sad victims of this heinous crime sometimes took their own lives having seen their dreams that they worked decades for go up in smoke. And in smoke-filled halls could be heard the despicable laughter by the villainous minions of the devil himself. Laughter at the expense of their fellow human.

No such laughter was ever heard at the expense of a fellow Siren. The sorrow or plight of any siren was the sorrow or plight of all sirens. It was beyond a brotherhood of bloodline or ideology. There was never any question that a siren in need would freely seek and receive the immediate assistance of their fellow man. It was a blueprint for mankind that was enjoyed by Siren, but not afforded to Earth.

Through no fault of their own, mankind on Earth was the victim of a powerful wave emanating from far out in space. It was a wave that was the result of a conflict of two very different and warlike worlds. A bloody war escalated between the two worlds for eons until the discovery was made how to collapse the sun of the enemy's solar system. Their star was collapsed into a white dwarf for less than a second before it imploded into a black hole creating a quasar pulse escaping on the light side of the dark matter. The quasar eventually pulsed with gamma radiation and the hapless planet Earth fell within its path. Siren, being on the opposite side of their sun at the time, was spared the gamma wave radiation. Upon realizing what had happened, *Preculis*, the victorious planet in the age-old bloody conflict, recognized a responsibility to their fellow members of the galaxy known as The Milky Way. Knowing that the gamma wave would produce a warlike nature in mankind of Earth, they chose to intervene. They knew that Earth would pose a direct threat to Siren when they gained the ability to travel in space and detect the presence of their benign sister planet. It was therefore determined that two things must happen to ensure the safety and peaceful existence of Siren. Mankind of Earth must not be able to overcome the combative nature that was accidently thrust upon them. And secondly, Siren must construct a *great shield* to completely hide its presence. The shield was designed by the engineers of *Preculis*, but over time, constructed by the sirens. The shield was constructed of six planes anchored by eight satellites orbiting around Siren in a geosynchronous orbit of sixteen thousand miles above her surface. They were initially powered by nuclear fuel supplied by the planet *Preculis*, but eventually had to be replenished by fuel from one of Earth's space probes called Cassini.

Aside from rendering the planet Siren invisible, there remained one other stumbling block that had to be addressed. The planet's mass had a magnetic signature in that it would affect light and vectors of nearby celestial bodies. It was for this reason that a huge circle or *belt* of ionized gas was suspended above the planet in a counter rotation around its axis. The counter-rotating gas belt cancelled out the magnetic signature of the planet. The gas was encased in clear aluminum tanks strung together in a train-like straight line, which stretched forty-five thousand miles and were suspended ten thousand feet above the surface of the planet.

No expense was spared by *Preculis* to protect Siren from the warlike nature of planet Earth. They had created a monster and felt that their souls remained in the balance. They are all too aware that they, as all of us, have to answer to our creator. They believed that eternity was at stake.

The Grand Counsel of Regents was meeting for the first time of the year and for the first time in centuries there was much excitement in the air.

"Fellow Regents," began the Master Regent to the four remaining members. "This is a great day indeed." The four Regents waited breathlessly for the news that had so elated their chosen leader. He continued, "Our creator has given us life and the great planet *Preculis* has given us protection by way of their spectacular technology, which led to the construction of *The Great Shield* and *The Great Belt* to cloak our magnetic field. But what is even more fortuitous is the fact that their science has now ultimately led to our deliverance."

The counsel exchanged some mumbled confusion as to what the Master Regent was referring. He continued, "I would like to introduce the Head of the Institute for Siren Scientific Studies, Dr. Stephen J. Hawkins." The collective Regents then lightly tapped their coffee cups onto the table as a show of respect.

"Gentlemen, and Lady," he added referring to the lone female Siren Regent, "I have come here today with superb news. As you know, for over a thousand years we have been studying the possibility of a matter energy transfer with little or no loss of cohesion to the molecular structure. In short, we have been trying to *exchange space/time,* for lack of a better definition and explanation. Our goal had been to quantify a particular place in the space-time continuum and exchange it with an exact measure of space-time over a distance through the ether, or on a beam of light, if you will.

For the first time, *The Preculians* have been successful in doing so and have discovered why we were not in all of our previous attempts. Their discovery has opened the door to vast new applications of travel and commerce, but most importantly, it has done away with the necessity of *The Great Shield."*

The Regents were immediately skeptical and were abuzz with objections regarding the holy grail of all imperatives of their planet's history. *The Great Shield* was the most important consideration of the planet Siren throughout all recorded history. Dr. Hawkins let them ramble for a few minutes before holding up his hands and saying, "If you will, please let me explain." The counsel settled down as did their subordinate staff members seated around the perimeter of the chamber. The doctor continued, "*The Great Shield* was our protection against warlike worlds like our sister planet Earth because it employed cryptic imagery. We were for all intents and purposes invisible. Now, let me state for all time that we do not need to be invisible any longer. The perfection of matter energy transfer puts *The Preculians* eons ahead of any world that might be a threat to us. Consider this scenario if you will: Let's say that a warlike planet, like Earth, decides to travel the necessary distance to visit our world. In this case, with the present Earth technology, they would be required to be in space for nearly fourteen months. Not an inordinately long amount of time to be in a weightless environment, and you may very well think it is well possible to achieve. Well, I would have to agree with you." Dr. Hawkins paused to let the scenario set in.

Then he continued, "Well, now let's suppose that upon entering our atmosphere, *The Preculians* located their vessel and determined its place in the space time continuum. It is a very rudimentary procedure, I assure you. Then by extrapolating the position of the Earth's atmosphere, which is a sister to our own, the *Preculians* now have the ability to *exchange space/time.*

"After fourteen months of space travel, the vessel from Earth would find itself right back where it started from, just entering Earth's atmosphere. I think that it would only take one such example to end all attempts in the future to invade our world. We have been assured that our friends from the planet *Preculis* will remain duty bound to protect the planet Siren from invasion by any hostile species. I must add, however, that this new discovery of theirs is so consequential that it must never leave the planet *Preculis.* I can't overstress the importance that this technology must remain off limits to all other worlds."

The council members were very excited and elated by the news given by Dr. Hawkins. They knew the implications of the discovery. Their little planet now had the power to remain completely protected and oblivious to any presence that might somehow happen upon them.

"And I have more good news," the doctor continued. "For more than four thousand years, some of our brethren were forced to live among the human population to assist us in stalling their awareness of Siren and to facilitating our need for nuclear fuel for *The Great Shield*. Indeed, these people are heroes of our planet and will soon be welcomed home."

Cheers broke out among the assembly and the periphery of counsel member subordinates began clapping and whistling. The Regents were banging their coffee cups on the table and some were seen to have tears in their eyes.

Hawkins continued, "The first *exchange* of *space/time* transfer is due to take place in seven days. This will give us time to prepare for the momentous occasion of their arrival."

Again there were more cheers throughout the chamber as Dr. Hawkins left the podium and headed for the exit.

~

Chapter Twenty-eight

Matthew rolled off of Alankha and said, "You are insatiable."

"I am young and I have a need for love."

"You sure do."

"Is that such a bad thing?" she asked with a wrinkle in her brow.

"It works for me," he said honestly. "Tell me more about this hidden room at Khufu. You mean there really is another room behind the West wall of the Queen's chamber?"

"Not exactly. It is to the West, yes, but it is below the Queen's chamber. Such a silly name. There was never to be any queen at Khufu's tomb."

"I know," he said, "it was misnamed by the British."

"What else do you know about Khufu?" asked Alankha.

"The usual stuff. I've studied it and read a few books."

"Then you know about the pyramid shaped rock that once capped the top?"

"Sure, the pyramidion."

"And what covered the pyramidion?"

"It was a shiny metal made of silver and gold," said Matthew.

"Yes, the metal is called electrum. Do you suppose it looks anything like this?" said Alankha as she let loose her charms on him and held him with her eyes. He could clearly see the silver and gold in her eyes.

"Yes, now that you mention it," he began numbly, "I'm sure it looked precisely like that." It was like a window to understanding the sirens, indeed his own origins were opening up before him.

"And what do you know about the first excavation on the north side of the pyramid?" she pressed his knowledge just for the fun of it.

"OK, in the ninth century, a guy named Caliph al-Ma-moun and his men broke through seven courses up and tunneled in about a hundred feet. There they found the descending corridor, which branched off about eighteen meters in. How'm I doing so far?"

"Go on," she said slyly.

"Well, the upper corridor, or shaft, went up from there to the King's Burial Room and what they now call the Queen's Chamber."

"Very good," said Alankha and then continued, "what about the lower corridor?"

"It led to the subterranean chamber and further west to what they call the dead-end corridor."

"And what did Caliph find at the end of the dead-end corridor?"

"Legend has it that he found a large key and some gold coins."

Alankha leaned over to the bedside table and picked up a satin covered box and handed it to Matthew. She then asked him, "Do you suppose the key looked anything like that?"

Matthew was dumbstruck. When he finally found his voice he said, "Yes, I'd say that it probably looked exactly like this . . . but how?" He let his question trail off into the night.

"My uncle is Zaphi Hanass, the Chairman of the Egyptian Supreme Council of Antiquities."

"Naturally," said Matthew shaking head. "That's exactly how the dream would go. Please don't wake me up."

~

Chapter Twenty-nine

Alex looked across the table at Durbah in the soft glow of the candlelight of Missy Kathryn's Hideaway's dining room and again noticed her eyes. She was unfamiliar with the feelings that she had for him. She found herself having to forcefully reign in her natural impulse to attract him to her. She wanted to let herself go and find the depths and limits of her abilities for the first time in her life. In the past, she was always aware when her charms were having an effect on the men around her, and she was always quick to hold them in check or make up an excuse to leave the room. Now she was a different siren. She was curious just how far it could go. She was feeling an attraction to Alex that taunted her to abandon all safeguards. Her psyche was daring her to let loose the pheromones and capture him with her eyes and her body and drive him mad with desire. She knew that she could assault him with her magical beauty until he lost all power to reason. She knew he would crave her like a drug in which he was powerless to let go. She wanted to climb inside his mind and take root and find a home there looking out through his eyes – be one with his thoughts and be centered in a universe for the first time in her life.

No one else whom she had ever met, neither siren nor human could hold any bond to her that was similar to what she felt for Alex Jansen. She knew for the first time a relationship was beyond her control. She had always been in control, and it always seemed like a necessity for her own safety to never let herself go and feel the depth of total abandon, to lose oneself in another's soul. But now the closely held safeguards were coming off. Her caution was coming off, and she was looking forward to the thrill of selflessness in the throes of passion.

But there was an important task laid down before she could realize any of her urgent needs and expectations with her first ever real love interest. She needed him to understand what she was and what he was bargaining for. And she needed to try to convince him to leave his world and come to Siren with her. For the first time in her life she had a mission she was unprepared for. She had no idea how to go about it. Finally, love found a way, "No tricks," she said simply.

"What did you say?"

"I said no tricks, Alex." Durbah looked almost sad in the candle light reflecting in her blue-green eyes.

"I have a lot of respect for you, Durbah. I hope I'm not playing any tricks, but if I am, please understand that I've never met anyone even remotely as charming as you and . . ."

"Shhhh." She sat quietly for a few moments and lowered her head with her eyes closed. She stayed in that posture as she continued, "Not you, Alex, me. I can't look at you now because I can't control myself. I can't trust myself not to cloud your mind."

"My mind? What are you saying?"

"I'm saying that I have to be totally honest with you, Alex. You deserve that, if nothing else."

"I'm sure that you are being honest with me, Durbah. I don't understand."

"Let me help you try to understand." She was very near tears, and Alex could sense it and had to hold his protective nature in check. He let her continue, "You find me attractive, Alex."

"Yes, indeed I do."

"Beyond that, you are enchanted by me. You find me irresistible, isn't that so?"

"Yes, I'd have to say that I honestly do."

"You see, now, that is the problem. Honesty."

"I don't follow," he said.

"I haven't been completely honest with you, so far."

"I'm a big boy, Durbah."

"You haven't been given a choice. I want to give you that choice. I want you to see me and make the choice to love me or not."

"I think I know what my choice would be."

"I have purposely tried to enchant you."

"Well, I'd have to say that you succeeded."

She lifted her eyes, and Alex could see the beginning of tears. His heart became heavy, and he wanted to comfort her. He began, "Hey, what's bothering you? You look so sad. We're here to have fun, right? So, relax and let's just have some fun." He motioned for the waiter to bring their check.

"You're right," said Durbah. "I guess I got a little bit too heavy there for a moment."

"This is all pretty new to us. Kind of a whirlwind encounter, wouldn't you say?"

"Yes, definitely," she said. "I've never let myself get so close to someone, let alone so soon."

"I think we have something special here, Durbah. I want to protect whatever that is. I want to hold it close and never let go."

"Well, I hope you feel the same way an hour from now."

The waiter brought their bill and Alex handed him his credit card. When he left their table, Alex asked her, "An hour from now?"

"Yes, an hour from now. An hour from now you will know everything."

"Don't tell me you have some deep, dark secret. I'm not sure I can handle that right now. I have a pretty darned good feeling about us, Durbah. Please don't take that away from me. There's not a whole lot going right for me, and you're pretty much it."

"I feel the same way, Alex. That's why it's so important that you know what you're getting into. What I am."

"What you are is beautiful."

"No tricks. Not this time."

"I don't know what you're talking about. You are a mysterious lady. Maybe that's what I find so attractive in you."

"You don't know the half of it, but you will."

The waiter brought back the bill, and Alex signed it and stood to pull back Durbah's chair. He led her out of the dining room, and they made their way up to their room. Alex slipped the card key into the slot and opened the door. Before she stepped inside, Durbah looked him in the eye. Her eyes were blue green and not a hint of silver or gold could be seen in them. She said to him, "Your life will never be the same once you walk into this room. I just want you to know."

"My life hasn't been the same ever since I saw you in traffic court the other day."

"That's exactly what I'm talking about." She closed the door behind them and turned off the light. The room was nearly lightless except for the moonlight coming in through the window. Alex's eyes adjusted to the darkness, and he could see the beautiful form of Durbah standing before him. She began to take off her clothes. Alex did the same and soon they found themselves standing before each other totally revealed. He closed the distance between them and for the first time, he kissed her. It was a long passionate kiss that held them both for what seemed like an eternity. His mind was swimming with desire and passion as their lips blended together and became one. His hands caressed her firm body and found the softness of her round supple breasts. She moaned with pleasure and his hands searched for the rest of her.

The language of love fell from their fingertips, and they explored each other in the moonlight as they made their way over to the bed. Their lover's embrace was quick to find them locked together in a motion of mutual desire fitting together like a finely crafted sword finding its scabbard. Excalibur from its stone destined to come to rest in the Lady of the Lake. Their lovemaking went on and on and was the only word between them. Their bodies said what their lips could not, and it seemed that time was slowing down just for them. They felt that they would wind the clock at a time of their own choosing or perhaps let it stop altogether as they found new ways to bring pleasure to each other. When at last they lay spent with a cool breeze bringing gooseflesh to their heated bodies on the bed, Durbah said to him, "I knew it could be like this, and I'm glad that I was right."

"What an incredible beauty you are."

"Yes, you really think so, don't you?"

"I certainly do. You are a goddess, Durbah."

"I have something to tell you, now that we have been true lovers. I'm afraid that I'm going to shock you, but I don't care. I have to let you know who I am and what I am. I don't care if you run from me and I never see you again, but what I feel for you is so important that nothing matters anymore except the truth."

"You're getting me a little scared, Durbah," said Alex with a nervous chuckle.

"You should be scared. I was scared, too. When I became aware not long ago."

"What are you saying, Durbah. Tell me now."

"I am something other than you. Something other than human." She held up her hand to stop Alex from commenting and continued, "Many thousand years ago my ancestors came to this planet and have procreated very sparingly, resulting in people like me. Sirens. We are from the planet Siren. We are not of Earth. We are not human. There, I have said it and now my heart is in your hands. Hate me if you choose, but I couldn't continue with you not knowing who I am."

Alex said nothing. He appeared to be trying to take in the information and was coming up empty. At first he thought that Durbah was delusional and cursed his rotten luck to fall in love with someone who had a mental illness. But he did love her. He was enthralled and enamored and hopelessly enchanted with her. Her beautiful body fit so well together with his. She quenched his desire like no one else he had ever imagined. Perhaps Durbah could undergo therapy, and they could have a happy and healthy future together. She could read his thoughts and said, "I'm not delusional, Alex. I am a siren. I can shape your will, but I choose not to. I want you to love me for the woman I am and for the heart that I choose to share with you. No tricks."

"What do you mean tricks?" he asked her.

"OK, Alex. Eyes wide open, let me show you." She then climbed on top of him and put him inside of her. His excitement grew, and he felt himself filling her. She said to him, "I love you, Alex. I want you to see me as I truly am. What do you see?" She rocked back and forth making love to him and let her charms become visible in her eyes. Alex could see the silver and gold electrum in her irises and was enraptured by her pheromones, which she loosed upon him. His desire was nearly beyond any satiation as he was fully taken by her. He managed to say, "My God, you weren't kidding me. You aren't delusional. You have captured my soul. I can't resist you. What have you done to me?"

But Durbah didn't let him loose from her spell. She held him captive and rocked him and rolled him and loved him and spent him until he was drunk with ecstasy and his mind was swimming hopelessly around in circles of unrequited desire. He literally couldn't get enough of her to satisfy his longing. It was almost painful to contemplate the limitations of his physical being. He wanted to climb insider of her and become one with her. Finally, he said, "Enough. Please, Durbah, let me go. I believe you. Please let go of my mind."

Durbah did let him go and then was moved to tears. She cried helplessly, tears falling from her blue-green eyes to her breasts. Her nose began to run, and she was having trouble catching her breath.

"I'm so sorry, Alex. That was what I had to show you. I am a monster." She continued to cry and lowered her head to his chest, her tears freely flowing.

"I'd hardly say you are a monster. But you surely are dangerous. What did you do to me?"

"I attacked you emotionally. I shaped your will."

"I've never felt anything like that in my entire life. It was incredible. The feeling was like distress. Not in a harmful or bad way, but I was distressed that perhaps I couldn't give you enough joy somehow. Like I would do whatever it takes in the world to make you happy."

"That is what a siren does. It is what is unfair, and I don't ever plan to do it to you again."

"Now, hold on. What is this never stuff? I didn't say that it wasn't fun. It's just kind of intense, that's all."

"Yes, but the point is that it is not your mind that wants to please me. It is not your mind giving you those thoughts. It's mine."

"It's a very powerful feeling. It's an intensity that I don't think can be experienced any other way. I've never had that kind of desire."

"But you desired me without any electrum or any charms. You desired me for just being a woman, and you made love to me when I showed you just a woman."

"It was wonderful. It was every bit as good as when you held me in your magic."

"Yes, it was wonderful," she said holding back tears. "I became fully a woman in every sense of the word. My body came alive with needs and was satiated and felt like it was placed in the center of the universe with everything spinning about me. And there is something else that I think you should know. It was my first time ever being intimate with a man."

"Now I know that there really is a God," he said.

~

Chapter Thirty

Sarah turned around and reached up to kiss Brad Early. The cool sand between her toes sent a chill up her spine and her lips found his eager to meet hers. She kissed him deeply for nearly a minute before breaking away and lightly biting him playfully. I have something that I need to talk to you about, but first, make love to me."

"What? Here?"

"Right now. Take me now. Right here. Fill me with your love right now, right here." She began shedding her clothes. She placed them on the ground covering the smooth black granite rocks that eons of waves have caressed on the shore. Then she lay down and was a vision of beauty before him. At first he was startled and then quickly followed suit - shedding his clothes and lying down next to her to take her in his arms. He leaned down and with his lips rescued her small elegant breasts from the chill of the night. Then he entered her, and they rolled together to the rhythm of the waves losing themselves in each other beneath the glistening canopy of stars. She moaned to him, "Oh, why have I hidden this from my life for so long? Love me, Brad. Love all of me. Love every inch of me as though all we will ever have is tonight."

When they finally lay still on the shore in that starry night, Sarah said to Brad, "I'm glad we could share that."

"So am I. It was unbelievable. I've never felt like that. You are some kind of sorceress."

"That's what I need to talk to you about. You're partly right."

~

Matthew Winter was holding Alankha against his chest in the Presidential Suite of the Cairo Hilton when he asked her, "Well?"

"Well, what?" she teased him.

"What do you mean, well what? What does the key open?"

"What do most keys open?" she said mysteriously.

"OK, a door. But which door?"

Just east of here down Pyramid Road is a small house. It is a house of legend in its neighborhood because there is a mystery behind it. The locals call it '*The House That Grows.*' She said giggling. "They say that because it is a small house, and yet many people enter it twice a year and no one knows where they all can fit. There is, in fact, a door in the basement that leads to a tunnel. The key opens that door."

"And the tunnel leads to Khufu?"

"Precisely. The tunnel was constructed before Khufu was even begun. My ancestors, in fact your ancestors, were the architects who designed Khufu's tomb."

"They were some very smart people," said Matthew.

"Yes, but they had a lot of help. The stones were actually quarried and moved by the guides of a planet called *Preculis*. They are the ones who brought our ancestors to this world."

"I remember learning from a sensor named Jonah that there was another race that brought the sirens here."

"Yes, it is ironic, no?"

"What do you mean?" asked Matthew.

"It is ironic that such a peaceful group of people were charged with pouring fuel on the fire. They were a force for turmoil."

"I'm still not exactly sure why," said Matthew.

"It is the same with any directive regarding our home world. All they ever wanted was to be left alone. Mankind has a hard time leaving anything alone. But now we have been given our deliverance."

"What do you mean? I don't understand," said Matthew.

"We have been given word from Siren that the Earth is no longer a threat to them. They are even dismantling *The Great Shield.*"

"Do you know the particulars? Why they are finally safe from Earth?"

"Not exactly, but we have been told it is the source of great celebration on Siren. Something about exchanging space and time."

"Well, I guess we'll find out eventually. When did your *sensor* say you could begin the exodus?"

"Very soon. I think we only have to wait about twenty days at the most."

"That's what we were told, too. The *space-time exchange chamber* would be ready in about seven days to start taking sirens back to Siren."

"Yes, it is not a ship, but merely a room."

"I'm not sure I fully understand it."

"It is a room that exchanges space with another on Siren. When something or someone is placed in the room, they are exchanged as well."

"Kind of like teleportation," said Matthew.

"No, that is exactly what it is not like. No two things can occupy the same space. That is a constant. No matter what world you are on, no two things can occupy the same space. If you were to teleport an object to a different location, the new location is already filled with substance, even if it is only dark matter. There is simply no room for anything else to be. That is the flaw in teleportation. You could never push *essence* out of the way in order to occupy its space. However, you can exchange space if you have like amounts of essence. You can move *what is* to another location as long as you vacate *what is* from another location in order to make room. Understand?"

"Yes, I think so. So, what now? Are you going to show me your alpha omega meeting place?"

"Certainly, but first we have love to make. Don't we?"

"Somehow I knew you were going to say that."

~

Chapter Thirty-one

Cathy Ellis was joined by Bonnie Smith during her follow-up meeting with Johnny Poole at his Vero Beach home. Kathryn Poole met them at the door, "Please come in," she said. "John is in his room. Would you like me to bring him down?" she asked.

"That won't be necessary, Mrs. Poole. We're just here to ask you a few questions if you don't mind."

"Not at all."

"This is going to sound a little strange, but have you noticed that your son had any kind of psychic abilities in the past?"

"I'm sure I don't know what you're talking about," said Kathryn.

"Well, Mrs. Poole, I'm sure you're aware of Mrs. Bloome's account of the statement that Ben Farmer made regarding your son's awareness of Cindy's disappearance."

"Oh, nonsense," said Kathryn.

"It's not nonsense," said Bonnie Smith and then Detective Ellis put her hand on her arm. They weren't there to brow beat the Pooles.

"Mrs. Poole," began Cathy, "whether or not you want to admit to the facts, your son told me matter-of-factly that Cindy Bloome would turn up safely the next day while she was still missing. Now, I'm not saying that he had anything to do with it, but the fact remains that he made the statement. Do you have anything to say about that?"

"I have nothing to discuss with you Detective Ellis."

"Yeah," she said. "I've heard that before. Let's go, Bonnie. Sorry to have troubled you, Mrs. Poole." They showed themselves out. When they got to the cruiser, Bonnie said to Cathy, "What do you think?"

"I think it's downright creepy, don't you?"

"Yup. That's what I'd call it. Creepy. You really think the kid is psychic?"

"I'd bet my life on it. When I first interviewed him at the center, he gave me the impression that he knew clearly that Cindy would be taken and that she would be returned safely. And that's not all. He ain't no normal nine-year old. He talks like he has the wisdom of the ages."

"Do you think he can tell me tomorrow's lottery numbers?"

"That's not even funny, Bonnie."

"Who's kidding," she said. "I could use the money."

Sarah looked up at Brad and seemed to have a slight tear in her eye. The stars at Sand Beach on Mount Desert Island were the most brilliant cross section of the galactic equator she had ever seen. But she had no interest in the stars at the moment. She told him, "I'm really going to miss you, Brad."

"Why do you have to miss me?" he asked. "I'm not going anywhere."

"That's why. Because I am going somewhere and you're not."

"Well, maybe I could come and visit you."

"I don't think so. When I tell you where I'm going, you won't think so either."

"Where are you going to, Mars or something?"

"Oh, much further than Mars. I'm going to Siren."

"Siren?"

"It's a planet. My home planet, but I've never actually been there."

"What are you talking about?"

The cold chilled their bodies, so they shook out their clothes and hastily put them back on. He put his arms around her and began rubbing her back hoping that the friction would bring them both some heat.

"I'm going to tell you, and then I'm going to ask you to do something and you won't have any choice but to heed my wishes."

"If you say so." he said simply.

"My ancestors are from another world. A very peaceful world known as Siren. It is Earth's sister planet and is on the other side of our sun. It is a hundred and eighty-six million miles from here. It would take light or a radio signal sixteen minutes to get there. For thousands of years, we sirens were in fear of Earth and for good reason. Earth passed through a wave of dangerous gamma radiation, and it changed the nature of its inhabitants. There is a dark nature to humanity that is not present on Siren. That is why I am choosing to return there now that I have been given the chance. My only regret is that I am going to miss some of the people here on this planet, and perhaps you most of all. You have awakened something in me that I didn't know was there."

"Why can't you stay if what you're saying is true?"

"Do you think you would stay?" she asked him.

"I don't really know. All I know is that I've just found you, and I don't want to lose you."

"Look at me," she said. Her eyes began to fill with the visual properties of electrum, and Brad was quickly mesmerized and lost in the sight. His mind was spinning, and he had trouble bringing words to his mouth. Sarah spoke for both of them, "I don't want to lose you either, Brad, but I have to leave this planet very soon. I won't be coming back. Now look me in the eye and tell me that you can deny me anything that I ask for."

Brad looked in her eyes and his own began to fill with tears. Sarah was crying as well when she continued, "You are a beautiful man, Brad Early, and I will always have love in my heart for you. I will always be grateful to you for loving me tonight and raising a fire in my flesh that I have never experienced before. I have never made love with anyone, and I am glad that I got to share the experience with you.

Tomorrow you will wake up and the fire that you feel inside for me will be less than it is now. With each passing day, you will think about me less and less and soon will forget that I was ever in your life at all. She released all of her pheromones and held his will in her caprice. You don't have any choice in the matter, Brad. You cannot deny me what I wish for and what I now wish is that you will forget about me and anything I have told you. Will I get my wish?"

Brad Early found his voice briefly and said, "Of course."

"Thank you, Brad. Thank you for everything. Thank you especially for loving me. Tomorrow I will take myself away from you, but for tonight, only for tonight, you can have all of me and share all of our tears."

~

Chapter Thirty-two

Shelly Simon was sipping on a bottle of Perrier in the backseat of Alyssa Grant's limousine. The outside temperature in the Washington area, which was indicated by the thermometer over the rear view mirror, was a cool dry fifty-two degrees. That was as high as would be expected because the sun was already slipping into the western sky. Shelly turned to Grant and said, "Jesus, it's cold in this city."

"It's the river, dear. The Potomac is one cruel indian," She giggled at her little joke.

"I'd like to ask a favor, Ms. Grant."

"Go ahead."

"I need a couple of days off."

"What? You mean besides the weekend?"

"I'd like Monday and maybe Tuesday if it's all right with you."

"This isn't the best of times, Shelly. You know that the D.E.C. is about to propose regulation of the consortium. In case you have forgotten, I'm a major player in the dispute."

"I haven't forgotten, Ms. Grant. In fact, I was hoping that you'd let me work the issue from another angle."

"I'm not following you, dear."

"I'd like to pay a visit to Walter Purness."

"The lobbyist?"

"That's right. The V.C.C. is a huge factor in the coal consortium. I'm hoping to soften his position on supplementing the hydro-electric plants on the east coast with equal BTU's of natural gas. Senator Blake is about to get his pipeline and could very well contribute to a price war."

"What makes you so interested in the Virginia Coal Collective all of a sudden?"

"I'm just trying to do the right thing, Ms. Grant. Call it paybacks."

"It seems to me you'd be just adding another evil. Both coal and natural gas contribute to greenhouse gasses. We're boiling our planet as we speak, dear."

"Oh, horse pookie."

"Excuse me? What did you say?"

"You heard me. I said horse pookie. You keep blowing so much steam up everybody's ass I'd say *you* are contributing to global warming."

"What's gotten into you, Shelly? You can't talk to me like that."

"The Earth has been steadily getting warmer since the ice age. Look around you. See all those homeless people freezing to death out there on the street. Go tell them how warm it is."

"You're about to lose your job, dear," said the congresswoman with an icy stare.

"Look at me," said Shelly turning toward Grant and glaring into her eyes. The silver and gold flecks of electrum began to take form around the edges of her irises. She released a chemical spell as well in the form of a powerful pheromone and continued, "Look, Ms. Grant. I want to make a difference to the atmosphere of the east coast to make amends for some things that I have done in the past. The burning of coal is producing acid rain and effectively defoliating the region."

Alyssa Grant just sat back in her seat with a far away expression on her face. Shelly continued, "Do you realize that the South Carolina walnut trees have all but disappeared? Even the wildlife is suffering. There have been multiple bird kills and fish kills, and it's all preventable. Senator Blake is actually doing the environment a favor with his company Energix; however, I'm sure that that is the last thing on his mind. Now what I want is to go down to Florida where Walter Purness spends his winters and see if I can do something good for a change. You agree with me one hundred percent and in a few minutes you will think that it was *your idea* to send me to Vero Beach, Florida. Do you understand?"

Grant brought a sleepy smile to her lips and said, "Why, yes, dear. By all means, please take the next few days off. Go down to Florida and get a tan. And while you're at it, see if you can get in touch with Walter G. Purness. He lives on John's Island in Vero Beach. See if you can soften up the position of the consortium. You know natural gas would be a good substitute for bituminous coal in the hydro-electric plants."

"I think that's a very good idea, Ms. Grant. I'll call you when I get to Melbourne Airport."

Shelly released her spell on the congresswoman who then pressed the down button on the back window of her limo for some cool air to clear her mind. She then said to Shelly, "I don't know what's wrong with me, dear. My head seems to be spinning. I thought I was through with menopause, but apparently not."

~

Chapter Thirty-three

Alankha arranged for a taxi to meet her and Matthew Winter under the portico of the Cairo Hilton Hotel. She instructed the driver in the Arabic language Farsi to take them to 1800 East Pyramid Road, which was on the southernmost outskirts of the city. The dust was raised off the hard pan desert road by the constant traffic down the main artery to the Giza Plateau. Tourists and scholars came from all over the world to visit Khufu's tomb as well as the other two smaller pyramids built by the pharaohs of his bloodline.

Khufu, or Cheops as the Greek like to refer to him, became king of Egypt after the death of his father Sneferu. But there was no convenient place in Sneferu's burial complex at Dashur to build his own tomb, so Khufu moved his court and residence further north to Giza where his prospectors found a secure limestone outcropping for a suitable foundation. When Khufu's son Khafre succeeded him, he built the second large pyramid at Giza for his tomb. When Khufu's grandson Menkaure finally succeeded his son Khafre, the third and smallest pyramid was built for his tomb. Legend has it that Khufu's mother was a woman of great beauty whose eyes could command the attention of the men around her and shape their will. It is said that she was born of a bloodline that descended from the heavens to rule over the people of Earth. This was the time of *The Old Kingdom of Egypt*.

One theory is that Menkaure died before his pyramid could be completed, and the remaining construction was hastily done to finish it in time for the burial. It is also not along the diagonal line that runs through the Great Pyramid and the Second Pyramid, but instead is nearly a hundred meters to the southeast. This offset, which was obviously done on purpose given the mathematical skill known to have been possessed by the ancient Egyptians, speaks to the fact that the three large pyramids of Giza are actually meant to be in an alignment resembling that of the three "belt" stars in the constellation Orion: Alnitak, Alnilam and Mintaka.

This fact is no small coincidence. There are two shafts in the Great Pyramid that lead from the burial chambers directly to the sky. Some experts think that these are ventilation shafts, while others would see an astronomical function. Arab legend suggests to the possibility that the shafts were built to enable the king's dead body to ascend into heaven. Little did they know that the king's *live* body, at least in Khufu's case, made the journey to the heavens by way of the planet *Preculis.* The north shaft is aligned with the circumpolar stars Minoris, Ursa and Beta, while the southern shaft is aligned with Sirius. It is through this southern shaft that the sirens of Earth will travel to their home planet. Every five days, for nearly a month, twelve sirens will travel through the tunnel underneath 1800 East Pyramid Road and assemble in the chamber of Khufu's Horizon.

The belt stars of the constellation Orion point to Sirius, which is the brightest star in Canis Major or *Larger Dog*. The small Earth-like planet *Preculis* is the sole satellite that revolves around the smaller star of this binary system. Aside from being the sole satellite around Sirius, *Preculis* is also the sole survivor of a great war between their people and those of *Xeries*. *Xeries* paid the ultimate price to be engaged in a war between two star systems. They were obliterated by the scientists of *Preculis*. They had found a way to accelerate the nuclear fission *Xeries'* sun produced from reducing hydrogen to helium, helium to carbon and carbon to iron. The subsequent collapse of their sun into a white dwarf was followed instantly thereafter by the formation of a black hole producing a quasar pulse on the opposite side of the dark matter. As luck would have it, although Einstein once said God does not throw dice, Earth was the unfortunate recipient of a very strong pulse of gamma wave radiation. Siren, being on the opposite side of our sun at the time, was not.

When Matthew and Alankha reached the residence at 1800 east Pyramid road, they were greeted by an old woman in a dark blue robe. She wore a veil over her eyes, but Matthew could still see the suggestion of electrum on the edges of her irises. He was getting good at recognizing his fellow sirens; however, Alankha had taken him completely by surprise. Alankha greeted the old woman, "Old Mother, how you always look like a young mother. What is your secret?"

"I don't listen to the foolish ravings of young beautiful women."

"May you sleep with a camel that has fleas."

"May you sleep with a flea who cannot afford a camel."

The two women laughed and embraced each other warmly. Alankha continued, "Mother Bakhawi, this handsome young man is one of us. He is also a student of antiquities, and I promised to take him on a walk through the ages."

"Yes, by all means, Alankha. You know the way. Do you need my torches for this evening?"

"Yes, please."

The old woman left the room and returned shortly with two large flashlights. She held them out to Alankha, "These should last you for about five hours. Will that be sufficient?"

"Oh, yes, certainly, Mother Bakhawi. We won't be gone more than two."

"Give my best to the emperor," she said cryptically.

"I surely will," was Alankha's equally cryptic reply.

Emperor? Thought Matthew. *Don't tell me I'm actually going to see Khufu's tomb. There isn't supposed to be anybody buried in the Great Pyramid. I don't think it's very likely that such a huge secret could be kept from humanity for four thousand years.* He would soon learn that the revelation to be received was surely even much greater than that.

They made their way down a narrow staircase and came upon a curtain of rough burlap laid flat against one wall. When Alankha pulled aside the cloth, there was revealed a small doorway no more than four feet high. In the exact center of the door was a keyhole, but there was no handle visible. Alankha produced the large key she had shown Matthew earlier in the evening from a small bag hanging from her shoulder to her waist. She handed it to Matthew and said, "If you please."

He took the key from her and said, "Yeah, I definitely please." Thoughts were spinning around in Matthew's head. As a student of archeology and Egyptian antiquities, he knew that more discoveries were happening every day and that most of them were by accident. This was certainly no accident. He was standing before a door that would lead him to a tunnel into Khufu's tomb. A French antiquities scholar speculated that two of the descending shafts would converge at a place roughly fifteen meters beneath the base of the pyramid and that a tunnel should be constructed to reach that point. What no one in the world except the sirens of Egypt knew was that the idea was certainly not a new one and had in fact been put into place before the construction of the tomb had ever begun.

Matthew placed the key into the door. It opened easily inward by the slight press of his hand. The air that wafted out of the tunnel was stale, but also held a fragrance of sandalwood and rosemary as though a fair amount of the two herbs were strewn across the thousand meter expanse between the house at 1800 and the base of Khufu's tomb itself. He clicked on his flashlight. Alankha didn't follow suit as she was undoubtedly very familiar with the tunnel and the contours of the landscape between Khufu and 1800 East Pyramid Road. She needed no artificial light to guide her. Alankha couldn't help herself as she started to crave the closeness of Matthew again. She backed her way against a wall in the dark tunnel illuminated only by Matthews's lone flashlight. She began to unbutton her shirt and fired up her eyes with electrum until Matthew said urgently, "Enough, Siren, I beseech you to release me."

"Oh, you are no fun at all."

"Listen, we don't have time for this, Alankha. But I promise you, when we get back to the hotel, I'll be in a different mood."

"I'm going to hold you to it, Matthew."

"I wouldn't have it any other way."

They made their way along the tunnel, which featured many primitive hieroglyphics depicting the planet Siren and the planet Earth and *The Great Shield* and the *The Great Belt* of ionized gas. It reminded Matthew of the ride Space Mountain at Walt Disney World in Orlando, Florida. Often there is such a long wait, riders are herded through a labyrinth of ropes and hallways intended to stack the masses who unfold their hard earned money with abandon.

Matthew considered the ridiculous difference between some Hollywood contrived yarn about a planet making contact with Earth, and the actual circumstance he now felt himself encompassed within. He was charged to become more than he had been before. He imagined the tunnel filled not with humanity, but rather *sirenity* on a long train of souls twice a year making a pilgrimage to the meeting hall within the Great Pyramid of Khufu.

After walking at least a full kilometer, they came upon another door, which was identical to the one in the basement of Mother Bakhawi's dwelling at 1800 East Pyramid Road. Matthew took the key from his back pocket and it slid easily into the lock. He tried to turn it clockwise and when nothing happened, Alankha said, "Opposite ends of the tunnel turn opposite locks."

Matthew turned the key counter clockwise and the door swung silently open. The air was again sweet with rosemary and sandalwood as if it had been placed across the dusty floor for eons. At first Matthew thought they had come to a dead end. He remembered the description off the subterranean chamber of Khufu as being *the dead-end corridor.* But that couldn't be right. Alankha was familiar with the hidden chamber twice a year since she was sixteen years old. She merely waited silently until Matthew could figure out which way to go. He probed the walls with his hands while Alankha held the flashlight in a still position so as not to aid him with any kind of clue. The walls were rough in comparison to the polished pink granite that was usually used for blocking stones of the King's burial chamber. Then his hand loosened some clay packing a crevice to reveal what must be a hand hold. He reasoned how far a person could reach from one hold to the next and could see another depression in the rock about thirty inches above him. Then he looked lower on the wall and could see a depression clearly intended to be a foot hold. He reached down and dug out the clay in the foot hold and put his right foot in the opening. Reaching up with his right hand, he found the first hand hold and pulled himself up. Further up the wall on the left side, he found another hand hold and dug out the clay. Once he pulled himself up another thirty inches, he put his right foot in the original hand hold on the right.

"Very good," said Alankha. "It took me twice as long when my *sensor* first brought me here as a young woman."

Making his way up the wall, Matthew found a ledge and eased his body over until he was lying on his side looking down at Alankha roughly three meters below him.

"What now?" he asked her.

"Maybe you are not as good as a young girl of sixteen," she said tauntingly.

"Hang on," he said, "I can get this." He rolled over and into the darkness reached out with his hand. The wall wasn't rough stone as it was below him, but rather a series of smooth bamboo shoots bound together with papyrus strands. It was another door. He called down to Alankha, "Throw me up a flashlight. I think I've got it." The beautiful Egyptian siren instead climbed easily up beside him and produced a flashlight that she had secured in her belt. When Matthew shined the light on the door, he could see a handle but no lock. He grabbed hold of the handle and pulled toward him. It wouldn't budge. He heard a soft giggling behind him and said, "OK madam siren, what now?"

"All doors *open* in, my darling, and then all doors *close* you out."

Matthew pushed on the handle and the door fell easily away and lay flat on the floor before him. There wasn't enough head room to stand, but he managed to crawl on his knees over the flattened door and gain entrance to the chamber. Alankha followed him and made her way over to the wall on their right. She produced a small lighter from a pouch at her waist and lit a torch that was attached to the wall. Then she crossed the room to her left and lit another torch as well. The two flames grew large enough to illuminate the entire room. It was huge in terms of known chambers held within burial tombs. A typical chamber documented by Alankha's uncle of the SCA, or Supreme Council of Antiquities, was twenty meters across. This chamber was twice that and equally as high. Matthew looked up and was astonished to see that there was a clear opening in the ceiling by a shaft in direct alignment with a bright star in the heavens.

"Do you know what you are looking at?" she asked him.

"Yes, a star."

"And which star do you suppose it is?"

"Well, by its size I'd say it's a pretty major one. Is it Polaris?"

"You have your directions crossed. You are facing south, not north."

Matthew's mind was spinning out of control with the speed of the revelations this night was bringing him. He couldn't focus his thoughts for a moment and then it came to him, "Sirius. The star is Sirius."

"Yes, the faithful pup of Orion the hunter. His belt points directly to it."

"He's not much of a hunter without his bow."

"Oh, so you know the story well, do you?"

"His bow fell into the lake."

"And what was the fate of the hunter?" she teased him.

"He swam way out into the sea and was just a dot on the horizon."

"Go on," she said.

"Generally speaking, Orion was known as the *"dweller of the mountain",* and was famous for his prowess both as a hunter and as a lover. But when he boasted that he would eventually rid the earth of all the wild animals, his doom was sealed. It might have been the Earth Goddess herself who sent the deadly scorpion to kill Orion. Or possibly Apollo, concerned that Orion had designs on his sister, Artemis. Apollo may have told the Earth Goddess of Orion's boast. It seems clear that it was the Earth Goddess who sent the scorpion on its mission.

Some stories have the scorpion killing Orion with its sting. However, the general consensus is that he engaged the scorpion in battle, but quickly realized its armor was impervious to any mortal's attack." Alankha clapped her hands and said, "You know your mythology, but do you know it is based on truth? Perhaps you believe that truth is based on mythology."

"Nothing would surprise me tonight, Alankha."

"Please, go on with your story."

Matthew continued, "Orion then jumped into the sea and swam toward Delos. But Apollo had witnessed Orion's struggle with the scorpion and would not let him escape so easily. He challenged his sister Artemis, who was an excellent shot with the bow. He told her of an infamous and treacherous villain, and that the small dark spot on the horizon was his head. Artemis struck the object with her first shot. She then swam out to retrieve her victim's corpse and discovered she had killed

Orion. Artemis implored the gods to restore his life, but Zeus objected, so she put Orion's image in the heavens.

In his eternal hunting, Orion is careful to keep well ahead of the scorpion. In fact Orion has disappeared over the horizon by the time Scorpio rises in the east, as it becomes his turn to rule the evening sky."

Alankha looked at Matthew and brought the silver and gold to her eyes. She took hold of his hands and pulled them toward her eager flesh. He could feel her hot breath on his neck as she told him, "Unlike Artemis, I always aim for the heart. And I am also a very good shot."

Matthew was soon looking up at the beautiful face of the Earth Goddess Alankha and just above her head he could see a very bright star called Sirius.

Chapter Thirty-four

Brad Early held Sarah Poole in the starlight at Sand Beach and she could feel his hot tears on her cheek. He sniffled and rubbed the back of his hand across his runny nose, "I don't know what's the matter with me, Sarah. I'm sorry to be acting like this."

"I know what the matter is. It's what's wrong with me as well. It's love. Love is the matter."

"But that doesn't make any sense. Love should only bring joy to us."

"And it does. But it also brings sorrow when we lose it."

"I never thought I'd be saying this, but I'm not sure it's worth it."

"I'm sure. Take me to your home, Brad."

"What? You want to rub some salt in the wound?"

"There will be no wound, Brad."

"But there is pain. The pain of losing you. I know that you will soon be gone from my life forever."

"But you won't know it forever. There will be no pain. You will miss me only tonight, while you have me tonight."

"I don't understand," he said miserably.

"I will make you understand. Take me to your home and love me once again."

"You know I can't refuse you," he said wiping tears from his eyes.

"Yes," she said simply, "I know."

~

"You've honestly never been with a man before?" Alex was taking in the beautiful form of Durbah lying across the bed of Missy Kathryn's Hideaway.

"Never."

"But you're so beautiful. I'm sure it's not for lack of opportunity."

"It just never seemed important to me until now."

"Lucky me."

"Lucky you."

"Don't take this the wrong way, but, I mean I know I'm not chopped liver or anything, but why me?"

"Why not?"

"Why do you all of a sudden have this fire in you – like the fire you have in your eyes."

"My eyes are a trick of light. The fire in my heart is no trick."

"Again, why me?"

"I guess I've changed. I guess now it's important to me to have love for the first time."

"What changed you?"

"This might sound a bit strange, but I feel like it was something from the sky. Some kind of energy raining down on us."

"Well, I read about something in the newspaper recently. Some telescopes were damaged by some kind of wave. Could that be it?"

"Possibly, but in my case I'm not damaged. I think whatever it was made a definite improvement in my life. I have feelings now that I never had before and I like it. A lot."

"So what now, miss alien monster from outer space. Shall we have some little green babies?" he teased her.

"Something like that."

~

Chapter Thirty-five

Shelly Simon landed at Melbourne Regional Airport at 10:05 A.M. on Saturday morning. She rented a car and drove south on I-95 for thirty-five miles until she came to route 60 and took that over the causeway into Vero Beach. She stopped briefly at the Shore Break Bed and Breakfast, where she had reserved a room, to drop off her bag and hang up her clothes. Her hosts, Robert and Beverly Jones, seemed very pleased to have her staying with them and asked if she would like to join them for dinner.

"That's very sweet of you, Mrs. Jones."

"Please call me Beverly."

"I'm not sure of my plans just yet. I have to visit a man who lives a short distance from here. I'm kind of still working. But as soon as my mission is accomplished, I'd love to join you. Please don't blame me if it's just for dessert and not dinner."

"Whatever, dear," said Beverly. "Just know that you are always welcome."

"Thank you, Beverly. You make me feel very welcome."

"It's our pleasure, Shelly," said Robert. Shelly had no doubt that he meant every word.

She left the parking lot of the Shore Break and traveled north on A-1-A until she came to a traffic light and turned left for the up ramp of an exclusive community called John's Island. It seemed like it was one step up from a gated community because it effectively had a mote surrounding it. It was literally an island with a small fixed bridge that could not open to allow any tall boats to go through. The clearance was only thirteen feet from the water during most of the tides so the larger sport fishing yachts had to make their way around the island to gain access to the Intra-coastal Waterway.

John's Island had more than their share of seaworthy craft. Post, Hatteras, Ribovich, Chris Craft and Sea Ray were all represented in all their glory and splendor. A typical John's Island yacht would boast a price tag of many millions of dollars. One such yacht was owned by a lobbyist for the Virginia Coal Collective named Walter G. Purness. He was the yachtsman whom Shelly Simon sought on that particular Saturday. She drove up to the security gate and addressed the guard, "Hello, my name is Shelly Simon, and I'm here to visit the Purness family."

The guard looked down to his clipboard and checked to see if her name was on a list of expected guests. He then told her, "I don't see your name here, Ms. Simon. Are they expecting you?"

"Nope."

"Let me give them a call. Please pull your car up and park to the side of the road." The guard walked back to the guard house and picked up a cell phone from his desk. He dialed the Purness residence, and Shelly could tell he had made the connection as she could see him talking. She wasn't even sure if Walter Purness was in Florida or not.

Shelly pulled her rental car up and parked to the side. She kept her engine running as she didn't expect to be there for very long. After a few minutes the guard walked up to her car, and she rolled down the window. He still had the cell phone, "That's right, Mrs. Purness, Shelly Simon."

Shelly then said, "Tell her I'm from the alpha omega conference."

When the guard related that information he nodded his head and said, "Yes, Ma'am, I certainly will." He switched off his phone and said, "Go right ahead, Ms. Simon. The address is 1400 Green Turtle Lane. It's the second left, you can't miss it. Biggest house on the block."

No doubt, thought Shelly as she pulled the car out and said, "Thanks," to the guard waving kindly in her rear view mirror. When she found the house, she could see Edith Purness standing in her driveway. She had a big smile on her face, and she came forward as Shelly was pulling in to her guest parking spot. "Welcome, Shelly. I'm Edith Purness."

"Shelly Simon," said Shelly reaching out to shake her hand. "I'm very glad to meet you. I've seen you at the alpha omega retreat recently and I know your daughter Durbah from Washington."

"Now that you mention it, you do seem familiar. Please come in and make yourself comfortable in our home."

"Thank you, Mrs. Purness.

"Edith."

"Thank you, Edith. You have a lovely home."

"Actually, I think it's a bit much," she said jovially, "but Walter likes to do things in a big way."

Shelly smiled, but couldn't quite get herself to laugh at the expense of the lobbyist. Walter Purness was nearly as rich as God, if only half as powerful.

Edith went on, "This place is really too much for me to handle. I want Walter so sell it. Especially in light of recent events. You know what I'm talking about, don't you?"

"The exodus."

"Precisely, the exodus. It all sounds very exciting, and I can honestly say I'm sorry that I will have to miss it."

"Oh?" posed Shelly. "You mean that you are not going to make the journey?"

"I'm afraid not, dear."

"Afraid to fly?" asked Shelly jokingly.

"It's hardly that, Shelly. I thought you knew."

"Knew what?" she asked.

"Walter won't go. He isn't one of us. I don't want to put him through the screening process. It would break his heart to be rejected. I'm afraid he's going to miss Durbah terribly."

"Oh, I'm so sorry to hear that. Yes, I can imagine it would be very hard to let go of your child like that. But Durbah will certainly go, won't she?"

"I can't imagine how she could pass up the opportunity, as I'm sure you won't as well."

"Oh, I'm going all right. I hope to be one of the first to enter the exchange chamber."

"It's all so thrilling," said Edith, "walking into a room and walking out again on another world."

"They say it looks very much like this one," said Shelly.

"Yes, I've heard that, too."

"Edith, is your husband home?"

"Almost," she said. "He's out on the dock playing with his little toy."

"His toy?"

"An eighty foot Ribovich. She's docked behind the house."

"Cool," said Shelly. "I've heard that they actually have a resonance in their planking that brings up fish."

"Yes, I suppose. I don't know very much about boats."

"You're not a fan of boats?"

"No, I'm just a fan of Walter."

"Actually, it's your husband that I came to see."

"You plan to put a spell on him, no doubt."

"Just a little tiny one if it's OK with you."

"Help yourself, dear. But just make sure he keeps his clothes on."

"Oh, Edith," laughed Shelly. "You know it's not that kind of spell."

"I know you want him to scale down the production of coal in favor of cleaner burning natural gas."

"That's amazing, Edith. Are you a *sensor* or something?"

"No, dear. I may not know much about boats, but I know a lot about Washington."

"Can I ask you how you feel about it?"

"You mean scaling back coal production?"

"Yes. Are you in favor of it?"

"Yes, I am. I've tried to influence Walt, but he has always resisted me. I can understand his position."

"Economics, right?"

"You're a smart girl, Shelly. And a very beautiful one as well."

"Thank you, Edith. That's a lovely thing to say."

"I'm sure you've heard it before. Look, you're welcome to make your point to Walter, but I wouldn't get your hopes up."

"I'm not sure I see the problem the same way as you do," said Shelly.

"Well, let me just say that coal has been very good to this family. It's made Walter a very rich man, and he denies me nothing. I am very well cared for, and I mostly have coal to thank for it."

"You're concerned about the miners and their families. Is that it?"

"Yes, mostly that. I know all about acid rain and defoliation, but I also know about starving families and how hard it is to make a living digging coal. Those men, *and women*, deserve something more than a place in the unemployment line."

"I have an idea Edith. There may be a way around the problem."

"Well, I'd love to hear it."

"Subsidies."

"You mean paying people not to mine coal."

"That's right."

"That sounds a bit like socialism to me, dear."

"Wait, just hear me out. For decades, wheat and corn farmers were given subsidies to scale back production in order to maintain a stable price for commodities. If we were allowed to flood the market with corn, the price would have dropped so low as to be nearly worthless. Now they are using the excess corn and other starches to make ethanol. Subsides are no longer necessary in those arenas. I'd like to convince your husband that subsidies for the coal industry along with unilateral tax cuts could scale back production to half and keep the workers in meatloaf and potatoes."

"That's a very ambitious plan, Shelly. And not, I would imagine, very attractive to the Republicans of Congress. It sounds like tax increases for the general public to benefit a very small sector."

"But that's just the point. The benefit is for all of us. The EPA has an agenda and they have a fairly healthy budget as well. Resources from the Clean Air Act and a number of other environmental concerns would do well to get behind the idea."

"And just what is the idea, Shelly? Give me the nut shell version."

"Funny you should use that term given the plight of the East coast walnut trees. OK, here it is: All we're talking about here is the price of electricity. Coal is used in hydro-electric plants to heat the water and make steam, but it also releases harmful elements into the atmosphere. Natural gas is much cleaner to burn and will heat the water just as well. There is also a growing industry that powers fuel cells with natural gas to create electricity. A unit no larger than a shoebox could power even a house of this size."

"Yes, dear," said Edith. "I'm familiar with the technology. It's been somewhat of a thorn in Walter's side."

"Well, the electric companies don't care how they create steam or power fuel cells as long as they can stay focused on the bottom line."

"I'm still not following you."

"What I'm suggesting is that the consortium actually raises the price of coal forty percent, and the electric companies commit to buying sixty percent of what they do now. The shortfall will be supplemented by natural gas at a much cheaper price, and the bottom line stays the same. Your electric bill doesn't go up. The air gets cleaner, and the Virginia Coal Collective still makes the same amount of money. Get it?"

"I think I do. You're a very smart girl as I said before. But I'm not sure how you could push this through Congress."

"I'm sure. That's where the sirens come in. There is a well placed siren in nearly every office of our Congressional leaders. That was done by the *sensors* to expedite the decision to use nuclear fuel in our space probes like Cassini. The sirens were stealing it to power *The Great Shield* as you well know. Now the shield is unnecessary due to the same technology that will bring about the exodus. Now the sirens have a much more noble cause. We can leave this planet a better place than how we found it nearly five thousand years ago."

"Why don't you go out to the dock and meet Walter. I'm sure you'll be able to find something worthwhile to talk about."

"Thanks, Edith. I'm sure we will."

When Shelly found Walter hosing off the large deck of his sport fishing yacht, he stopped briefly and said, "Well, hello there." Extending his free hand he said, "I don't believe I've had the pleasure. Walt Purness."

"I'm pleased to meet you, Mr. Purness. I'm Shelly Simon."

"Friend of Durbah's?"

"And your wife, Edith. I was hoping to become your friend as well."

"Well, I've always said, you can't have enough friends. I'm pleased to meet you, too, Shelly."

"That's a great boat, Mr. Purness. What's her hull speed? About forty knots?"

"Forty-eight. You know boats?"

"Not a lot, but I can see that yours is a beauty."

"The birds think so, too. Whenever Edith is around, all the herons and pelicans and seagulls flock around like she's cleaning fish or something. We even get the neighbor's dogs digging out and coming over to visit Edith. I don't know what it is about that woman, but they all seem to love her. I can't say that I blame them." He chuckled.

"So they make you have to hose off the deck, is that it?"

"Yeah, but it's only feathers. I suppose they can't help it, and it really doesn't hurt anything. Listen, I just got my engines tuned up, and I was about to do a sea trial. Would you care to come along?"

"Sure, that would be great," she said. "I wish I had a bathing suit with me so I could work on my tan."

"Go on up to the house and ask Edith to give you one of Durbah's. I'm sure she wouldn't mind."

"Thanks, Mr. Purness. I will."

Shelly found Edith in her kitchen making a pitcher of fresh lemonade. She said, "Oh, hello, dear. I was just going to join you two with some drinks. Can I get you a glass?"

"That looks wonderful."

"Fresh squeezed. One of the perks of living in Florida."

"Your husband said you might be able to lend me one of Durbah's suits."

"Don't tell me, let me guess. Walter wants you to be his first mate."

Shelly laughed and said, "I don't mind telling you I'm looking forward to it."

"I'll get you a suit. Here," she said handing her the pitcher of lemonade. "Please take this out to Walt."

Shelly walked back out to the canal behind the house and saw that Walter was sitting high atop the flying bridge loosening up the throttles and gear shifts. He turned on the blower for the engine compartment to get rid of any potentially explosive fumes. Shelly was carrying the pitcher in her left hand and waved to him with her right. She called up to him, "Permission to come aboard?"

"Permission granted," he said to her and then added, "spoken like a true yachtsman, Shelly. Not many people would have asked that. I guess you really do know your way around boats."

"A little. I used to sail when I was younger."

"Well, you might find this a little less peaceful."

"I'm sure I'll love it."

"I wish I could get Edith to love it," said Walter.

"You mean she doesn't like to ride with you?"

"Only if we're entertaining."

Edith came out and walked up to the side of the yacht. She handed up the bathing suit to Shelly and said, "Here you go, sweetie, you'll find glasses for the lemonade in the galley."

"What? You're not coming?" she asked.

"No, dear. I'm a big fan of dry land. You saved me."

Shelly took the suit and noticed that it was new. It still had the price tag attached. She said to Edith, "You're sure Durbah won't mind?"

"I'm sure. You can keep it," she lowered her voice, "it was a gift from her father and I don't think she likes it. It's not her color."

Shelly laughed and said, "Thanks, Edith. I'll try to do something nice for Durbah when I get a chance."

"I know you will. Have a nice cruise."

Soon Walter Purness and Shelly Simon were putting the newly tuned engines through their paces in the Intra-Coastal Waterway. They were running at two-thirds power and had planed off throwing out a huge wake and rooster-tail behind them. Shelly's long dark hair was pulled forcefully back by the wind, and she had a huge smile on her pretty face.

All of a sudden they both heard a loud rumbling thunder over their heads. Shelly was startled, but Walter just smiled knowingly and winked at Shelly. He brought the engines down to an idle anticipating her question.

"What the hell was that?" she asked.

"A rocket launch from Canaveral," he said smiling.

"But there wasn't anything in the news about a launch happening today."

"It's a military mission. They didn't announce it because they rarely do when it's military. Happens all the time."

"But you knew about it, didn't you? I could see it in your face," she told him with certainty.

"That's right."

"Well, spill it," she said giggling. "What's it all about."

"Do you remember the launch of the space probe called Cassini?"

"Uh huh," she said. "They made a big deal about the nuclear material that it contained if I remember correctly."

"That's right," said Walter. "That was my baby."

"What do you mean?"

"I'm on the president's committee for space development and operations. I was instrumental in pushing it through congress."

"And was it really dangerous?"

"Not in the least. It was nuclear powered, but it was not a bomb."

"So what is it that we just heard?" asked Shelly.

"It's a space craft being launched into Earth's orbit. It looks like a miniature space shuttle, and it's called the X-B 37."

"Is it a weapon?"

"My guess would be yes, but I don't know for sure. Even though I'm on the presidents committee, there are some things that they don't even tell me."

~

Chapter Thirty-six

"Little green babies, huh?" asked Alex jokingly.

"Count on it," said Durbah. She wasn't letting him off the hook so easily. "You know that if I had your child, it would be a siren," she declared.

"But I'm not one of you; at least I don't think I am."

"No, you're not. If you were, a sensor would have explained it to you on your sixteenth birthday."

"So then why would my child be a siren?"

"Our child. The siren traits are carried by the female. A male siren can take a human wife and have human children. Only the females carry forth the bloodline."

"What happens when two sirens marry and have children?"

"Well, it happens, but it is pretty rare. Many times in that instance the progeny is a *sensor* or *seer*."

"What? You mean like a psychic?"

"Something like that, but not exactly. A sensor is able to recognize a siren right off the bat. Even if he is not shown the electrum in their eyes."

"Electrum?"

"The silver and gold I can bring to my irises."

"It's beautiful. I've never seen anything like it."

"I have a small confession to make."

"What is it?"

"That day in the courthouse. I let you see a bit of electrum then. It's the reason why you chose to call me."

"I still think it was my idea."

"Of course, you do."

"So what is the purpose of your power if not to seduce a poor sucker like me?" he asked jovially.

"I had many purposes in my life that I was not even aware of."

"I don't get it."

"It's like I was controlled through my subconscious and given a directive twice a year since the age of sixteen."

"What kind of directives?"

"Well, you remember the work you did for Senator Williams about the ban on Blake's pet project?"

"Yeah, so?"

"Blake's pipeline project was my idea. I put it into his head."

"But why?" asked Alex.

"I have no idea. It was all from a *sensor* who got his directive from Siren."

"Why do the sirens care about natural gas?" wondered Alex.

"I think it's more about a power struggle than the actual gas."

"That's what you meant when you said, *'pouring fuel on the fire,'* isn't it?"

"Uh huh. We siren are instigators. We stir up the pot."

"So what now? What directive do you have?"

"None. I am cast now. At least I think I am."

"I've heard you use that term before. What does it mean?"

"When we were born, we were *cast* among humanity to understand their behavior and their motives and were essentially human. Then at the age of sixteen, a *sensor* explains to us the power that we might wield over humans and how we can influence them. This is thought to being *un-cast*. Think of it as a fishing line that was cast out and then at sixteen, reeled in."

"And now you're casting yourself out again among humanity, is that it?"

"Yes, but not for long. That's what I have to discuss with you. Soon I will be leaving Earth. It's time for me to take my place among my fellow sirens on our home world."

"Somehow I knew this would be too good to last," he said.

"Who said it can't last? I'm hoping that you will be able to come with me." Alex opened his mouth to say something and then closed it. His head tilted to one side, and Durbah could see a far-off look in his eyes. She thought that she could see the wheels turning in his head. After about a minute of contemplation, he said, "I think my main focus is staying with you, Durbah. If it has to be on another planet, I can live with that."

"I was hoping you would say that. But I want to make a promise to you. The decision will always be yours and yours alone to live with. I will use no tricks on you. I could shape your will and make you think that it is your idea to be so shaped, but I will not do it, ever."

Chapter Thirty-seven

Sarah and Brad arrived at his house in the sleepy tourist town of Bar Harbor. It was off season and the streets were quiet with some of the shops closed down with decorative iron gates covering the doorways. The season would open back up at the end of April and run through September, but the winters were relatively peaceful. Brad preferred the off season even though his job as a ferry boat captain was non-existent for five months of the year. During the months of October through March, he worked as a handyman doing home repair and maintaining the security of vacant properties. He would often move his residence throughout the town - house sitting for his various clients. But this night he wanted to be in his own home and share it with his new lover.

Sarah quickly took to the place and though she thought it could definitely use a woman's touch, she could see that it was extremely well cared for. The ceilings all had cove molding, and all of the finely crafted door casings and baseboards were newly painted with a loving attention to detail.

"I love your house, Brad."

"And I love you, Sarah."

"Show me."

Brad showed Sarah just how much he loved her. And then he showed her again.

~

Alankha lay next to Matthew Winter and looked up through the shaft in the ceiling of Khufu's tomb. Sirius, being a binary star system seemed to be pulsing with a barely discernable flicker of energy. It was hard to imagine how very far they were from the distant star and its sole revolving planet of *Preculis.* The actual distance is eight and one-half light years, but considering the fact that light travels over fifty billion miles in one hour, the distance that light travels in eight and a half years is unfathomable. The human mind is simply unable to get a handle on it. Fortunately, the *Preculian* mind is not. The *Preculians* found a way to boost light speed by collapsing the ether in on itself. The ether is the medium that light travels on or through. That is why light can travel through a vacuum. It makes its own vehicle during its procession forward through space. The *Preculians* found the mystery behind speeding up the vehicle of light rather than light itself. Were it not for this discovery, they would have been unable to come to the aid of Siren as the distance between the two worlds would be too great. Two very grateful sirens were looking up at their benefactor at that very moment.

"It's beautiful," said Alankha.

"It sure is," said Matthew.

"What can you tell me about it?" she asked.

"Well, Sirius is actually two stars, Sirius A and Sirius B. Sirius B is a very dense white dwarf or small star that's only about four times the size of earth. Sirius A is three times the size of our sun."

"That's why it flickers, no?"

"Yup" said Matthew. "It's also the brightest star in the sky."

"It is where our savior lives. Did you know that?" asked Alankha.

"Our savior? You mean Jesus?"

Her laughter had a sweet musical tone to it, "Perhaps, but that is not what I meant. I meant the savior of Siren is a planet that revolves around the smaller of those two stars. My ancestors were always in much reverence to the bright star, and perhaps it is because they were aware of our benefactors on the planet *Preculis*."

"I've heard the name before at an alpha omega conference in America, but I don't know the whole story. Perhaps now you can educate me."

"Well, I don't know very much, but Arabic legend has it that there were two worlds at war. Their names were *Preculis* and *Xeries*. I am not sure of the reason behind the war, but some say it is believed to be a jihad or religious conflict of some kind. The war went on for over a thousand years when all of a sudden one of the worlds, *Preculis,* found a way to put out the star of *Xeries*. That in itself is a very tragic occurrence, but that is not the end of it. When the star collapsed, it produced very harmful energy to an area of space many light-years across. Earth fell in the way of that harmful energy, but Siren did not."

"And do you suppose that's the main difference of our two worlds?" asked Matthew.

"I do not know. For many years I have known contentment and peace, but lately I have had urges and cravings. It is like a fire has come alive in me."

"I've noticed," he said with a wry grin.

"And are you glad that I have this fire?"

"As I said before, it works for me," he chuckled lightly stroking her long dark hair that lay across her chest.

"I don't want to surrender this fire, Matthew. I have gotten used to these new feelings."

"I know what you mean. I feel the same way. But I'm not sure we can bring these feelings back to Siren. I think they are human feelings."

"Oh, nonsense. My body is my body and my mind is my mind. Do you actually think when we get to Siren that I won't wish for you to make love to me?"

"You make a good point. I want to continue what we have together. It's something that has been missing my whole life," said Matthew. "The sad thing is that I was never really aware of it."

"Well, we are aware of it now. Isn't there something that your body wants to say to me now?"

"As a matter of fact there is.

Chapter Thirty-eight

Charles Donovan had the overwhelming impulse to get in touch with a long time rival of his former employer Senator Williams. Williams' rival was a Democratic senator elected by the State of Florida over fourteen years ago named John Poole. He knew the senator's daughter and recently saw her and the senator's family at the alpha omega conference under the mountain in West Virginia. It is said that he is so well-liked by his constituency that no one ever bothers to challenge him for his seat. Senator Poole is known to be a good man and Charles always regarded him as such; however, Charles also just recently retained the knowledge that he is, in fact, not a human. He is a siren as is his wife, daughter, and son. Charles also learned at the conference that John Jr., being the progeny of two sirens is also a *seer*.

Although a *seer* would be instrumental in revealing the very pleasurable events of his near future, it was not what Charles sought in the home of Senator Poole. He sought an opponent of his former boss. Senator Poole, aside from being a champion of rights for the elderly, was a major force in the campaign to reduce the numbers of American forces in the Middle East. Charles was there to offer his support. Having driven the twelve hours from Washington, D.C., to Vero Beach, Florida, Charles had a lot of time to reflect on his friend Durbah Purness and her human friend Alex Jansen. He found that his anger was waning and that his urge to reverse his position on troop deployment gave him a sense of peace. He was, in fact, reversing his position regarding Durbah's relationship as well. He had learned that the Purness family lived a short distance away from Senator Poole on the same island. He thought that if he were able to get in touch with Durbah through her family, he might even offer her support. He had a sneaking suspicion that Durbah intended to make a case for the sirens to allow Alex to travel to Siren with her. Now that he had time to reflect on the matter, he had to admit that he didn't see the harm. Soon Earth will be in contact with the planet Siren if for no other reason than to exchange artifacts or medical advances. Now that the threat of violent behavior on the part of humanity was reduced to impotence, the benevolent nature of the two societies could be a benefit to both of them. If Alex Jansen is, as Durbah suspects, a new breed of humanity with a peaceful spirit although being cast on Earth, perhaps he could be installed on Siren as Earth's Ambassador. *Alex Jansen, Earth's Ambassador to Siren*, he chuckled at the thought.

Charles found himself at the front gate house of John's Island much the same as Shelly Simon did a mere three hours earlier. He told the guard, "I'm here to visit Senator Poole."

Charles was told that he was expected and was instructed to drive on ahead and that he would be warmly welcomed. *Expected,* he wondered. *Was it Williams sensing that I might visit his rival senator when I jumped ship?* When he reached the Poole residence, he parked in the circular driveway which surrounded a huge fountain that boasted a half dozen large ceramic fish spouting water from their mouths. He walked up and rang the bell.

Johanna Poole answered the door in a bright red kimono. Her face was white painted and powdered in the style of a geisha, and her long, dark hair was piled on the top of her head and held in place by what looked like ivory chopsticks. In her hand she held a fan in front of her face and peered over it with a seductive look in her electrum colored irises. She began to laugh, "You should see your face, Charles. It's priceless."

"Mrs. Poole?"

"Yes, Charles, I'm Johanna Poole. Forgive the outfit and the makeup. My husband John and I are preparing for a costume party. This time we're doing Shogun."

"Well, you make a beautiful geisha, Mariko, Mrs. Poole."

"Thanks," she laughed. "Come on in, John's been expecting you."

When Charles Donovan was shown into the senator's library, he was surprised to find him dressed as Lord Toranaga. He wore what looked like an authentic ancient samurai outfit in the style of the Bushido Code. He addressed Charles, "Konishiwa, Charles san."

"Konishiwa, Senator san," answered Charles.

"The senator laughed and said, "How was your trip down?"

"Uneventful. Just the way I like it. It gave me some time to think."

"You're thinking of coming over to our side with regard to cutting back troop deployment, aren't you?"

"As a matter of fact, I am. How did you know I was coming?"

"My son, John Jr."

"Oh, yes. I remember your daughter talking about him at the conference."

"Some pretty wild stuff, wouldn't you say? I've just been able to realize for the first time outside a retreat who and what I am."

"You and your wife both."

"That's right. Johanna is a siren, too. Go ahead, you can say it. Siren is not a dirty word in this house," he gave a small chuckle. Can I make you a drink?" asked the senator.

"Saki?" asked Charles facetiously.

"Hate the stuff. How about some twelve-year-old scotch?"

"I'd love one. It's cocktail hour somewhere, right?"

"Right here and right now." The senator rose from his futon on the floor and made his way over to a wet bar near a large window that looked out on the canal that surrounds the island.

"You take soda, Charles?"

"Just ice, please."

"Ahh, a man after my own heart," said the senator.

"How well do you know my daughter, Charles?"

"Not well, really. I've only really talked to her a couple of times at the retreat."

"Well, she's a beautiful soul."

"She certainly looks beautiful."

"Thanks, Charles, but I think you should know she's taken."

"I know she was close to Matthew Winter at alpha omega."

"I don't know much about that, but she called us recently and said she's fallen pretty hard for a guy named Brad Early, a human, no less. She says that if he can't join the exodus, she might not go."

"I think I know another one of us who feels the same way."

"You're talking about the Purness girl, or I should say woman. What is she about twenty-five?"

"I guess. How do you know about Durbah's love life if you don't mind me asking?"

"Oh, her dad and I are fishing buddies. We go way back. He said she's called him recently and told him she's in love. They're pretty happy for her."

"Even though her man is a human?"

"Now, don't be a bigot, son. Sirens end up with humans all the time, in fact, most of the time."

"But you married a siren, Sir."

"That I did. I think she put a spell on me," he said with mock seriousness.

"You're a lucky man, Senator."

"Yes, I am. So what brings you here? Young John said you would come, but he didn't say why."

"I'd like to help, Senator, if I can. If there's anything that I can do to further your agenda for the reduction of troops overseas, I'd like to know."

"Well, now that's very kind of you, Charles. If I think there's anything you can do, you'll be the first to know."

"I can be very persuasive if I have a mind to."

"No doubt. And you don't have a problem with the morality of that?"

"Lives are ticking, Sir."

"I think I like you, son."

"Thank you, Senator Poole. I like you, too, even though I've been kind of confrontational in the past."

"Forget about it, son. That's all water under the bridge. And besides, my office was quick to undue any of your boss's dirty work. You guys were harmless. We just made a lot of noise so you'd think you were gaining ground."

"I'm familiar with the rules, Sir."

"I know you are, Charles. And by the way, you can just call me John in private. All this, Sir this and Senator that, can wait for Washington."

"Thanks, John. Good scotch," said Charles.

"I'll bet they don't have anything like it on Siren."

"I hope you're wrong on that count."

"I think there's something else you should know, or at least you'll find out soon enough."

"Oh? What's that?"

"You're about to get another letter. So are we."

"John again?"

"That's right. John said it will come in tomorrow's mail. An alpha omega letter. I'm sure you'll get one also for the retreat in West Virginia."

"Did John say what it's all about?"

"I'm sure he doesn't know. A *seer* has visions, I'm told, but I don't think they can actually know what the future holds."

"I think it's fascinating. I'd like to meet him sometime."

"Oh, I think that can be arranged," said the senator. "I suppose I can drag him away from his video games. I can tell you that he was very relieved when he found out from Jonah that they have them on Siren." The senator chuckled and said, "As if his life won't be exciting enough traveling to another world. But I guess a nine-year-old is a nine-year-old whether he is a *seer* or not." The senator left the room briefly and when he came back, John Jr. was in tow. "John, meet Charles Donovan," said the senator. John Jr. reached out his hand for Charles's and said, "I'm pleased to meet you, Mr. Donovan."

"Charles is a siren, John," said the senator.

"That's right, Dad, he is."

Senator Poole caught himself remembering that John could *see* sirens as well as the next day ahead of him. That skill is the principal reason behind them becoming *sensors* to guide the sirens from their sixteenth birthday on. But all that is changing now with the exodus and the end of the directives to manipulate mankind in Siren's interests. Siren doesn't need their special skills anymore. The senator wondered what that implied for the future of his talented son. He was told by Jonah that the art of *seeing* is a lost one on Siren, and he wondered if and what young John would *see* when he got there.

"Charles is interested in your gift, son."

"So am I," said John. "As far as I can tell, I've only come aware of it in the last week or so."

"I'll bet you were kind of scared at first," offered Charles.

"I don't think so."

Senator Poole then said, "John has never been your average boy, Charles."

"Thanks, Dad," said John sourly.

"Oh, you know what I mean, John. You've always been very special, especially to your mother and me and your sister Sarah as well."

"I know, Dad."

The senator continued to Charles, "What I meant to say was that not much can shake John up. He's always been a pretty level-headed kid. There've been some episodes when his gift sort of got him some attention, but we were never really aware of the reason behind it. We always thought it was just kid's stuff, if you know what I mean."

"Sure, I can see that," said Charles.

"Would you like to see a demonstration?" asked the senator.

"Aw, Dad."

"Come on, John. Is it time or not?"

"No, Dad. Siren won't be lined up for another twenty minutes or so."

"Well, go on and play your games, John, but come back in twenty minutes and do your stuff."

"OK," said the boy hanging his head clearly tired of all the attention and confusing feelings that he had connected with his gift.

"He's quite a guy," offered Charles.

"Johanna and I worship him, but if you tell him that I might have to use this sword on you," he said gripping the hilt in the scabbard at his waist.

"Have no fear, sir. My lips are sealed."

Chapter Thirty-nine

Sarah Poole was lying in Brad Early's arms on the couch in front of a crackling fire. Brad's house in Bar Harbor was a bit drafty that time of year, but they didn't seem to feel the cold at all. They had just made good use of a lamb's wool rug before the fireplace. The fire heated their bodies on the outside, and their love for each other heated them from within. She took hold of his hand, "Brad, I'm not going to go anywhere without you."

"What? Did you just say what I think you did?"

"I said if I can't get you to be part of the exodus, then I'm staying right here on Earth with you."

"You would do that for me?" he asked hopefully.

"Yes."

"But think about what you're saying. What if we were to fall out of love, and you had missed your chance to return to Siren?"

"That's not going to happen, Brad. I don't think sirens *can* fall out of love."

"Maybe not sirens, but what about humans?"

Sarah looked him deeply in the eye. He took in her beauty, and she had a sure feeling that no tricks would be needed to drive home her point.

"Never mind," he said simply.

"Then you agree with my decision?"

"You know I can't refuse you anything. Even if it means having to be selfish enough to keep you all to myself."

~

When Alankha and Matthew got dressed, she used the flashlight to show him the reliefs on the walls in Khufu. The story of the journey to Earth with the aid of the *Preculians* was depicted as it was on the walls of the tunnel. In a niche halfway around the room, there was a large rectangular granite box that Matthew was quick to identify as a sarcophagus. He made his way over to it and shined his own flashlight on the inscription on the pink granite slab that was the lid. He could make out the Arabic symbols for supreme ruler and the depiction of a funeral procession that traveled over a long distance. He said to Alankha, "That isn't what I think it is, is it?"

"That all depends," she said. "What is it that you think it is?"

"That's not Khufu?"

Alankha's laugh echoed throughout the chamber and she said, "No, Matthew. Khufu is not buried in Khufu's tomb."

"But the symbols. It says supreme ruler."

"And so he was, and a very brave warrior as well, but it is not Khufu buried in the sarcophagus."

"If not Khufu, then who?" asked Matthew.

"Alexander," said Alankha simply.

"Remember when I said nothing about this night could surprise me?'

"Yes."

"I think I spoke too soon.

~

Charles Donovan was looking anxiously at his watch noticing that nearly twenty minutes had passed since young John Poole left him and the senator to resume his video games. He knew he would be back shortly to give a demonstration of his gift. He asked the senator, "What did you mean when you asked your son if it was time?"

"It seems the timing is critical, Charles. John says he can see tomorrow when the Earth lines up. It only lasts about a half hour or so."

"What do you mean lines up?"

"I think he means when the Earth lines up with Siren. When they are in synch physically, there is a brief window when he has the gift of sight into the next day."

"Did you ever ask him how a Senate vote would go down?" asked Charles jovially.

"I would have if I knew he could've told me," said the senator laughing. "All's fair in love and politics. Isn't that how it goes?"

"Something like that," said Charles and then took a large pull on his glass of the senator's expensive scotch. Just then,

John Jr. entered the room. His father asked him, "Is it time, John?"

"Yes."

"What would you like to know, Charles?"

"Maybe we should give a heads up to Durbah about the upcoming conference under the mountain. Can John tell us where she is?"

"Go ahead," said the senator.

John Jr. sat down on the soft leather couch and leaned back against the headrest. He closed his eyes briefly and then opened them again. "Tomorrow Ms. Purness will be standing in front of a sign that says *Missy Kathryn's Hideaway."*

"Hmm, a sign," said the senator thoughtfully. "It must be a place of business. I'm guessing a motel or a bed and breakfast. I think the internet can give you a quick answer, Charles. Just do a search when you get back to your hotel."

"That's pretty amazing, John."

"Isn't it?" The senator was taken aback, as well.

"What about me, John," said Charles to the boy. "Where do you see me tomorrow?"

The boy again sat back against the couch and closed his eyes. When he opened them his eyebrows shot up into his forehead and a rush of color came to his cheeks. He quickly got up off the couch and scurried out of the room. Charles felt a chill run down his spine and said to the senator, "What's that all about?"

"I haven't a clue, Charles. I guess something he saw shook him up."

"Why am I not so glad to hear that, John?"

"Relax, Charles. It's probably nothing."

"That's easy for you to say. Mind if I make myself another drink?"

"Sure, go ahead," said the senator laughing.

"I'm glad you think it's funny, John, but I don't mind telling you I'm a little worried about what your son saw."

"OK, just make yourself a drink, and I'll go find out." The senator left Charles in his study to his thoughts of pending doom and gloom. When he came back shortly thereafter, he was shaking his head and chuckling. Charles was literally sitting on the edge of his seat of the leather winged-back chair and asked, "Well?"

The senator continued to laugh and said, "Like I said, a nine-year-old is still a nine-year-old, gifted or not."

"Don't keep me in suspense, John. What did he say?"

"He said that when he looked at you tomorrow, you were in your birthday suit."

"So he was embarrassed, is that it?" asked Charles with some relief.

"That's right, he was embarrassed. I guess that's the price of his gift. He never knows what he's going to see."

"Well, I'm glad that's all it was. He had me scared there for a minute." Charles took a long sip on his drink, exhaled and wiped his brow.

"Uh, Charles, there's something else that you might like to know."

"Something else?" Charles was suddenly alert.

"John said that you . . . uh . . . were not alone." The senator raised his eyebrows and lifted his drink in a silent salute.

~

Charles knew that Durbah's parents, Walter and Edith Purness, were also residents of John's Island. When he mentioned this to Senator Poole, it was he who mentioned that Charles might like to drop in on his old fishing buddy and inform his wife Edith that a letter might soon be forthcoming.

When Shelly Simon and Walter Purness returned from their sea trial, they found Charles Donovan sitting with Edith on a pair of lounge chairs on the dock. The first thing that Charles noticed was the fire-engine red bikini that Shelly was wearing. He had a vague recollection of her from the baths beneath the mountain retreat, but this vision that he suddenly had was infinitely more alluring. She filled out the suit in a way that he had never quite seen before. The scant few square inches of cloth seemed to reflect the afternoon sun and accentuated her body revealing the unbridled shape of her lovely breasts. He couldn't imagine what in the world was keeping the suit on her. Gravity certainly wasn't doing its job. As the boat docked, Charles sipped on his scotch on the rocks, and Edith sucked at her frozen margarita from a straw.

"Ahoy there," said Charles. It wasn't only his second drink of the afternoon. He learned that John Poole liked his good scotch, and he also liked company.

"Help us with the lines, son," said Walter as he eased the large boat between the pilings and reversed the engines to come to a halt. It was an impressive display of seamanship, and Shelly and Charles had little trouble securing the lines both fore and aft as well as attaching a spring line to keep it suspended in the middle of the mooring.

When Walter came ashore, he shook Charles's hand, "Thanks for the help, son. Walter Purness," he gave his name and added, "have we met before?"

"No, Mr. Purness, but I know your daughter Durbah."

"She certainly gets around," he said with a slight laugh.

"We run into each other occasionally in Washington."

"Durbah has informed us that she recently left her job."

"I did, too," said Charles. "There didn't seem to be much point considering where I'm going." Charles mistakenly assumed that *both* Walter and Edith were sirens.

"Oh, and where is that?" asked Walter.

Shelly and Edith were both quick on the uptake instantly and changed the subject. Charles caught Edith's forceful glare, and he quickly realized what he had done. *My God, he doesn't know,* thought Charles. *How could I have been so stupid!* He tried to cover his tracks, "I'm thinking of accepting a position overseas. Hong Kong, actually. I have a friend in international finance who might have a position for me."

"Well, let me know if I can open any doors for you, son. The V.C.C. and the consortium do a lot of business over there."

"Thanks, Mr. Purness. I will."

"Looks like you're enjoying my scotch. I think I'd like to join you. I've had enough lemonade for one day."

"I think I'd like one of Edith's margaritas," said Shelly. "Cruising is thirsty work," she said smiling at Charles. He found himself fighting to contain the electrum in his irises as he returned the smile. Shelly was doing the same and was comically thinking that if they weren't careful, they just might blow each other up. She, too, was seeing Charles Donovan in an entirely new light. She had always appreciated his good looks and devilish grin, but until now they had little effect on her. Now she was suddenly thirsting for stimulation instead of denying herself the pleasure. When Walter walked out of earshot, she asked him, "So what brings you here, Charles?"

"I thought I'd deliver a message to Edith."

"So you were just in the neighborhood?" she asked slyly.

"Something like that." Charles again took in the vision of Shelly in Durbah's bathing suit. "I don't mind telling you that the message is what got me here, but that suit is what's keeping me here."

"Why, Mr. Donovan," she said coyly, "you just might turn my cheeks the same color."

"Sirens don't blush," he said quietly.

"Well, I'm sure they're willing to learn," she said in her sexiest voice.

"Seriously, Shelly, you look fantastic. The sun and sea agree with you."

"Thank you, Mr. Donovan. You can sail with me anytime." She made no attempt to reign in her electrum following that statement. Charles could clearly see it in her eyes. He excused himself briefly to go and throw some cold water on his face. The scotch seemed to be getting to him, if not the sight of Shelly Simon. When Walter came back outside to where Shelly was sitting, he said to her, "Charles seems like a very nice fellow. Have you met him before?"

"We've attended some of the same functions in Washington. This is the first time we've run into each other outside of work."

"That's a pity," offered Walter. "You both seem like very nice kids to me."

"Your daughter is really a sweetheart, Mr. Purness. I can tell you that she will be missed in Washington."

"Well, then we'll just have to change her mind, won't we?"

"I think she knows what she wants, and I for one am very happy for her."

"You mean her young man. No doubt Edith mentioned him to you."

"Yes, but Durbah talked of him, as well. It was during a conference that we both attended. We talked like a couple of schoolgirls comparing notes," she said jokingly.

"Well, all we really care about is her happiness. I don't need to tell you what she means to us. She's our only child," said Walter smiling.

"She deserves to be happy, Mr. Purness."

"You all do, dear," he said sincerely.

Shelly wondered how the news of Durbah leaving would affect him. She found herself holding back tears knowing the depth of his love for his daughter. Perhaps Edith could convince Walter to make the journey. He seemed to be in good shape for a man of his age. Wouldn't he be amenable to making the voyage to a new world if it meant sharing the experience with Durbah? Shelly made a mental note to try to broach the subject with Edith when they got a moment alone. She found herself feeling emotions much more strongly than she ever had before. It was as though a curtain had been lifted from in front of her revealing a part of her mind that she had kept locked up in a box. Now that the door was open, she knew she would forever throw away the key. There was no going back. Freedom is something that can be denied; however, once it has been fully tasted, the desire for it can never fade. Desire was a word that she suddenly associated with Charles Donovan. At first, that seemed very surprising to her. She had known him for years, but had never actually seen him for the beautiful man that he was. She was newly exploring the freedom to feel an attachment that had always seemed to elude her. It seemed to come easily to her all at once. She wondered if the feeling was new to him as well. Could they explore the newness together and perhaps take it with them back to Siren? She had no way of actually knowing, but it seemed to her that Siren promised comfort and equality, but also held something else in check. It was as though there was some kind of safeguard for putting a limitation on extreme emotions. But extremes can be very addictive she was realizing. And once you felt the breadth and width of their powerful influence, all bets were off.

Chapter Forty

Edith Purness asked Charles and Shelly if they would care to stay for dinner with her and Walter. They eagerly accepted. It proved to be a wise decision because after an appetizer of New England steamed clams and a Caesar salad with garlic and herb croutons, the main course proved to be fresh Maine lobsters that had just been delivered by a truck that was painted with the name *Mainely Lobster*.

It was all delicious and afterward topped off with glasses of Walter's favorite port imported from Spain and Edith's home-made key lime pie. When they brought their port out to the screened-in porch overlooking the canal, Charles and Shelly settled into cushioned Adirondack-styled chairs and put their feet up on the coffee table.

"It doesn't get any better than this," announced Charles.

"I could get used to this. Can you believe Walter's boat?"

"And Edith's cooking? We really lucked out, Shelly."

"We sure did. They're very sweet people."

"So, what do you think?" he asked.

"About what?"

"Siren."

"I guess I won't know what to think until I go there."

"Then your mind is made up, is that it?"

"Oh, yes. There are things here that give me pleasure, but nothing to really keep me here."

“No one special in your life? No human?”

“I’m afraid not.”

“Do you feel a void? Like something is missing in your life?”

“Of course, I do. I didn’t used to feel this way, but I certainly do now.”

“As of about three days ago, right?”

“Exactly.”

“Why do you suppose that is?” he asked her.

“I don’t really know.”

“I guess we’ll find out.”

“What do you mean?”

“Come on, Shelly, it has to be connected to the mountain somehow. You feel it, Durbah feels it, I feel it and so does Sarah Poole. What are the odds? It has to be something that affects only sirens.”

“Has Edith mentioned it?”

“Not so far. But I’m pretty sure she feels it, too. When she mentioned Durbah and Alex, I could sense her sort of cheering them on.”

“I’m glad she found someone.”

“He’s human. Did you know that, Shelly?”

“I have human friends,” she said. “Until last week, I didn’t even know *I* wasn’t human.”

“But you’re not really close to anyone, are you?”

“No, not really.”

“Me neither,” he said. “Maybe it’ll be different on Siren.”

“I hope so.”

~

Alankha and Matthew left Khufu's tomb and made their way back through the tunnel to Mother Bakhawi's home at 1800 East Pyramid Road. When they came up the stairs and through the doorway in the basement, Mother Bakhawi was sitting at a table drinking a glass of wine. She said to them, "How was your journey to Khufu?"

"Fabulous," said Matthew. "I'm very grateful to you for letting us use the passage way."

"It is my pleasure, Sir. Can I get you a glass of wine?"

"That sounds wonderful, Mother," said Alankha.

"Yes, I'd like one, too, if you don't mind," said Matthew.

"Not at all." The old woman got up from her chair and pulled a dusty bottle of red wine from a rack in the corner of the room. She brought it over to Matthew and handed him a corkscrew, "Would you please assist me, young man."

"I'd be happy to." Matthew noticed by the label that it was a Chateau Laffite Rothschild. The date on the bottle was 1993.

Edith Purness left Walter in their living room where he was watching a basketball game on the television. She walked out of her French-style patio doors and joined Shelly and Charles on the porch.

“That was a close call earlier, Charles.”

“Edith, I’m so sorry. I nearly blew it.”

“Well, he has to know sometime, but I thought I would let it come from Durbah.”

“You’re right, of course,” said Shelly. She looked over at Charles and giggled, “I thought you were going to faint.”

“So did I,” he said shaking his head. “I had just come from the Poole’s house and I just assumed . . . I don’t know.”

“That Walt was a siren, too. Afraid not,” said Edith raising her eyebrows and shaking her head. “But he acts like one of us. He doesn’t have a mean bone in his body.”

“Yes, he’s very sweet,” agreed Shelly.

“How was your cruise, dear?”

“It was great. Your husband is a terrific captain.”

“Not only that, he brings me fish,” she said happily. Charles and Shelly laughed along with her. “Edith, that dinner was to die for,” said Shelly.

“It sure was,” agreed Charles. “I wonder if they have lobster on Siren?” he posed.

“I’m sure they do,” said Edith. “Well, I’ll leave you two alone,” she said getting up from her chair and walking back inside.

“She’s such a sweetheart,” said Shelly. “Leaving us alone like she doesn’t want to crowd us.”

“Uh huh,” said Charles.

"As if she thinks we're going to get intimate with each other."

He reached over and took her hand in his and said, "I've heard of worse ideas." Shelly leaned over and kissed him.

Later that evening, they both slept at the Shore Break Bed and Breakfast. At least for a little while.

Chapter Forty-one

When Matthew and Alankha finished their wine, they thanked Mother Bakhawi and made their way up the stairs and out into the street. No taxi cabs were in sight, so Matthew clicked open his cell phone and tuned on the power. He noticed that he had one missed call. The name read J. Riley. He said to Alankha, "I missed a call from Joanne."

"The woman at the dig," stated Alankha matter-of-factly.

"I should call her."

"You're not going to work the dig, are you?"

"What? After tonight? I think you just blew my socks off as a lover *and* an archeologist."

"Then you're saying I shouldn't be jealous," she said.

"Sirens don't get jealous, Alankha."

"I'm willing to learn."

He dialed a taxi company and called for a car from a number he had stored on his phone. While they were waiting, he dialed Joanne's cell phone. She answered on the first ring, "Hello, Matthew," she said coldly. "I hope you had a nice trip to the states."

"Do you, Dr. Riley?"

"Oh, so now it's Dr. Riley. It was Joanne the night you got me drunk and took advantage of me."

"You were drunk before I got there."

"Yes, I suppose I was. I'm sorry."

"What's the matter, you sound awful."

"You really know how to charm a girl."

"No, really, what is it?"

"The scrolls were damaged. They're useless now."

"Oh, what a shame," said Matthew honestly feeling sorry if not surprised by her news. He knew they were damaged and that the deed was done by him.

"Yes, it is a shame. They're saying it's my fault."

"Who?" asked Matthew.

"The SCA."

"That's ridiculous. Why would it be your fault?"

"They're saying I didn't control the climate. The humidity."

"But weren't they sealed in the vases like the first one?" he asked knowingly.

"I know, I know. But they're blaming me. Forty-eight hundred freakin' years they're fine, and then they dissolve in my tent. Go figure."

"Oh, Joanne, I'm so sorry," he said honestly.

"I'm closing the dig."

"And what are you going to do, teach?"

"Not at first. The SCA authenticated the first scroll. I'm going to ride that wave for a while and lecture."

"Well, do you need me to help you close the dig?"

"There's really nothing to do, Matthew. I'm sorry. Go home."

"Go home," he repeated dully.

"Yes, actually there is a letter for you that came from the states."

"A letter?"

"It looks like it's from your fraternity. There's a stamp on the outside of the envelope that say's alpha omega."

"Just throw it away, Joanne. They just want money."

"OK, if you're sure."

"I'm sure. Good luck with your lecture tour."

"Thank you, Matthew. I'll look you up when I get back to the university."

"Take care, Joanne. Safe travels."

"Thanks," she broke the connection.

Alankha asked Matthew, "What did she say?"

"You need to check your mail."

"My mail?"

Matthew looked back at the front door of 1800 East Pyramid Road and said, "In a few days, I think you'll be going back through that doorway."

"You got a letter."

"It came to the dig. Listen, could you do me a favor?"

"I will do anything you ask."

"Call your uncle and see if you can get him and the SCA to take the heat off Joanne. You know the damaged scrolls aren't her fault."

"Yes, I know. And so does my uncle Zaphi."

"What makes you say that?"

Alankha gestured to Mother Bakhawi's door and said, "Because both Zaphi and his beautiful wife, my aunt, will be going back through that door with me in a few days. Are you going back to America?"

"Apparently, but I'll be back. You've put a spell on me."

"As you have also put a spell on me."

"Ask your sensor if we can make the journey together from Khufu."

"I will. I will miss you while you are away from me."

"I'll leave you my heart, Alankha."

"I will watch over it carefully, my love."

~

Chapter Forty-two

Sarah Poole and Brad Early were lying on the couch and staring at the embers in the fireplace. Brad stroked her hair and said, "I should put another log on, but I don't want to move."

"I'll keep you warm. Just stay here with me under the blanket."

"You do keep me warm, Sarah. Just knowing that a beautiful creature like you can love me gives me all the heat in the world."

"It's a heat that will never leave you because my spirit will never leave you. I feel that I have been searching for a home for my whole life. I always was quick to make friends, but I never felt that I really fit in anywhere or within anyone else's life. You have given me that and for that I love you."

"I feel like I'm in heaven or something," he said honestly.

"Yes, we are in heaven. Our home is heaven, and it is not a place or time. It is a destiny to find our other self if we're lucky, and I think that finally in my otherwise placid existence I have found you."

"In Barnacle Bill's," said Brad; his voice thick with irony.

"Even Barnacle Bill's can't cheapen what we have, Bradley. Don't you feel how we have stumbled upon something magical?"

"The magic is all in you, Sarah."

"Maybe at first, but don't you think we've gotten beyond that now?"

"Oh, yes. I certainly do. I will do anything in the world just to be a part of your life. I have no other choice in the matter. I'm toast."

~

Durbah stroked the hair on Alex Jansen's chest. She had risen from her face down position on the bed at Missy Kathryn's Hideaway to her side. She lay with her long blond hair curled across her breast. The rise of her hips and downward slope of her torso was reminiscent of the graceful lines of a mountain that Alex was very familiar with in Marin County, California. She was called Mt. Tamalpais, or *The Sleeping Lady*. His mind was evolving into something beyond his control. It was careless, and all at once beyond care. He was feeling an intimate connection to a woman whom he couldn't imagine a mere week earlier. His marriage to Brianna was always good. Good, but not great. They both felt that their union was a success in that it produced a very valuable person in Billy Jansen, but that was all. They knew that their chemistry fell short of the ideal that may or may not even exist in the world. But in the interest of trying to find the penultimate soul mate before it was too late, they felt that what they shared together aside from Billy was something they were settling for and not satisfied with. They would always remain friends, but both Brianna and Alex knew there was still a chance to really find the right place for their heart and perhaps an uncomfortable separation was not too much to pay for that privilege.

Alex gave Durbah a long and loving kiss. When he broke away, he said, "You'll never use your charms on me to shape my mind, is that it?"

"I've been totally honest with you, Alex. I've told you what I am. I'm not perfect, but I can assure you that I will try to be responsible with respect to how I know I can affect you."

"I think I like the way you affect me."

"But the power can be abused. All power can be abused."

"I don't have a problem placing my heart in your hands."

"But your mind? Do you trust me to always know what is best for your mind to hold true. I'm not sure that I trust myself, Alex."

"I know what I feel. That's all I have to go on. If you love me, I don't think you have it in you to purposely cause me harm."

"I'm not a saint, just a siren."

"Somehow I feel that a siren is enough."

"I hope you're right. But you know that I've changed recently."

"You've said it is a change for the better, and I'm sure of it."

"I hope so. If I were to ask you to be screened by the *sensors* to insure that you have a benign nature and are no threat to Siren, would you agree?"

"You know I can't refuse you anything. Why would you even ask?"

"No tricks, remember? I will not try to shape your mind even in that decision as much as I want you to go through with it."

"I only want to find ways to please you, Durbah. If a screening process will clear me to join you on your journey, nothing would make me happier. It's almost like judgment day. It's something that everyone considers sooner or later. I want to know as well, whether or not I will be acceptable to the people of Siren."

"Well, as far as I'm concerned, you're more than accepted. You are preferred and revered over any other man I've ever met on this planet, either human *or* siren."

"And that's how I can't help but give you all of my heart. I simply have no choice in the matter."

"But no tricks, remember?"

"Perhaps love *is* a trick."

"If so, then you're the best magician I know." She kissed him.

When Alankha reached her home at the western edge of the city of Cairo, there was indeed an alpha omega letter in her mail slot. She didn't need to read it past the date in the heading. Her directive always required her to merely add three days to the date and that was the scheduled time for the conference. She called her uncle's cell phone, "Dearest Uncle Zaphi, are you well?"

"I am, Alankha. You are calling me to tell me of the arrival of your letter, isn't that so?"

"Yes, Uncle, and to also ask a great favor of you."

"Anything that is in my power to do, I shall," he said.

"I have found love, Uncle Zaphi."

"And?"

"I would like him to make the journey from Khufu instead of a different chamber location designated as E. C.-2."

"Ahh, an American."

"Yes, he is."

"So your lover is a siren."

"Yes, Uncle Zaphi."

"Then I don't foresee any real problem. All he has to do is let his *sensor* know."

"I was hoping you could ask his *sensor* for him since you are my *sensor*."

"Very, well, Alankha. You know I can never refuse anything asked of me by my favorite niece."

"Thank you, Uncle Zaphi."

"What is your lover's name?"

"Matthew Winter."

"I know of him. He is famous on Siren for destroying the scrolls."

"Yes, I know, Uncle, though he is sad that it caused pain for his friend Dr. Riley."

"The pain will not last, my child. I will take responsibility for the scrolls in a letter to be opened after the exodus."

"Matthew will be glad to hear that."

"What is the name of Matthew's *sensor*?"

"Jonah."

"I know Jonah. It will be done, my child."

"Again, thank you."

"You can thank me in person in a few days when we meet at the conference within Khufu."

"But there is one more favor I need to ask."

"What is it?"

"We want to travel to Siren together. In the same exchange chamber."

"Very well. Your names will be placed in the same slot for the exodus schedule."

"Oh, you have made me so happy. How can I ever thank you?"

"When you and your love have a child, he will grow up to be a "*seer*" because both his parents are sirens who have developed on Earth. Siren has no such thing as a "seer" anymore so he will be an important member of their society. Perhaps he should also have the name Zaphi."

"Yes, of course, Uncle."

"That will be thanks enough."

~

Chapter Forty-three

The Planet Siren 3700 B.C.E.

The Great Hall of The Council of Regents was located on the East Coast of a continent in the northern hemisphere of Siren. On a cool and crisp spring morning, there came a great ship from the heavens, and it landed on the lawn in front of the Council's Hall of Monuments. The sight brought great excitement because never before had there been any contact with beings outside of their world. There were many stories depicting the occurrence, and they were many times thought to be the result of prescient dreams by the *seers* of Siren. In time the very art of *seeing* would become a vestigial ability of the society of Siren because its benign nature had little use of the knowledge of future events. Today, like tomorrow, is a mirror of yesterday in a world that enjoys perfect balance. But never had there been an actual ship descended from the heavens until that day.

Sirens came from all walks of life and corners of the globe to pay tribute and worship the great craft. Artisans brought their finest work and laid it before the sleeping ship hoping to gain favor. The finest wines and sweetest ambrosia were placed on tables before the ship, and many animals were offered as sacrifice as was their custom. But after a week, still the ship remained idle and completely silent. The sirens, at moments of spiritual weakness, sometimes began to doubt that the great ship was there to commune with them at all. Some would call it *the great accident* and give it no more significance than a tree falling in the forest or a great wind whipped up from the city of Atlantica in the middle of the ocean to the East. And then it happened. After 60 days and 60 nights, the great ship came to life, and a portal became visible with a ramp leading down to the lawn. A procession then came forth of beings identical in appearance to those of Siren who stood before the great masses assembled to worship that day. One of the newcomers stepped forward, and it was clear that he was to be the voice of the visitors to the people of Siren. The first words he uttered were, "We come in peace to your world and have the unfortunate responsibility to deliver grave news."

The sirens didn't take this news as welcomed, and many immediately bowed down in prayer. Some began a soft wailing cry as though the Gods themselves would deliver them from their apparent predicament, although they knew not what they were actually to be delivered from. They were soon informed by the new visitors and learned that indeed their prayers were going to be answered in full.

The next words that the leader of the newcomers said were, "We are the *Preculians*. We come from a planet that revolves around a binary star that your people call *Sirius*. We call it *Preculis*. It is located to the right of the constellation of the great hunter whom you call *Orion*. If you follow the line that is formed by his belt, you will see *Preculis* just past the tip of his bow." There was a general murmur among the sirens as they recalled the constellation that they knew very well. They had always believed it was the source of their creator and that it held the gates to heaven and the afterlife. The leader of the *Preculians* continued, "We are very sad to bring you the news that a great conflict between our people and a world called *Xeries* has come to a horrible conclusion. As sometimes happens beyond the will of the great creator, scientific advancements outrun their application of practical wisdom. We, as a people, sought to end the great conflict, which had raged on for over a thousand years, by releasing a catastrophic technology upon our brothers. The act was done too swiftly to consider the possible outcome of our actions. We have turned back the will of our creator and destroyed the fruits of his labor. For this we are truly sorry and will surely meet our just reward upon the Day of Judgment. We, as one, are prepared for this with the greatest sin to atone for."

The Grand Regent of Siren, who had been called forth to greet the newcomers when they appeared from the great ship, listened to the words of their leader and then asked him, "Why do you bring us this news of your atrocity? We do not stand in judgment of our brothers from other worlds."

"No, it is our belief that you do not. We know of your race and that you are a peaceful people and truly some of the creator's greatest work. Our news comes to you not to stand in judgment, but to deliver you from a potentially harmful enemy." Again the general assembly of sirens around the great ship mumbled in confusion and voiced many questions that they all hoped would be soon answered. The *Preculian* leader continued, "Our enemies from the planet *Xeries* were a very warlike race, and all we ever sought was to be left in peace. Now through a tragic cosmic accident, we have thrust the same conflict upon you. When our scientists collapsed the sun supporting the planet called *Xeries* . . ."

There was a collective gasp among all the sirens assembled. The *Preculian* repeated, "When our scientists collapsed the star called *Xeries* that the planet *Xeries* was a satellite of, a massive wave of gamma radiation was produced and emanated forth throughout the cosmos. A nearby world was flooded with a tide of negative energy that changed their very nature, which had been designed by the Great Creator. In destroying a warlike world, we have brought about another one. Perhaps that is what plagued the nature of *Xeries* to begin with. There is a sister planet of Siren that revolves around your sun in exactly the same orbit, although it is on the opposite side. It is called Earth and will one day detect your presence and seek to conquer your world. We will assist you in constructing a great shield, which will render your planet virtually invisible. However, this in itself will not allow you to completely escape detection. Your presence can be detected by your magnetic signature or *"field"* in space. It is therefore necessary to construct a giant ring around your planet of large gas-filled canisters tethered together and launched in a counter rotation of Siren's natural rotation. We know that the news of this potential conflict that we have brought about brings you great sorrow. For that reason we are truly committed to come to your aide and neutralize the threat. There is one consolation to this tragedy: The great shield and ring of canisters will not have to be operational for nearly five thousand of your years. That is the rough estimation by our scientists of how long it will take Earth inhabitants to conquer space flight. We hope you will forgive us, as we hope that our creator will as well. We will do everything in the power of *Preculis* to set things right. Now we will give you many gifts, which you will find useful. Crystals that will give you great power as well as the secrets to manipulating great blocks of masonry to build structures that will last many thousands of years. Now, one of our most prominent Shamans would like to give you the gift of his wisdom. It is believed that he is able to channel from the Great Creator of all things. We hope that you relish his spiritual insight as we do."

An ancient *Preculian* man with brown skin, a bald pallet and a long gray beard was dressed in a simple tan muslin robe and wore no shoes or sandals on his hard leather feet. Around his neck was a silver and gold rope, which served to hold a bezel, containing a perfect jade egg.

He smiled and then addressed the sirens, "From the Great Book of Proverbs: *Prudence will watch over you; and understanding will guard you.* We have resolved ourselves to be your window to the threat that will eventually come upon you. It is of our making and we will not falter in our efforts to protect you.

Do not plan harm against your neighbor who lives trustingly beside you. Do not quarrel with anyone without cause, when no harm has been done to you. Do not envy the violent and do not choose any of their ways; for the perverse are an abomination to the Creator, but the upright are in his confidence.

What this means is that you cannot adopt to the ways of your enemy or else you become them. We will deal with them because they are of our making.

A scoundrel and a villain goes around with crooked speech, wrinkling the eyes, shuffling the feet, pointing the fingers, with perverted mind devising evil, continually sowing discord; on such a one calamity will descend suddenly; in a moment, damage beyond repair.

What this means is that the design of your retribution will become your own undoing. To love your enemy will reap its own reward tenfold in the eyes of The Creator.

Do not rejoice when your enemies fall, and do not let your heart be glad when they stumble, or else the Creator will see it and be displeased, and turn away his anger from them.

Let your enemies churn in a miasma of their own making. Neither should you add to it, nor take any of it away. The Creator knows what is deserving of all of his creatures."

The Shaman then put his palms together and closed his eyes. He raised his arms over his head and said, "*The Creator is the Great Architect of goodness. May his goodness and mercy follow us all the days of our lives.*"

Chapter Forty-four

Shelly Simon and Charles Donovan didn't rise from the bed at the Shore Break until well after they had missed Beverly Jones' sumptuous breakfast. They slipped out the door stealthily avoiding the apology for doing so. Beverly would understand. Robert certainly did when he saw them turn in the night before. He successfully restrained himself from offering a knowing smirk when Shelly introduced him to Charles in his study. Robert offered them a glass of port and they politely refused, clearly having other cordials on their mind. *Ahh, to be young again,* thought, Robert. And then he corrected himself getting up from his chair to join Beverly upstairs, *What's being young have anything to do with it?*

When Shelly and Charles once again found themselves at the Purness house to say their good-byes, they were alerted by the raised eyebrows of Edith when Walt was out of the room. Shelly quietly inquired, "Edith, what is it?"

"I got my letter. An alpha omega. Yours, no doubt, are waiting for you back in Washington."

"I wonder why they came so soon?" commented Charles shaking his head. "It's only been about a week since the last time."

"I'm sure it has something to do with the changes going on."

"Yes, maybe we'll get some answers, not that I'm complaining," Shelly added reaching out and taking Charles's hand in hers.

"Walt and I are very happy that you two found each other in our home," said Edith. "Some people never do find someone to be close to."

"We're happy as well, Edith. We just wanted to stop by and thank you on our way back to Washington."

"Walt will be happy to hear it, but he won't be happy about losing his first mate."

"Sorry, Edith. You've now got your job back."

"I may learn to forgive you, Shelly. But just maybe not today."

They all got a good laugh at that one in spite of the fact that the news about the letter had them a little uneasy. This is the first time that returning to the mountain included the full knowledge of what they would find there. Shelly suddenly realized what was left unsaid, "You're not going, are you, Edith?"

"To the mountain? I don't really see the point," she said sadly. It was almost as though she was disappointed that her life wouldn't contain any more directives affecting the movers and shakers in Washington. Even though she was unaware of her role in the unspoken imperative of the sirens, she knew her life and actions had a consequence that was now coming to an end. She gathered Shelly and Charles into her arms for a quiet conspiratorial group hug. "Love you guys."

"We love you, too, Edith," said Charles.

"And Walt, too," added Shelly.

Just then, Walt entered the room and said, "What's all this hugging going on without me?" A mock anger painted his brow.

"The kids are leaving, Walt. Going back to Washington."

"So soon? I'm sorry to hear that. Perhaps we can hook up next week after the DEC conference. In fact, I'll probably see you there, Shelly."

"That sounds like a fun idea," said Shelly honestly. She had grown to love her all-too-human captain, Walter Purness, and her fellow siren Edith.

~

Chapter Forty-five

Sarah found her letter sticking out of the screen door when Brad Early dropped her off back at Mrs. Eldridge's house. Her mood was suddenly very serious, and she took both of Brad's hands in hers and said, "I knew this day was coming, but I had no idea when. I have to go away for a while."

"I miss you already, Sarah."

"I know you do, and I miss you, too. But at least I can give you some relief for the time being. Remember what I told you about thinking of me less and less with each passing day?"

"I know what you said, but I think it's impossible."

"No, it's not. Trust me. Do you love me?"

"You know I do."

"Can you refuse me anything?"

"Never."

"It's time to break your mind and heart away from me, Brad. That is the only thing that will make me happy. How much happiness do you want for me?"

"It's all I want, Sarah. It's what I live for, and yet I've known you such a short time. My mind is a blur."

"It will be clearer tomorrow. But the image of me will not be. It will begin to fade. But fear not, my love, if there is any way on this Earth that you can come with me to where I have to go, then you will. It is my promise to you. Now give me what I want most of all. Release me from your heart and mind until I come back for you."

Brad closed his eyes and took a deep breath. When he opened them again, he said, "Good night. I had a nice time."

"Me, too, Brad," said Sarah holding back tears. "Let's do it again sometime."

"Yeah, I think I'd like that."

~

Durbah rose from the sleep-warmed bed and slipped on one of the complimentary terrycloth robes with letters *M K H* embroidered on the right breast. She picked up the phone and called the front desk of Missy Kathryn's Hideaway. "Are we still in time for breakfast?"

"Is this Durbah?" asked Alice.

"Hi, Alice. Yes, it's me."

"Let me bring it to your room."

"Please don't go to any trouble."

"No trouble at all. Belgian waffles and Canadian bacon sound alright?"

"That sounds like heaven, Alice."

"Coffee or cappuccino?"

"Coffee's fine. You're a dear."

"Believe me, Durbah, it's my pleasure. I also have some fresh-squeezed orange juice. *Please* tell me that you're here for another night."

"That's the plan."

"I'm very glad to hear that. Let me know if I can make your stay more enjoyable. Anything you want. I mean, anything, OK?"

"OK, Alice, I will."

"Oh, I forgot to mention, you had a telephone call while you were at dinner last night."

"Last night?"

"Yes, that's right. He left a message for you."

"Who left a message?"

"A Charles Donovan. He said he is a friend of yours."

"What was the message?"

"He sounded kind of mysterious to tell you the truth. He just said that you need to check your mail."

"Thanks, Alice." Durbah broke the connection and said to Alex, "Alice said I got a call from Charles Donovan."

"I thought this place was called a hideaway."

"I think he found me through John Poole, the senator's son."

"What makes you say that?"

"His son is a *seer*."

"Just what is a *seer?*"

"Well, what does it sound like?" asked Durbah chuckling.

"You don't mean he's clairvoyant?"

"You guessed it. He can see tomorrow. I guess yesterday he saw us in front of the sign for Missy Kathryn's Hideaway. That's the only way I can figure that he could track me down. I don't think Charles could have found us by himself. I don't have to be a *seer* to know what he was calling about."

"What is it?" asked Alex with concern on his face.

"He said to check my mail. The sirens must be getting alerts. The alpha omega letters."

"Which means?"

"I've got to report to the sirens under the mountain in West Virginia."

"Well, you knew that was coming, didn't you?"

"Yeah, eventually, but it's only been about a week since I was there. We were told that the first exchange chamber wouldn't happen until about two weeks."

"Seems like something stepped up the timetable."

"I guess so. It's just as well. Now I can make my case for you to undergo the screening process."

"It makes me kind of nervous, Durbah."

"Don't be. You'll be fine. I know it in my heart. But if you are really worried, we could always ask John," she said jovially.

"Don't be surprised if I take you up on that."

"Just relax, Alex. You know, I have powers of my own," she said cryptically.

"Oh, really?" he said with a chuckle.

"Yes, really," she said with mock severity. I can send you my thoughts through telepathy."

"Uh, huh," came his dubious reply.

Durbah stood at the foot of the bed and let the terrycloth robe slip from her shoulders to the floor. Alex threw the bed sheet aside and said, "Wow, you weren't kidding. I'll never doubt you again."

"Then you got my message?" Her heavy lidded eyes holding his.

"That's the best offer I've had all day."

"It's early, Alex. I think it's going to be a *long* day."

~

Chapter Forty-six

Under the Mountain at E.C.-2

Matthew Winter arrived early on the Friday morning that the conference was called in West Virginia. His flight from Cairo via Frankfurt was uneventful, just the way he liked them. He found his steady cat naps at thirty thousand feet often included the beautiful body and soul of his precious Alankha. He missed her terribly, but the knowledge that she would be waiting for his return to Egypt was a constant beacon to keep him focused and ever moving forward. He had no doubt that her dreams were filled with his image as well. If someone had told him a month earlier that he would be filled with passion regarding another person, he would have said it was impossible. But Matthew was a different person than he had been a month before. He lived in an entirely new world – one of exciting discoveries and fantastic revelations. He found himself waking from his dreams and taxing his conscious mind to digest the facts that he had actually been underneath the great pyramid, the supposed burial tomb of Khufu, and instead found the burial tomb of Alexander the Great. He knew from his exhaustive study of the subject that Alexander's tomb had never been discovered and deemed to remain a mystery since the fourth century. Alexander's long funeral procession snaked back and forth from his beloved Alexandria to Ammoneion where he had requested to be buried while on his deathbed.

Why the tomb never surfaced there is anyone's guess except Matthew Winter's and the sirens of the Khufu conference chamber. He knew that if he were to make the claim to the Egyptologists of the day, he would be met with ridicule as well as derision. The location will be his last parting gift to Dr. Joanne Riley in the form of a letter mailed well after the departure of the last siren from Earth. The most fantastic find in the history of archeology will no doubt make up for her ignominious reputation having damaged the two remaining lost scrolls of Cleopatrah. Once Joanne identifies the location of Alexander the Great's tomb, she will become the most famous archeologist of all time. This will derail the ongoing misconception that names Siwa Oasis as the likeliest resting place for Alexander among archeologists. In the Western Desert there is the temple of the god Amun Ra, who proclaimed Alexander to be a god himself. The mountain in question is one of thousands in the Siwa Oasis and is called *Mount Khamisa or Gebel Ghaffir*. Alankha had learned from her uncle Zaphi, the Chairman of the SCA, or Supreme Council of Antiquities, that Khamisa did not hold any great secrets within its many caves and caverns, but a lake called Birket Zaytun, which covers about 32 square kilometers and features an island in its center where the saber and seal of the Prophet Mohammed are buried. Another treasure on an island in Lake Arachie is the resting place of the sword and crown of King Solomon. When Alankha asked her uncle Zaphi how he knew of these hidden treasures, she was told that Mohammed, as well as Solomon were two of the first sirens to come to Giza along with another man who would become known as the Prophet Krishna.

These facts were purposely laid to rest when, in the 1920s, Byron Khun de Prorok, a notable archeologist who also happened to be a siren, documented a journey to the islands and determined that there was evidence of human habitation, but sadly, no treasure was to be found.

~

When Sarah Poole entered the portal into the mountain retreat, she was greeted by her good friend Matthew. He then wrapped his arms around her and said, "Sarah, dear, I've missed you very much."

"I've missed you, also, Matthew. How was your trip to Egypt?"

"I've fallen in love."

"Well, I guess you can't ask for any more than that. How wonderful," she said honestly. "I'm very happy for you, Matthew. And I can honestly say that I know the feeling very well myself."

"You've found someone also?

"Yes, I have. I've met a wonderful man in Bar Harbor. I'm sure that you would like him."

"A man. Then you mean a human."

"That's right."

"Interesting," said Matthew.

"Then your lover is not a human?"

"No, she is siren. We're going to make the exodus together from her conference chamber in Egypt."

"That sounds very romantic, Matthew."

"You don't know the half of it, but somehow I think you will."

"You mean this conference?"

"Yup. I think we're all in for some revelations, Sarah."

"I'm sure it will all be for the best. I'm going to petition the sensors to allow my human lover to come with me to Siren."

"I'm not surprised. Love is a powerful thing."

"Passion is even more powerful, Matthew."

"I wholeheartedly agree. I feel like my whole life has been changed, and my heart is no longer asleep."

"That's a wonderful way to describe it, Matthew. I feel the same way. It's totally different than the way I have loved you here under the mountain. I will always love you that way, but now my senses reach out further than my own mind and body."

"I feel like I'm living the life of my soul mate as well, but tell him from me he's a lucky man."

"Thank you Matthew. Your lover is lucky, too."

"I'd love you to meet her. Perhaps on Siren."

"I'm sure we as the newcomers will be in contact with each other when we complete the transfer. It seems like a dream come true."

"Will you go if your human friend is not allowed to go?"

"What do you think?"

"I know how you feel. Some things are just too important to be ignored. Passion is certainly one of them."

Sarah took Matthew by the hand and said, "Let's see who else has made it here so far."

"Are your parents here with John?"

"Not yet. But I'm sure they're coming."

"Then they're going to make the transfer?"

"Certainly. They wouldn't deny John the experience, and they would miss him horribly if they sent him off with me and stayed behind."

"I suppose you're right. I guess there will be more than a few mid-term elections to make up for the shortfall of elected sirens in the political machine of Earth."

"Not only Congress, but the president of Chile, too, I'm told."

"Things will be turned upside down for a while. My lover's uncle is an exciting siren, and he is the Chairman of the SCA."

"That's bound to turn a few heads."

"Then you know what the SCA stands for?"

"The Supreme Council of Antiquities. I'm a librarian, Matthew, remember?"

"Right, right, I knew that," he said chuckling.

~

When they reached the great hall of the conference center, they could see small groups of sirens chatting and sharing pictures and artifacts they had brought along from their walks of life among the human population. Leishia was there showing some of her paintings to a few well known celebrities from the motion picture industry. They, no doubt, would soon become collector's items if they remained on Earth. Matthew and Sarah were thinking they might even give Van Gogh a run for his money at Christy's in London. They looked toward the entrance just as Durbah was entering the room. Sarah smiled and waved her over to their table. Durbah was dressed in a long green dress with a revealing neckline. A long string of exquisite pearls hung from her neck. She greeted them with a warm smile and said, "I have to show off my trinket." She brought attention to the pearls that she fingered with her right hand.

"They're real?" asked Sarah.

"That they are. I wonder if there are oysters on Siren."

They all chuckled and were enjoying her pride about the fantastic necklace. Matthew asked, "A gift from a friend?"

"A very good friend," said Durbah. "And a human as well."

"There must be something in the air," said Sarah. "And I have to say that I'm very glad that there is."

"You, too, Sarah?" asked Durbah.

"Guilty as charged. We've just got to get these beautiful men of ours to Siren."

"Hey, you two," complained Matthew, "what am I, chopped liver?"

"Oh, be quiet, Matthew," said Sarah with false anger. "You've got your siren, don't you? We can't let you have all the fun."

"Ooh, a siren," said Durbah excitedly. "I'm sure there've been a few fireworks going off in Egypt lately."

"You can say that again," said Matthew.

"Braggart," laughed Sarah. Durbah laughed as well.

A short time later, the group was joined by Shelly and Charles who were holding hands as they entered the room. Durbah said, "Is it me, or do those guys look like the handsomest couple in the room?"

"I think the temperature just went up," joked Matthew.

They were all laughing as Shelly approached them and said, "What's so funny, and I sincerely hope it's us."

"Oh, it's you alright," said Sarah. "You guys look like you're on fire or something."

"Something like that," said Charles. "Try as I may, I just can't seem to put her out."

"Oh, shut up, Charles. You're the one with the nuclear half-life. It's all Durbah's fault. By the way, I owe you a bathing suit."

Durbah laughed and said, "Not the red one. Can you believe my father bought me that?"

"Well, I think he did me a big favor," said Charles as he kissed Shelly on the lips.

"Get a room," said Matthew jokingly.

"We intend to," said Shelly when she broke off the kiss.

When the hall was nearly full, the E. C.-2 *sensor*, Jonah, entered through a door off to the left side of the stage and stepped up to the podium. "Welcome, welcome fellow sirens. It's good to see you all here again. I know that you may have been surprised to be summoned so soon after our last meeting, but some things have come to pass that we, your *sensors*, feel you should be made aware of. First and foremost are the changes that you have been experiencing in your own bodies. They are the result of a shower of gamma radiation, which fell upon the earth for approximately forty-six hours shortly after our last conference. You may be alarmed about the possibility that harm has come to you, but I assure you that the radiation is harmless other than the fact that you may now be feeling some emotions more intensely. You may in fact find the changes very appealing for one reason or another. Our scientists on Siren have detected another more intense shower of gamma wave radiation due to impact the Earth and Siren on December 21st, 2012. You will be pleased to know that they have reconfigured the Great Shield's photo-reflective properties to protect the planet Siren from the upcoming wave. Earth will have no such protection. This fact may play a major part in your final decision to join the exodus to Siren or to stay behind on Earth. As you know, the collective population of Earth fauna experienced this radiation many thousands of years ago. They are now essentially immune to the effects, but we sirens are much more sensitive to changes to the pituitary gland as it effects the secretion of hormones and pheromones. You've heard of "*love potion number nine?*" well just consider this little episode "*love potion number 2010.*" I can assure you that the next wave will be considerably less benign.

We *sensors* felt that it was our responsibility to call together the conference members of each chamber to explain the circumstances. We want to alert you to the possibility that your judgment could be clouded with respect to your decision to leave the planet. We will begin the screening of human applicants shortly to determine their compatibility with respect to the general population of Siren. We are aware of many instances where sirens have been emotionally tied to humans lately, and we whole heartedly encourage the connections you have made. We are confident that the merging of our two species will take the best of both and produce a progeny that is greater than the sum of the parts. We expect great art and great science to be the result. Very often the union of sirens and humans has produced such offspring, and we have both species to thank for it.

The baths will be available for the next three days for those who wish to energize with the crystals. This will be your last opportunity here on Earth because the crystals will be returned shortly to their origin within the lakes in Egypt called Birket Zaytum and Lake Arachie. They will not be purging your recent memories as they have done in the past, but will offer the same revitalizing effect. This evening's entertainment will feature two of your favorite Canadian performers. Comedian Stephen White will open the show and then we are proud to have the poet laureate John Lightwing performing his greatest hits of the last quarter century. We hope you enjoy the performances and by all means feel free to take the CD's provided in the baskets as you leave the theater. Thank you all, and again a very warm welcome from all the *sensors* of Siren."

The nearly fifty sirens seated in the conference room gave a small round of applause as Jonah left the podium. Many rose to leave the room in search of some exercise in the gym or a late lunch in one of the many cafés beneath the mountain. The sirens from Washington were the last to leave as they considered what they had just been told by their *sensor*. Matthew Winter said, "Gamma waves, huh? I knew it had to be something. Not that I'm complaining."

"I wish it had happened a long time ago," said Sarah Poole.

"Me, too," offered Shelly. "Look at all the time we wasted, Charles."

"Better late than never," he declared.

Durbah asked the group, "What did Jonah say about the screenings? Did he give any kind of timetable?"

"I don't think so," said Sarah and then added, "that's what I'd like to find out, too. Come on, Durbah, let's find Jonah and get some specifics."

"Lead the way," said Durbah rising from her seat. The others remained seated while they left, and Shelly called out after them, "You go, girls." Then Matthew and Charles joined in, "Yeah, you go, girls." They all raised a fist in the air as a salute.

~

Alankha was joined by her uncle Zaphi and Aunt Sophia in the conference chamber within Khufu. They were assembled with nine other sirens and Zaphi, their *sensor,* had just finished delivering an address very similar to the one Jonah stated in West Virginia. Afterward, Alankha went up to her uncle and asked him, "Uncle Zaphi, have you informed my lover's *sensor* that he will be making the exodus with us?"

"Yes, Alankha. It is all arranged. There are twelve names in each group that will be picked at random. Your names are in the same group."

"Thank you, Uncle. Little Zaphi thanks you, also."

Alankha's aunt Sophia then asked, "Little Zaphi?

~

Chapter Forty-seven

Sarah Poole and Durbah Purness caught up with Jonah in the small room he had entered just left of the stage. He was sitting at a small desk recording a pulse message to be delivered to Siren via a way station set up by the *Preculians*. The electromagnetic signals could not travel through the sun to Siren and therefore had to be relayed from a mid-point satellite far out into space. This same satellite was to be used in the chamber transfers that would facilitate the exodus to Siren. Although the chamber transfers would use a retarded light speed, the simple pulse messages could travel to Siren in just under seventeen minutes. Jonah held up his hand to the two women as they entered the room as a gesture to excuse him for a moment while he completed his task. It seemed little more than pressing a key on a laptop computer and very well might have been just that. When he was sure the pulse was away, he motioned for them to come forward, "Durbah, Sarah, please come in and have a seat," motioning to a small couch opposite his desk chair. "Is there anything I can do for you? Please don't hesitate to ask."

"Thank you, Jonah," said Sarah. "Yes, you can do something for us, you can . . ."

"Wait, Sarah, of course, I know what it is you want. You are looking for a timetable for the screening process."

Realizing that Jonah, as a *sensor*, could, of course, *sense* what they were concerned about Durbah said, "I'm sure we're not alone. You weren't very specific in your address to the conference members."

"Yes, I suppose I wasn't. I apologize. It's really very simple. Your candidates are welcome here anytime as long as they are accompanied by you or another siren. We feel sure that if they have a strong connection to a siren that they are no threat to us here. There is a *sensor* here who has been specifically trained for the psychological screening process. His name is Raphael. He will be very helpful in welcoming your friends to the world of Siren."

"That's very good to hear, Jonah," said Durbah.

"I have to admit, I've been a little nervous," said Sarah.

"Well, you shouldn't be. We sirens are not worth our salt crystals if we cannot embrace our brothers who would join with us in a mission of peace."

"God bless you, Jonah," said Durbah.

"Yes, I am pleased to say that he has."

"So what now?" asked Sarah.

"Just give me the names of your candidates for fellowship among the sirens. A first name is all that we need."

"Alex," said Durbah simply.

"Bradley," said Sarah.

"Now you have only to bring forth your friends and the rest will be taken care of. And have no fear that we will not embrace them as you have. We have the utmost faith in you and your judgment. It is our belief that our gain on Siren will be Earth's loss."

"I can't believe that it's this easy," said Sarah.

"You have served your home world well, Sarah. They owe you a great debt. You will find yourself *and your friend* well taken care of."

"Thank you, Jonah. I will bring Bradley here as soon as possible."

"Just relax, Sarah. The hard work is over. It's all downhill from here."

"It seems too good to be true," said Durbah.

"Maybe here on Earth, but on Siren, all things are possible Durbah. All we need is the freedom from opposition. Peace has always been the answer and always will be."

Durbah looked around the room and was surprised how similar it was to an ordinary corner office. It had two large windows with holographic images that gave the impression that they were overlooking the shoreline from the highest building in Dubai. "This room is remarkable, Jonah."

"Yes, it's my favorite. I love working from here."

"You mean communication, don't you?"

"That's right."

"With Siren?"

"Sometimes. Often I'm in communication with other conference locations. And we all are able to send messages to Siren. There are a lot of details to oversee with the exodus."

"I can imagine." She motioned to his computer terminal and asked, "Is your computer online with the internet?"

"In a sense, yes and in a sense no."

"What do you mean?"

"Well, Durbah, sometimes we send messages of a sensitive nature, and we have to encrypt them and then the other parties decode them. It's all like being a secret agent of sorts."

"That's pretty cool. So I could go online or send an email from this office?"

"You could," said Jonah. "Want to check your email or something?"

"No, not really. I was just curious," she laughed.

Sarah said, "I feel like I've been dreaming for a couple of weeks and will soon wake up, and it will all be gone."

Jonah laughed and said, "The only thing that will be gone is us." Suddenly there was a deep rumbling vibration beneath their feet. The images of the windows began to flicker and fade into a soft blue blurry mass of concentric rings and suddenly went totally black.

"Wow, that's a first," said Jonah.

"What's going on?" asked Durbah.

"I don't really know. This office has lost power from the main and is in emergency mode. I'm sure it's nothing serious, but we are on a battery backup for the moment. The power should be restored soon. If I didn't know better, I'd think we were going through an electromagnetic buffeting from sunspot activity. Usually it just wreaks havoc with radio signals, but some fear that the 2012 activity will affect electromagnetism."

"Which means?" asked Sarah.

"That things will cease to function from electricity. Motors, lights, generators – the scary thing to contemplate is being in an airplane if it were to happen. Imagine a total engine failure at 30,000 feet."

"Scary is right," said Durbah.

"Why don't you two just sit tight and let me go find out what's going on." Jonah rose out of his chair and crossed the room to the door that led to the conference hall. When he opened it, no light entered the room from outside. Jonah came back in and opened his desk drawer and took out a flashlight. He said to the two women, "I'm sure there's nothing to worry about. It's just a little dark out there."

Durbah and Sarah waited until he left before offering their opinions. "I don't like the sound of what happened underneath us, Sarah. I've never been in an Earthquake, but I'll bet that's what it feels like."

"Jonah was trying to exude confidence and a relaxed demeanor. I don't think he'll ever win an Oscar."

"You felt it, too? Man, that's scary. If Jonah is shook up, we should be shaking in our boots." They both felt a chill down their spines. A short time later Jonah came back, and they noticed a light from the conference hall shining weakly into their room. "Come ladies, we are gathering in the main room to decide our next move."

"Next move?" asked Sarah.

"Yes. I'm afraid that the entrance doors to the compound are temporarily out of order. They are powered by the main power line, and the emergency power isn't opening them just yet. We may have to do so manually."

"Oh, this just gets better and better," offered Durbah.

"It's not time to panic yet, ladies," said Jonah.

"But when it is, I'm sure we'll be the first ones to know, right?" Her biting sarcasm was clearly evident in her tone.

"That's right," he said nervously. "You'll be the first to know."

Alankha was holding onto Zaphi's arm with both hands in the darkness that was the west chamber of Khufu's Horizon. "Uncle? What's going on? Why have the torches gone out?"

"I am not sure, my child. I felt a great disturbance beneath my feet. Did you feel it also?"

"Yes, Uncle. I'm afraid. Perhaps we should leave and come back when we are sure that it is safe."

"Stay where you are with your Aunt Sophia for the moment, Alankha. I will make my way over to the door and return in a moment." Zaphi left the two women briefly and then returned a short time later. He clicked on a flashlight and made his way over to the torches and relit them with a lighter. "It seems we are not able to leave for the time being, my dears."

Sophia asked nervously, "What are you saying, Zaphi?"

"The doorway is no longer opened, and what was once a wooden door is now made of very smooth stone. I fear that it may be the pink granite blocking stone that slides into place when the tomb is finally sealed."

"What do you mean finally sealed, Uncle?"

"Well, Alankha, it is believed that the great tomb of Khufu was flawed when it was under construction. A large crack appeared in the ceiling and construction was halted and taken up again at another location. Khufu was never meant to be buried here. However, if he ever were to be, the granite doors are the last to close in order to seal the tomb and protect the Pharaoh's spirit from the demons of the underworld. What they were really talking about was the tomb robbers."

"So we are trapped?" asked Alankha frantically.

"For the moment."

"Oh, Uncle. This is very bad."

"Yes, my child. Very bad, for now."

Matthew Winter was in a psychic connection with Alankha. Although he couldn't actually communicate, he had a distinct taste of her fear. What she feared most of all was what he himself was most afraid of - never seeing his soul mate again on this Earth. When Matthew reached the dimly lit meeting hall, he found Durbah and Sarah again seated at a table with Shelly and Charles. Sarah called to him, "Matthew, over here."

He walked up to them and took a seat, “Here we are again, one big happy family.”

“Not so happy, Matthew,” said Durbah. “Jonah said the doors are sealed, and they haven’t found out how to open them again.”

“Oh, swell,” was his sour reply. Although he feared for the safety of his friends and himself, his mind was constantly on Alankha. *Is she safe? Is she trapped in Khufu like we are here? Was this an isolated incident or is the power interrupted at all the conference halls?* His mind just couldn’t let go of his conspiracy fears. “This might not be an accident or a natural occurrence.”

“What are you saying, Matthew,” asked Sarah.

“I just don’t like it, that’s all. Why does the power go out now with all of us here assembled under the mountain? What are the odds?”

“It may be just a coincidence,” said Durbah. They all just looked at her for a long moment and were speaking volumes with the expressions on their faces. She continued, “Oh, I’m sure you’re right. Forgive me for wishful thinking.”

“Do you think that Jonah really knows what’s going on?” suggested Charles.

“I think we’re about to find out,” said Sarah. Jonah was taking the stage in the dim light and stood in front of the podium. He began, “Please come closer to the stage if you are having trouble hearing my voice. I don’t have a public address system now as we are on emergency power only.” He paused while some of the sirens moved up closer to the stage. “I would like you all to remain calm while we figure out our options during this uncomfortable situation. We are safe for the moment, although it seems there has been a seismological event directly below the mountain. An Earthquake, if you will."

"I knew it," said Durbah.

"Good call," said Sarah.

Jonah continued, "The doors at the entrance are powered by the main generators for the complex, and we are presently running on the emergency battery back-up system. Since this complex has been functioning for over three hundred years, there must be a manual operating system that predates electricity. It may just be a simple matter to find the system and physically crank open the doors. In the mean time, we have plenty of fresh air and provisions. If we were forced to stay here beneath the mountain for a prolonged period of time, I would guess that all fifty of us could survive for more than a year."

The collective consciousness of the hall was visibly aroused and unsettled. "A year?" Most of them commented."

"I'm sure that it won't come to anything so drastic," said Jonah. "I merely wanted to point out that our survival is not at issue. What is at issue is the timetable of the exodus. The exchange chamber was due to start its operation in about two weeks. Although the light pulse for the exchange is originated on a way station far out into space, a great deal of power is required to focus a beam of light directly into the sky above the mountain to pinpoint the progression of the Earth's rotation. If the pulse is interrupted, the sirens of E. C.-2 aren't going anywhere."

"I'm feeling a little claustrophobic all of a sudden," said Shelly.

"Don't worry, sweetheart," said Charles. "We'll get through this." He put his arm around her, and she laid her head on his shoulder.

"Yes," said Matthew, "we'll all get through this. It's just a little setback. I'm sure they will restore power to the mountain."

"Who? Who's going to fix the generators, or whatever else is malfunctioning?"

"I don't know, Sarah. Just have a little faith, OK?"

"OK, Matthew. I'm sorry; I'm just a little scared."

"How is your family holding up?"

"They're not here yet, thank God. They're still in Florida, due to arrive tomorrow."

"Well, when the senator finds the doors closed and all the cars parked on the road in, he'll make the connection. Especially if there is any news of the Earthquake in this area."

"Yes, of course," said Durbah. "Your father will get those doors open."

"I'm sure you're right," said Sarah. "Thank goodness for my little brother."

"What do you mean?" asked Matthew.

"I'm sure John saw it coming."

Chapter Forty-eight

Senator Poole drove his wife Johanna and his son, John Jr., to the mountain retreat in West Virginia on the day after the power breakdown occurred. When they arrived at the town closest to the mountain compound, the senator arranged for a room in the Radisson Hotel. He didn't intend to spend the nights beneath the mountain because he needed to remain visible through teleconferencing due to the upcoming Domestic Energy Commission symposium. As a member of the D.E.C., Senator Poole was expected to maintain a high profile if he were to have any effect on the reaction to the OPEC directives regarding the price of oil. His real agenda was the reduction of troops in the Middle East by demonstrating the reality that The United States could achieve oil independence if it could restrain itself from becoming the middle man for fossil fuels to China. Oil, as well as any commodity, is all too convenient to become a poker chip in the confluence of the global economy. If Congresswoman Alyssa Grant, also a member of the D.E.C., could track the particulars of the money flow for energy commodities, she would realize that America will soon become a minor player in her precious global warming agenda. China is not only second to America in the incidences of diabetes, but the thirst for internal combustion engines as well. They are, like the Japanese, extremely imitative, though exponentially more prolific with their progeny. Unlike Alyssa Grant, this was not something that Senator Poole lost sleep over. Indeed, he believed in his heart that global warming was a natural occurrence and mankind had a very small part in the overall scheme of things. What was of monumental concern for him was the loss of life, specifically young American lives in the interest of greasing the profits of large corporations charged with the rebuilding of third-world country infrastructures. For this reason, the Radisson Hotel would remain his base of operations for the near future. The first thing he attended to upon checking his family into their room was to ask his son John what he saw in the near future for the sirens in the conference hall.

John began to describe his vision into tomorrow, “At first there is a low rumbling noise and the ground starts to shake. Then there are some sparks and the ceiling starts to spray out water like the sprinklers on our lawn at home. The room then becomes very quiet and all the noisy machines shut down.”

“Go on.”

“Then, all the lights go out upstairs.”

“It must be the generators,” said the senator, “there’s going to be a power failure.”

“Then, they seem a bit worried, Dad”

“What do you mean worried, John?”

“Well, the entrance to the retreat is closed, and they can’t seem to open it.”

“Dear, God. Johanna, grab a jacket for John and yourself and let’s go. Something’s wrong. If John sees them trapped tomorrow, then there's going to be a power failure in the retreat between now and then."

"Good Lord, John, what could make that happen?" asked Johanna.

"We'll find out soon enough. Just go down with John and bring the car around to the front entrance."

"What are you going to do, John?" she asked.

"I'm going to get us some help. We can't go to the local authorities, but I have something better in mind."

"All right, dear. Meet us out front."

When Johanna Poole and John Jr. left for the parking garage of the Radisson Hotel, John Sr. made a call to a sensitive agency known only to himself and a dozen other Americans. When the call was answered he began, "Poole requesting priority delta "S" squadron West Virginia, specific Milton, Cabell County. Deployment ASAP minimal armament."

"Hold please," came the reply. After two minutes a gruff voice came back on the line, "John Poole, this better be a secure line."

The senator recognized the voice on the phone and said, "I'm sorry Bill, it's a cell phone."

"I'm hanging up in five seconds. Give me the location in Cabell County John."

"Let's go for the Waffle House on the exit for I-95 at Milton."

"OK, John, Nineteen-Hundred Hours. You're going to owe me the special."

"Thanks, Bill." The senator turned off his cell phone. His call was connected to a man who officially doesn't exist. His title was S.O.C. or *Special Operations Coordinator* for *The Scorpions*. The Scorpions didn't exist in any operations log or history of engagement of the United States military. They were not an elite group of highly trained military might like the Navy Seals or the Army Rangers or the Green Berets of the Marine Corps. They were civilian specialists who could be called upon for very sensitive operations and then forgotten and never spoken of ever on pain of death. The senator knew the rules well, as he was once one of their number.

~

Chapter Forty-nine

William J. Andrews was the legal name of the leader of the Scorpions; however, the word *legal* was rarely connected with any of their black-ops activities. He was known as and referred to simply as *Bill.* Bill had once served with Jonathan Poole in the Marine Corps twenty years before Poole became elected as the senior and presently sitting senator of the great state of Florida. John Poole and Bill Andrews were the founding members of *The Scorpions.* Officially, they didn't exist either independently or in connection with any branch of the armed services; however, they were often *"employed"* by The United States of America and Israel. One would seldom hear of their exploits within the general public or read about them in *Soldier of Fortune Magazine,* but nevertheless, they were the ultimate *mercenaries' mercenaries.* There were nine members, which constituted what they referred to as a *complete cell.* No operation was ever considered without the complement of a complete cell. For that reason, the nine operatives were extremely expensive to hire. A full 24 hours of the Scorpion's cell's fee was upwards of $100,000. It would cost John Poole breakfast for nine tomorrow morning at The Waffle House at the I-95 exit at Milton, West Virginia.

Two black Hummers were parked at The Waffle House at 8:23 P.M. as John Poole and his wife and son arrived in a dark blue Lincoln Navigator. The collective carbon footprint of the three vehicles was a whopping three miles per gallon, but this was not a night for going green with respect to emissions of greenhouse gasses. The Scorpions were going "red." Going red meant that they were presently on task, and as highly trained specialists for whatever contingency they faced, they would neither eat, drink nor speak until the mission was completed. The only voice was that of Bill. He left one of the Hummers and approached the senator's Navigator. Senator Poole flashed his lights once, which was an agreed upon form of communication that he and Andrews had drawn up twenty years earlier. Some lessons never fade. The silent message meant, *Greetings "S" I am your contact and I have not been followed and no one knows of my agenda at this time.* The senator rolled down his window and said, "Follow me, Bill."

Not another word was exchanged as Bill returned to his vehicle and both Hummers fell in line behind the Navigator. They headed East on Cabell County road for three miles and then turned south on a dirt road that was thickly wooded with smooth black saplings of the Black Locust and American Birch trees. There were also spindly vines of the Box Elder and American Hornbeam crushed flat on the side of the road as evidence of recent vehicle traffic. The road otherwise gave the impression that it was rarely if ever used and never trimmed of the encroachment of the foliage. The senator in the Lincoln led the way with his headlights on high beam defining the pathway to the foot of the abandoned mountain retreat. The Hummers behind him had no lights on and looked like dark, shiny waves of metal and glass that showed nothing of their interior and barely made a sound. Soon the road widened and the senator's Lincoln came upon the huge door to the retreat just on the other side of the tangled mass of field grasses. When he came to a stop, the engine was switched off. Leaving the lights on, the senator left his vehicle and approached Bill behind him in the lead Hummer. The smoky black driver's side window silently rolled down. The senator then said, "We're on site, Bill. We should be unobserved at this point."

"Should be?" The question hung for a long moment. "Getting careless in your old age, John?"

"I know the terrain, that's all."

"Are there civies in your vehicle," he asked referring to non-military citizens.

"My wife and son."

"Careless indeed."

"My wife or son could dispatch any of the Scorpions, Bill."

"Delusional, as well."

"Look, Bill, that's neither here nor there. Let me brief you and whoever your number 2 is in the cell."

Bill left his vehicle and raised his right fist in the air. A passenger side door of the rear Hummer opened and a man emerged in black face and camouflage fatigues and approached the two men standing beside the lead Hummer. There were no introductions. Bill looked at the senator and said, "It's your show, John."

He began, "This is a miniature Greek Island, although much more luxuriously appointed. Even Congress couldn't afford these digs, Bill." What the senator was alluding to was called *Project Greek Island: The Legislative Bunker under the Greenbrier Hotel.*

What was the Greenbrier's best kept secret has become one of West Virginia's top attractions. More than 65,000 tourists have walked by the decontamination chambers and dormitories of the recently uncovered bunker. The bunker was formerly called the emergency relocation center. The code name of the bunker was *Greek Island.* The 1,100 bed facility was intended to house members of Congress, their staff people and other officials connected with the Legislative branch. The Congressmen's families were provided with living space in the Conference Center of the hotel.

Between 1958 and 1961, the bunker was planned and built by the Eisenhower administration with Congressional approval. The West Virginia Wing of the Greenbrier Hotel was constructed as a cover for the bunker construction. The government paid for both the West Virginia Wing and the bunker. The total cost was $14,069,000. Although the siren's retreat under the abandoned coal mine was only a quarter of the size of *Greek Island*, the cost of its construction was nearly $90,000,000.

Although there is only one entrance to the alpha omega retreat, they used the same door design as *Greek Island* when they upgraded the facility in 1964. There are four entrances to the bunker under the Greenbrier Hotel. Each is sealed by a door that is 18 inches thick, weighs 25 tons, and is 12 feet wide and 10 feet high. These doors were meant to withstand a blast

15-30 miles away. The two hinges of the large doors are 4 feet long, 14 inches wide and 8 inches thick. Five feet of concrete and other steel reinforcements surround the doors. If you enter through the West Entrance, you travel down a long tunnel, which leads to one of two decontamination areas. In case of nuclear attack, persons entering the bunker would have to dispose of their clothes, shower and would be given new clothes before entering the main parts of the bunker. They would be issued garment packages containing khaki overalls, canvas deck shoes and underwear, and packages of toiletries.

Two of the four entrances to *Greek Island* had vehicular tunnels. The sirens' retreat had only one. There was only one way in and one way out. They faced the obstacle of the massive door to deal with in the event of a power outage. That was the reason for which Senator Poole called upon the Scorpions. A power plant contained in the retreat provided power needs for approximately 100 people for up to 40 weeks. A 360 day stockpile of food and provisions was housed in the main kitchen facility. Although the retreat was richly appointed, if the Scorpions could not open the massive door, the luxurious accommodations would effectively be a prison.

Contained within the retreat's first level is a conference hall, exercise rooms, dining halls and entertainment venues. The *sensor*, Jonah, also enjoyed a small administration control room where he met with Durbah and Sarah just prior to the seismic anomaly. On the second level, it housed a square floor of 48 suites used as living quarters for the sirens. Each suite had a television in both the living room and the bedroom, a computer and complete kitchen facilities. Senator Poole completed the briefing to Bill and his number 2 operative. “My daughter, Sarah, and nearly fifty friends are trapped beneath the mountain. Normally the huge door located just inside the entrance to the mine opens easily with the slight push of your hand. It is precisely balanced and assisted with powered gears from within the facility. There must have been some kind of power failure because they are running on emergency battery back-up. So far, they are remaining calm and are counting on us to affect their rescue. You’re familiar with the doors at Greek Island? That’s what we’re dealing with, Bill. What do you think?”

“Cut the hinges with oxy-acetylene. Should take about five hours, and then we’re home free. Is this a secure area?”

“It is. That’s what my wife and son are here for. I’ll assist them as well. You’ll have no interference with the operation.”

~

Chapter Fifty

The Scorpions worked silently cutting the hinges of the massive door to the retreat. No sound could be heard from inside. Andrews had posted four men along the road approaching the entrance to the retreat, and two more circled back around the rise of land to cover their flanks. The remaining two along with him began the laborious task of dismantling the massive door. After an hour had passed, one of the Scorpion guards from the road marched silently up to the entrance of the mine just behind a man he had taken prisoner. The man had both of his hands on top of his head, and the gun had been removed from his holster. He was a West Virginia State Trooper. Bill cursed his rotten luck at being visible to a member of law enforcement for any reason. The nature of the Scorpion's activities required their complete and total invisibility. This brought a very ugly scenario to bear. Bill said to the senator, "This is unfortunate, John." Then he turned to the guard and said, "Did he communicate after contact?"

A slight shake of the head was the only reply. Keeping to strict protocol, the guard knew better than to speak. Bill again addressed the senator, "You know the rules, John. You knew them before you ever made the call. Any prisoners taken during a mission have to be dispatched."

The Trooper spoke up for the first time, "You gentlemen are in a world of trouble. Your operation was detected by an extreme heat signature from a police helicopter about thirty minutes ago. If I don't report back shortly, these hills will be crawling with law enforcement. I recommend you just give yourselves up at this point. There's no real crime in lighting a fire as long as you have it under control."

"That will be enough out of you, officer."

"That's Sheriff, Sir."

"Whatever," said Bill. "John, you know there can't be any exceptions."

"Trust me, Bill. The rules have changed."

"The rules can't change, John. I'm sorry."

"Just give me a minute to make my case. A man's life is at stake here." The Trooper was beginning to look a little worried despite his boast of a backup. The truth was that the Sheriff's department was very short handed and his only backup would likely be a local black and white from the Milton Police Department.

"Johanna can erase us, Bill. She can shape his will and render him harmless."

"I don't think we're on the same page here, John. I'm on task with a complete cell, and you're still in your bed dreaming."

"Give me a chance, damn it!"

"How?"

"Let me prove it to you."

"By all means, go ahead. Prove to me that your wife can erase us from his memory."

"Give her one of your men."

Bill ran his palm up across his forehead and into his hair. He seemed very tired, and John could tell he wasn't happy about the prospect of dispatching one of West Virginia's finest in the interest of maintaining anonymity. But rules were rules. Finally, he acquiesced. "All right, I'll play along." He extended his hand to one of the guards closest to him and took the man's weapon. He pointed briefly to the Lincoln where Johanna was sitting with her son John and held up three fingers and then a thumb's-up gesture. The senator took this to mean that Johanna had only three minutes to complete her demonstration, and he hoped that it would be enough.

The guard opened the driver's side door of the Lincoln and climbed in next to the senator's wife. The rear passenger door opened, and John Jr. emerged and walked over to join his father. He said to him, "Sarah will be fine, Dad. She's with us tomorrow at the Radisson."

"Shhh," said his father. "Just be quiet for now, son."

The dome light of the Lincoln came on, and Bill could see the guard sitting very still looking into the eyes of the senator's wife. She seemed to be speaking to him, although they couldn't actually hear the conversation. After two minutes, they both left the vehicle and joined the others.

"Is it done, Honey?" asked the senator.

"Yes," was her only reply.

"Is what done?" asked Bill.

"Debrief your man, Bill."

Bill turned to the guard and said, "Although we are on task, Rudy, I want you to speak. Just this once."

"What would you have me say, Bill?"

"Tell me what we are doing here. Tell me where we are."

"I'm coming up empty, Bill."

"You mean you don't know?"

"That's right. The last thing I remember is getting out of that Navigator over there." He gestured toward the senator's Lincoln.

"And before that?"

"Nothing, Bill. I'm not feeling very well, either. I get the feeling that I'm forgetting something important, like I left the stove on or something."

"Forget it, Rudy. You're fine. Just return to the vehicle and close your eyes for a few minutes. I'll fill you in shortly." He turned to the senator and said, "That's pretty slick, John. Anytime you'd like to lend me Johanna, I could use her in the field."

"Not gonna' happen, Bill."

"I was only kidding. So what's our cover story?"

"I'm thinking kids with fireworks. A flare and some magnesium. It burns hot as hell."

Bill turned toward the Trooper and said, "You think you can sell that story to your buddy up there in the helicopter?"

"I could, but I don't know why the hell I should."

"To save your life, Sheriff."

"I don't know what you're talking about, Sir," he said angrily. "I don't take orders in my jurisdiction from citizens engaged in unlawful activities."

"Oh, yes, you do, Sheriff," said the senator. "That lady over there will explain it to you." He motioned to his wife who smiled at the Trooper. He could see something strange in her eyes. It was as though they glowed in the night with a light of their own, and it was silver in color and gold as well. His head was spinning, and he felt himself drawn to her as she beckoned him forward to the waiting vehicle where they would have a little chat. A few minutes later, they both emerged from the Lincoln and the senator's wife said, "You can give Bob his gun back. He needs to go home and lie down for a while."

Bill's raised eyebrows asked a silent question to his old friend, Senator Poole. The senator said simply, "Go ahead, Bill. He's on our side now."

"Incredible," said Bill handing the Trooper his gun. Without a word the Trooper turned around and headed back to his cruiser. A short time later, he radioed the helicopter and told the pilot that the intense heat signature was just a bunch of harmless kids in the woods. They were burning some magnesium with a flare.

~

Chapter Fifty-one

The sirens were remaining remarkably calm in the meeting hall under the mountain. Jonah was keeping them abreast of the situation and any changes that were happening by the minute. "As you know, the infrastructure of the mountain complex is maintained by a large service industry task force. There is one human worker for every siren here. They are isolated from our communication regarding the exodus and the particulars of your home planet and consider this complex nothing more than a luxury retreat for the very rich."

"Somehow, I don't feel very rich at the moment," said Matthew sourly.

"I wonder what the humans are thinking about the power failure?" asked Durbah. "I wish we could speak with them and give them some comfort. As though Jonah could read her thoughts, he answered them, "The service people are concerned about the power failure as is to be expected; however, they have been highly trained and briefed for every contingency. In fact, their main consideration at this time is the comfort of you. Each worker is able to do a number of different tasks with the proficiency of a consummate professional. The same woman who works in housekeeping to change the linens and dust and vacuum the suites is also capable of preparing a meal at a five-star restaurant. They are very highly paid for their skills and are resigned to the fact that they are here for the duration of the conference and will do anything in their power to make your stay more comfortable."

Some of the sirens at the table closest to the stage asked Jonah what the power failure meant for the exodus. He told them truthfully, "At this time, the exodus, at least from this exchange chamber complex is on an indefinite hold. We need a large amount of electricity to focus a beam of light for the purpose of targeting the pulse from the way station. It may, however, be possible to travel to other venues and make the chamber exchanges from there. This complex, E.C.-2 is one of six in the continental United States. There are two in Europe, two in China, and three in India and one in Egypt."

"I've been to the one in Egypt," said Matthew to the sirens at his table, "you're not going to believe where it's located."

"Where," asked Sarah.

"Khufu," said Matthew.

"You're not serious?"

"Serious as a heart attack. Or should I say, Sirius like the star."

"What is he talking about?" asked Shelly to Sarah.

"Khufu is what the Egyptians call the Great Pyramid. Matthew is saying that their conference room and exchange chamber is within the largest pyramid in the world. The Greeks called the Pharaoh Cheops, but the Egyptians call him by his Egyptian name when he was ruler of the world. They call the pyramid Khufu's Horizon."

"And you know how to gain access to it?" asked Charles.

"You betcha,'" said Matthew. "I might even be able to get you a glass of Chateau Laffite Rothschild on the way in."

"Incredible," offered Shelly shaking her head with a chuckle.

"When do you think we'll be able to get out of the mountain?" a siren asked Jonah. The question was on all the minds of the sirens.

"My guess would be that we will be extricated sometime tonight."

"Really?" asked Durbah.

"Oh, certainly. We're not a full compliment here. Some of the sirens haven't arrived yet, and when they do, they will find a way to open the door from the outside if we can't get it open from the inside."

"What are we doing about opening the door from here?" asked Matthew.

"The maintenance crew is going over the blueprints as we speak. As I mentioned, this complex is very old. There must be a mechanical operation to open the door in the event of a power failure. The issue has just never come up to my knowledge."

"When was the complex built?" asked Charles.

"I'm told that the mine was shut down just prior to the Civil War. The initial conference hall where we now sit was a secret meeting place of the Union Army. It remained as such for about forty years until the Rothschild family began pouring large sums of money into the complex. You could say that the mountain retreat was funded by World War I."

"Could you elaborate on that a little, Jonah?" asked Shelly.

"Sure. The Rothschild family leant money to both sides of the great conflict at a very low rate of interest. The loans were secured by very valuable assets, and there was never any doubt but that they would always be paid in full. No matter what side won the war, the Rothschild family won. They effectively did the same thing in World War II. As I'm sure you know from your history, war is very good business if you are a human. I'm afraid that the war machine and all of the financial ministrations and lobbying for leverage would be a dismal failure on Siren. Siren has never hosted an actual war."

"All the more reason to go there," said Shelly.

"Yes, you'll find it very pleasant there."

"You sound like you've been there, Jonah," said Durbah.

"Indeed, I have. I was one of the first *"test pilots,"* if you will, to make the exchange in a chamber as soon as the *Preculians* introduced the technology to Siren."

"Then Siren didn't come up with the concept?" asked Sarah.

"No, I'm afraid not. The technology is eons ahead of either Earth or Siren. That's why the *Preculians* are so confident that they have at last solved the dilemma of Siren's threat from Earth. They are merely lending Siren the technology for the exchange chambers and when the exodus is completed, they will dismantle the way station and both planets will remain isolated. That's why your decision to go to Siren is so crucial. There is no coming back. It's basically a one-time, one-way ticket, so to speak."

"Do we know yet what caused the seismic anomaly?" asked Matthew. Somehow he didn't believe in coincidence. The complex had run smoothly since the initial expansion during the Eisenhower administration, and it just so happened that the breakdown occurred when it was nearly full to capacity with sirens.

"Not yet," said Jonah, "but we are sure that there has been an Earthquake. We're just not sure of the cause. It could have been a shift of plate tectonics. We are operating the circulation fans and emergency lighting by a cavern of dozens of huge batteries. You will find that your electronic devices like cell phones and iPods will function, as well. You won't be able to get a signal here under the mountain, but they will still work. I'd like you to turn off any electronic devices at this time to conserve battery life. It may be possible to utilize them later if the need should arise. But rest assured, we will be rescued shortly by our fellow sirens on the outside of the doorway."

Bill and the Scorpions were just finished cutting through the first hinge. There were three of them, and he estimated that the whole operation would take upwards of seven hours total rather than five. The longer that the *cell* remained *on site*, the greater the chance they would be discovered, especially since seven hours would take them dangerously close to sunrise. The senator's wife was able to perform some kind of magic on the Trooper, but Bill was not in the habit of depending on the performance of any persons outside the cell. He felt that since the operation was taking longer than first planned, the loss of Rudy was surely to take its toll. He expressed the thought to Senator Poole.

"You can get him back, Bill. Johanna can reverse his will."

"His what?" asked Bill. He wasn't sure that he heard John Poole correctly.

"Never mind, Bill. All I'm saying is that my wife can get your man back, good as new."

"All right. Have her do it."

Senator Poole asked Bill to order Rudy back into the Navigator with his wife. His son, John, once again departed the vehicle and left the two alone in the front seats of the Lincoln. The dome light went on again, and the senator's wife was holding the Scorpion Rudy's hand in hers and talking very softly. They remained there for some time, and Bill was getting a little concerned. "Good as new, huh, John? I didn't like the look of that Trooper when he left us. He looked like he had a lobotomy or something."

"Relax, Bill. It's all very natural and harmless. I'd tell you the particulars of what's going on, but then I'd have to kill you."

"You ought to know better than to even joke with me, John."

"Yeah, I suppose you're right. It's been a long time for me, Bill."

"But I'm sure you haven't lost sight of the seriousness of what we do."

"No, of course not. I understand. I know what's at stake even though you can't talk to me about what you've been up to lately."

"Trust me, John, you don't want to know."

~

Chapter Fifty-two

Alankha was sitting on the floor of the conference room at Khufu holding the hands of her uncle Zaphi and Aunt Sophia. It had been five and a half hours since the rumble of the Earth beneath the chamber, and they were beginning to feel a chill as the heat of the plateau escaped into the night. They cuddled together for warmth and her uncle told her, "Just pray, my Alankha, and everything will be fine again. There are others who know that we were to convene here within Khufu, including your friend from America. When he finds the entranceway blocked, he will find a way to open it. We have not come so far in the history of this planet to have a useless end to our lives. There are great plans ahead for us on Siren. There," he said motioning to the air shaft directly above them, "do you see that star?"

"It is actually two stars, Uncle, as you have once taught me long ago."

"Yes, so it is. There is a planet not unlike this one that revolves around the smaller of the two stars, Sirius B. That is the home of the *Preculians*. Their powers are great, and they will be our deliverers to Siren. This very room will exchange place with a room on Siren sometime in the near future. We will be in the room at the time along with your friend from America. We will walk out of this room onto a new world full of wondrous karma, my dear. You will never want for spiritual peace and contentment."

"That sounds very nice, Uncle Zaphi, but what of my feelings for Matthew? Will the fire in my heart still grow as strong when we are together?"

"What do you suppose would put out the fire in your heart, my dear?"

"I'm not sure, Uncle. It's just that in the past, when I lay in the baths with the crystals at Siwa, my mind was free of all intense emotion. It was very restful, but I left something of my mind behind in the baths."

"But you will not go to the baths anymore, Alankha. Siren has dry crystals that resonate in the temples, but you are not required to go there if you do not wish to. There is total freedom on Siren. You are free to feel your intense emotion for your friend, or you may find some relief with the crystals if you are troubled by them."

"That makes me very happy, Uncle. I do not wish to live without the new feelings that have become a part of me. It is like I have been born two weeks ago instead of twenty-two years."

"And as a newborn, you must first learn to walk before you can run, my dear."

"What do you mean, Uncle?"

"Take things slowly at first, Alankha. A star that burns slowly lasts a very long time. A very large star burns itself out in a short while."

"I will burn very slowly, Uncle, and for a very long time."

~

Johanna Poole released Rudy's hands and kissed him on the cheek. "I have taken you on a little journey and your mind was at rest. Now I have returned you, and the fact that your mind is once again sharp and clear is very agreeable to me. In fact, the sharper and clearer you are, the greater pleasure it gives me. How do you feel, Rudy?"

"Like I've just had the best night's sleep in my life. I'm firing on all cylinders, Ma'am."

"That's good to hear. I'm sure that your leader will be pleased, as well."

"Am I dismissed, Ma'am?"

"You are."

Rudy left the vehicle and walked up to the large door where one of the Scorpions was cutting the second hinge with the torch. He motioned to Bill with a hand signal using his left fore and middle fingers. He placed them on his left cheek, which meant that he was ready as relief to the man with the torch. Bill gave a silent signal as well, and Rudy stepped forward and placed a welder's helmet on his head and reached for the torch. The Scorpion was nearly exhausted and grateful to Rudy for taking over. Having fresh arms and legs, he was able to focus the tip of the flame, which contains the greatest concentration of heat and was able to cut through the second hinge in under an hour. Two down and one to go. Rudy continued on to the third hinge and didn't show any signs of fatigue at all. Bill thought to himself, *the senator is a lucky man.*

~

Walter and Edith Purness were packing and making plans to return to their condominium at the Watergate Complex in Washington D.C. The D.E.C. was due to convene in two days in the capital building's main auditorium. His cruise down the Intra-coastal Waterway with Shelly Simon gave him much food for thought regarding the possible changes to the production of coal and the distribution for utilization in hydro-electric plants. He had contacted the Virginia Coal Collective's Vice Chairman and laid out the basics of the plan to scale down production with greater financial rewards. At first the Vice Chairman was skeptical, but after meeting in person with Walter and Edith over dinner, he was agreeable to proposing the changes to the collective. When Walter excused himself from the table for a short while, Edith assured him that there was a virtual sea of influential young people who would lobby for the tax breaks and increased profits for the V.C.C. There were a number of reasons she told him, but the most important one was the environment. It was fortunate that the universal consciousness regarding *carbon footprints* and *going green* was very instrumental in changing the minds and actions of some of the coal industries highly placed movers and shakers in Washington.

Chapter Fifty-three

The Scorpions were drawing in the perimeter of the site on a silent signal from Bill that was passed along to the six guard positions. They all maintained line of sight positions for that very purpose. When the Scorpions assemble a complete cell, they act as one mind and one body. That was one of the reasons that Bill discouraged and prohibited speech. They were forced to think and act as a unit, which saved their lives countless times in the past. The two black Hummers doors were opened, and the dome lights were turned on. The Scorpions racked their weapons in the rear compartments and carried only hand guns for the remainder of the mission. A large oxy-acetylene tank, along with fifty feet of hose was stored in the rear Hummer. The last hinge was finally severed and the remaining tank and hose were then packed up and stored.

The Scorpions were given another hand signal from Bill, and two of the cell members turned the Hummers around and backed them up to the entrance of the mine. Two long one-inch-thick towing chains were unpacked and laid out along the ground. The large hooks were attached to the towing packages beneath the rear of the Hummers and connected to two huge suction cups attached to the massive door. Each suction device could lift a Hummer with a full complement of passengers; however, they weren't required to lift the huge iron door, but rather simply create an opening on the hinge side large enough to admit a person. Two of the Scorpions then got behind the wheels of the two Hummers and gradually inched forward taking up the slack in the chains. When they were pulled tight, the Scorpions applied the parking brakes and placed the vehicles in park. Then they turned off the engines and waited for further hand signaled instructions from Bill.

Four of the Scorpions then walked to the front of the vehicles and two-by-two began paying out the long cables that were spooled around the large hydraulic winches. The cables were a quarter of an inch thick and over eighty feet in length. The men left the road with the cable hooks and attached them to the base of two large trees. After a hand signal from Bill, two of the Scorpions, who were manning the winch controls, began taking up the slack between the Hummers and the trees. All eyes were on Bill for a coordinated effort to exert a pulling force to the door of the mountain retreat. Although the Hummers were equipped with carbon steel plating and weighed over seven tons each, they would not be effective for pulling the door open because their tires would merely spin on the dirt road. That was the reason for the cables and winches. Bill walked up to the senator who was standing alongside his Lincoln Navigator with his wife and child. "We're set to go, John. Everything's in place."

"How confident are you?"

"Are you kidding? Did you see those trees? One is a Box Elder and the other one is a Black Locust. Their root systems are a mirror image of their canopies. It has to open, that's all there is to it."

"What about the suction cups?"

"They'll hold. Just say the word and fifteen seconds later, that door is open."

"OK, Bill. Just give me a minute. You guys will be out of here a few minutes after the door comes free, correct?"

"You know the answer to that, John. We were never here."

"OK, just a minute." The senator walked up to his son and asked, "Is it time, John."

"Almost, Dad. I can feel that it's just about a minute or so when we'll be lined up."

"Can you focus on the men in the dark clothing?"

"If you want."

"I need to know about the man who was doing the talking. Tell me where he will be tomorrow."

"OK, Dad. Here goes." Bill Andrews watched the boy as he closed his eyes and put hands behind his head. A minute later, he opened his eyes and said, "Egypt."

"Egypt? You're sure."

"Yup. Unless they moved that big pyramid someplace else."

"Interesting," said the senator.

Alankha and her aunt and uncle were with nine other sirens in the conference hall within Khufu. Three of them were sleeping, and the rest were praying on the rugs beneath the torch lit walls. Alankha was sitting with her back against her Aunt Sophia. Zaphi was lost in thought and pacing around the perimeter of the chamber. For the sake of his wife and niece, he exuded an air of a confidence he wasn't feeling. Although calling for help was always an option and might possibly lead to their extraction, he thought it was a very bad idea. The location of the meeting hall in Khufu was a precious secret maintained by a line of Egyptian *sensors* for thousands of years, and as the Chairman of the SCA, he didn't like the prospect of exposing it.

His old friend and fellow siren, Mother Bakhawi, was a very sweet woman, but she was getting on in years and she was often found sleeping soundly beside her empty wineglass. It could be days before she realized that she didn't see her friends make their way back into her basement from the hall within Khufu. And it was always possible with her failing memory that she might forget that they ever went in to begin with. She had decided not to make the journey to Siren because she had become very set in her ways and doubted very much that she could find fine French wine there.

Alankha's friend Matthew would, no doubt, be missing her very much and make the trip back from America as soon as he could; however, that might also be days away. They wouldn't starve to death in the meantime, but they might get a little thirsty. At last, he decided to heed the example of his fellow sirens and catch up on a little prayer.

Chapter Fifty-four

Senator Poole walked up to his old friend the leader of the Scorpions. He was chuckling and shaking his head. Bill was anxious to conclude the operation and leave the site before sunrise. Any further delay was reckless in his opinion. He said so to the senator, "We have to go now, John. First light is about twenty minutes away."

"Remember Giza, Bill?"

"This isn't exactly the time to catch up on old times, John. We're on site and past our deadline."

"Go ahead. Open it up."

Bill stood behind the two black Hummers. He raised his hands up over his head with his palms facing forward. When he closed his hands into fists, the lead men began coiling up the cables in the winches, and the drivers put the Hummers into gear. They pressed lightly on the accelerators, and the two vehicles began inching forward. Then as their tires lost their grip briefly, they spun on the dry dirt road, raising up a dusty cloud. Bill rotated his closed fists back and forth and the two Scorpions at the winches overcame the slack in the cables and the engines began to whine. The front ends of the vehicles began to groan and just when the Scorpions were starting to doubt the logistics of the operation, the door broke free. It slid easily across the concrete floor of the mine entrance and created a gap about four feet wide. Bill opened his hands with his palms forward again, and the vehicles stopped their advance. They backed up about fourteen inches to create some slack in the chains and cables so the hooks could be unattached. The Scorpions quickly winched up the cables on the spools in front of the Hummers, and the chains and suction devices were piled in the rear compartments next to the oxy-acetylene tanks. Without a word, they climbed into the seats and closed the doors, leaving the front passenger door open for Bill. Bill then said to the senator, “What about Giza?”

“Ever think about going back?”

“Not really.”

“Well, you will.”

~

When the senator walked into the entrance of the retreat with his wife and son, they made their way to the large conference room. Jonah was the first to see them and cried out, “Right on time!”

The sirens realized the implication of the arrival of three new people from the entrance hallway and rose up in a gratuitous cheer.

“Father,” called Sarah. “You are our savior.”

“No, Sarah,” said the senator, “it was your brother, John.”

Matthew rose from the table and approached the senator. “Senator, how did you get the door open?”

“Hello, Matthew. I uhh . . . had some help. I’m afraid the door is destroyed, or at least the hinges.”

“Well, I may have need of your help again.”

“Let me guess,” began the senator, “Egypt?”

“As a matter of fact, yes,” said Matthew. “How did you know?” The senator looked over at his young son and said, “Again, I had a little help.”

Matthew Winter was the only siren who knew the location of another conference hall and exchange chamber. Even the *sensor,* Jonah knew only of the retreat under the mountain in West Virginia. He knew the general region of some of the American retreats, but without specifics, there would be no way to discover their locations. They were often built hundreds of years ago by very skilled masons who were gifted with their sense of secrecy. The entrances could be anywhere and undoubtedly looked like something very different than an entrance. Jonah got the attention of the hall of sirens and then turned over the floor to Matthew, who briefed them all about the meeting hall within Khufu. He concluded saying, “Since we don’t know whether or not this facility will regain the necessary electrical power to focus the beacon from the way station, I think we should be considering making the exodus from Egypt.” A nervous chuckle escaped him and he added, “I guess history repeats itself.”

The sirens exchanged a few laughs as well and were visibly relieved by the news that there was another exchange chamber for their possible use. Matthew continued, “There is another issue that we may be facing. If it was not a coincidence that this facility was compromised during a conference, perhaps the meeting hall within Khufu is also compromised. I’ve studied the construction of the tombs, and there are always large pink granite doors that slide into place upon completion of a burial chamber. As of a week ago, there was no such door blocking the entrance to the chamber at Khufu. However, a seismic anomaly like the one we experienced here could easily trigger a closure of a suspended slab. I have an emotional connection to one of the Egyptian sirens and when the anomaly occurred, the first thing I thought of was that she might be in danger. I plan on making the journey to Khufu as soon as possible, and I suggest that we all keep in contact, perhaps with something as easy as email addresses.”

Jonah spoke up, “Make sure that before you leave this complex, you give me a way to keep in contact with you. If the exchange chamber in Egypt remains operational, we will request to be added to the rotation of their exodus schedule. I’m sure that the pyramid does not have a large power source to focus the exchange pulse from the way station of the *Preculians*. It’s my belief that the pyramid can be seen from space and therefore, needs no electronic beam to maintain a focus. I will try to contact Siren and get further instructions. This mountain is not the source of the message pulses used to communicate to Siren. I have been transmitting and receiving my messages from a booster station that I'm guessing is still operational. Keep in mind that Siren wants to welcome us home, and we will get there eventually if we just remain focused and keep in contact with each other. I will be the central contact address via my email address. I'm sure you are all anxious to vacate the mountain, and I'd like to thank you all for your calm heads and cooperation. If not in Egypt, I'll see you all on Siren."

Walter Purness was having dinner with his wife Edith when his cell phone began vibrating in the pocket of his sports coat. He looked at the caller ID and said, "It's John Poole. I wonder what he wants at this hour. It's a little late to talk shop. He might want to talk me into some fishing. Excuse me, dear." He got up from the table and walked toward the rest rooms. His good manners would never let him carry on a conversation seated at a table in a restaurant. His innate sense of good manners was one of the many reasons he was so popular with his constituency. He never took himself too seriously and usually put the needs of others in front of his own. Reaching the hall to the men's room, he answered the call, "What's up, John?"

"I am, Walt, when I should be heading for bed."

"Where are you calling from?"

"West Virginia. We're staying at the Greenbrier Hotel."

"Expecting some incoming missiles?"

"Funny."

"No, really, what's up? I left Edith at the table."

"I'm sorry, Walt. I need a rather large favor, actually."

"You know I'll help it I can."

"I need your plane." There was a moment of silence on the line.

"My plane."

"I know it's a big one, Walt, and I'll owe you big time."

"What on Earth do you need a Boeing 737 for, John?"

"I need to send about fourteen people to Cairo."

"Tonight?"

"That's right. Is she at Dulles?"

"No, there's a smaller field in Alexandria where she has just gone through her annual. I'm not sure my pilots are free for this evening. This is kind of sudden, John."

"I have my own pilots, Walt."

"And they're checked out on the 737?"

"Trust me, Walt. One of them is checked out on the space shuttle."

"I'll make the call. If my pilots are available, do you want them?"

"Sure, Walt, that would be great, and I know you'd sleep better knowing your baby is in good hands."

"I'll make the call."

"Thanks, Walt. I owe you big time."

"Yes, John, you do."

~

Alankha asked her Uncle Zaphi, "How long can we last here without food and water?"

"What makes you ask such a question, child? Do you not have faith in our benefactors from *Preculis*, if not your friend from America? They will discover our predicament and come to our rescue. Our paths have a great purpose on Siren, Alankha."

"I wish I were as sure as you, Uncle."

"Well, the difference is that I have been to Siren. I know the gentle and good nature of our future hosts."

"Tell me what it's like there."

"It is very much like this world. There are oceans and continents just like here on Earth. The only real difference that I can tell is that there is no moon."

"That's sad, Uncle Zaphi. I love the moon and how it shines on the sea."

"I'm sure that you will find it an equitable trade to have no moon, but also to have no hostility."

"Yes, I'm sure you are right."

"Are you thirsty, Uncle?"

"Not unless I think about it. If you were sitting beneath a waterfall, do you suppose you would be thirsty?"

"Thank you, Uncle. Your wisdom is a great comfort to me."

"And you are a comfort to me, as well, my dear."

"Why do you say that?"

"Because you are the future and I and your Aunt Sophia are the past."

~

The Scorpions arrived at the Alexandria Airfield with a complete cell ready and able to effect the extrication of the sirens at Khufu. When the senator briefed Bill on the intent of the mission he was dubious. "What you are talking about is fantasy, John. A hidden chamber in the great pyramid? Alexander's tomb? Do you know how that sounds?"

"Have your men filed a flight plan?"

"Yes, they have. Are you sure you're in your right mind, John?"

"What difference does it make? Your cell is promised at least three days deployment to the tune of $300,000. If I'm out of my mind, you still get paid. You're a soldier of fortune, so just do your soldiering and enjoy your fortune."

"You're seriously considering that there is a secret chamber within the Great Pyramid where Alexander the Great is entombed."

"You betcha'"

"I'd like to have some of what you're smoking."

"Look, Bill, you've made your point. If you're so sure I'm nuts, how about betting me double or nothing for the three days fee that I'm right?"

Bill considered the proposition and then said, "Never mind. After what I saw your wife do, I'm not sure of anything right now."

"Now you're finally making sense," said the senator.

"Yeah, go figure."

~

Sarah Poole did not make the trip to Cairo with the other four sirens. Matthew, Durbah, Charles and Shelly left her at the airfield with hugs and well wishes promising to meet up in Cairo as soon as she could reconnect with Brad Early. Durbah was able to reach Alex Jansen, and he met them at the airfield. He had a small suitcase and was well aware that those meager belongings might be the only things he takes with him from the planet Earth. He had met with his son, Billy, and told him that he was planning on taking a long journey and that he was now the man of the family. He outlined the considerable fortune he was leaving behind in his son's name. He told him that he was counting on him to take care of his mother, Brianna, and that he was proud to be able to count on him to carry on until he could return. What he didn't say was that he wouldn't be returning at all.

~

The Scorpions boarded the 737 owned by Walter Purness at 7:15 A.M. on the morning after their successful operation at the West Virginia mountain extraction of the sirens. They were unaware of the special abilities of their fellow passengers, but would soon learn of them in their entirety. When it came time to file a flight plan at the airfield in Alexandria, Virginia, they found out that there would be a six-hour waiting period to coordinate the collective air traffic control patterns and issue international transportation passes of venue. This was not acceptable to Matthew Winter and the rest of the sirens. The Scorpions doubted the merits of the sirens' confidence in their fellow siren Matthew; however, that was not an issue in their performance because all favors had been called in by Senator Poole, and they were now being paid $107,000 per day for the duration of the mission. Matthew ascended the stairs of the small control tower of the airfield and a short time later emerged and declared, "Our flight plan was filed yesterday and recently discovered by an oversight within this facility. We can leave at any time."

The Scorpions made arrangements for a Hummer and a panel truck to be available at the Cairo International Airport for the purpose of transporting them to the address with which Matthew supplied them. Again, 1800 East Pyramid Road would have a measure of activity not usually seen in that quiet neighborhood on the South side of Cairo. Mother Bakhawi would once again be able to share her stockpile of fine French wine with her friends. The sirens in Khufu were anxiously awaiting their arrival.

Chapter Fifty-five

Sarah Poole had another agenda. She needed to return to Bar Harbor and find her lover Brad Early. She arrived on the morning after her extraction from the mountain and drove directly to his home. He was there as opposed to bedding down in any one of the number of other options he had in the Bar Harbor area, being a trusted house sitter and maintenance professional. She knocked on the door, and he answered shirtless in his jeans. "I know you," he said. "You're Sarah, right?" He was feeling a little guilty for not being totally sure about her identity. He thought that his womanizing horns might be showing.

"Yes, Bradley, I'm Sarah."

He took in her beauty and had to take a well-needed breath to calm his heart. "Is there something I can do for you?" he asked hoping that indeed there was. He had never seen a more beautiful woman in his life. His heart began to beat faster.

"Yes, Bradley. You can love me for the rest of your life." She took his hands in hers and let fly the electrum in her eyes. Her pheromones were exuded in full force and a tear came to her eye. "God, I've missed you."

He began to cry as well and said, "Oh, Sarah, how I love you."

"Show me. Now," she said. She pulled her sweatshirt over her head and unclasped her bra. It fell away to the floor, and he cupped her breasts with his hands saying, "Is this a dream, Sarah?"

"Yes, it is, and with any luck we will never wake from it."

"How can I ever have forgotten what you mean to me? I feel so ashamed."

"Never feel that way, my love. You felt what I asked you to feel and nothing more or less."

"And so now what will become of us?" he asked.

"We are going to Egypt."

"Egypt?"

"Unless there's somewhere else you think you need to be."

"Egypt, it is." Bradley was quick to compose letters of explanation regarding all of the properties that were under his care. He placed them in his mailbox and put the flag up. A small carry-on suitcase was all he packed for his journey to Egypt. Somehow he knew that was all he would need. He was once again engrossed in the heights of a love that had heretofore escaped his life. He thanked his lucky stars and pinched himself on the way to the car. Yes, he was awake. Life was good. God was indeed in his court, and the prospects for the rest of his life were good. He thought to himself, *good things must come to someone, so why not me. I will do everything in my power to deserve Sarah.* He would be surprised to know that she was thinking the exact same thing.

~

The Scorpions were content to remain within the 737 until the customs agents had boarded the plane and cleared all the passengers. This was an amenity not afforded the general public; however, Senator Poole had been a frequent visitor to Egypt and personally knew the D.I.C. or Director of Immigration and Control for the country of Egypt.

Once they were all cleared, the two vehicles came directly under the large jet and waited until they would deplane using the ramps provided by the airport operations personnel. It was only a short time later when they found themselves at the address, 1800 East Pyramid Road.

Mother Bakhawi met them at the door and asked what their business was. It took a short while for Matthew to jog her memory about recently enjoying a glass of wine with her and she once again offered, "Yes, of course, I have just opened a bottle. Would you care to join me?"

"Perhaps later, Mother. Now, we have only to ask you to use the entrance of the tunnel to Khufu because we fear that there may have been a mishap there involving Alankha and her aunt and uncle."

"Oh, dear, I hope not," she declared. "Please, go forth and make sure of their safety. The wine can wait."

"Thank you, Mother Bakhawi. We will be back soon, I am sure."

The Scorpions were dressed in casual clothes and appeared to carry no weapons. They were all skilled in the art called *naked kill,* where nothing is more deadly than a creative mind.

According to the discipline, a room of any size with ordinary objects was said to contain over a dozen deadly weapons in the hands of a master. The Scorpions were all masters of *naked kill,* but their present mission was one of peace. It was a simple routine rescue mission. Usually there were much more complicated circumstances such as a standoff with hijackers who had taken hostages for bargaining purposes. Their record was 100 percent positive in that they had never lost a hostage or failed to return a kidnapped victim safely.

Three of the Scorpions stayed in the basement of Mother Bakhawi while three remained outside the house disguised as two street vendors and a beggar. Matthew and Charles went through the tunnel with Bill, Rudy and a Scorpion known only as The Scot. Durbah, Alex and Shelly stayed behind on the first floor of the house in order to run interference with any curious onlookers at 1800 East Pyramid Road. They would blank out the mind of anyone who was determined to discover the particulars of the operation. The first decent into the tunnel, and to the hidden chamber within Khufu, was only for the planning stage. Until they knew what they were dealing with, they had no idea of the tools they would need to open the chamber door.

When they reached the dead-end chamber with the foot holds to climb the wall, they knew at once Matthew had been right. Eight feet up the wall, where there once was a three-foot-square crawl space, was now a smooth, solid pink granite wall. Matthew's heart began to beat faster. He forgot himself for a moment and shouted Alankha's name as loud as he could.

Then he came to his senses. Naturally, even if they could hear him shouting, they wouldn't return his call. As a student of archeology, he knew the importance of keeping the location of the chamber a secret. He prayed that no one heard his foolish attempt to shout through the granite wall. He was fairly sure that neither the sirens nor anyone else presently within Khufu could hear his cry.

"How thick is the wall?" asked Bill having easily scaled the eight feet of hand and foot holds up to the ledge. He was holding his hand against the smooth stone.

"Probably about two feet," said Matthew. Rudy and The Scot looked at each other and raised their eyebrows in unison. They didn't speak because they were *on task* even though they knew that Matthew and Bill were the only persons who could hear their voices. Rules were rules, and the Scorpions never broke them for any reason. Bill gave a hand signal to Rudy who shook his head slightly back and forth. Then he gave a different signal to The Scot who reacted the same way. Bill's forehead and eyebrows painted a frown on his face, and he exhaled forcefully. This operation was going to be more difficult than he had imagined. According to the silent opinions of his two operatives, neither heat nor drilling was going to be an option. There was only one other way, and it would be both expensive and difficult. Lifting, cutting or removing the door was out of the question. Therefore they would have to make a new one. Fortunately the stone foundation was made of a softer limestone and could be compromised with EMR Pulse Sonics. Electromagnetic radiation was comprised of a spectrum that included both light and sound. Since light could not be concentrated enough to cut through even limestone, they had to rely on sound vibration to crumble the stone. One huge risk that they faced was the fact that millions of tons of stone were suspended above their position and might not react favorably to losing some of their foundation. But Bill believed it was possible with short, controlled bursts of EMR Pulse Sonics.

"What's the time frame," asked Bill to Matthew.

"Nothing critical. Air is not a problem. The only issues are food and water so they have a few days with only discomfort, but nothing life threatening."

"You're sure they have air?"

"I was in there last week. There is an airshaft directly above the chamber that opens in the South face of the pyramid."

"Can a man fit through the opening?"

"No, I'm afraid not. It's only about fourteen inches wide at the ceiling of the chamber."

"That's large enough to lower a rope down, though."

"Sure, but to what end? What good will that do us?" asked Matthew.

"We're not going to lower a man, just a message."

"What kind of message?"

"We need them to do two things. Number one is to protect their ears and number two is to stay far away from the wall next to the door."

Chapter Fifty-six

Walter and Edith Purness were having an intimate dinner party with John and Johanna Poole in a private dining room at HOTEL ROUGE located at 1315 16th Street NW, Washington, D.C. Usually, the senator had a hard and fast rule not to talk shop in front of the ladies when the venue was social in nature. This time he made an exception when Walter pressed him about his reason for borrowing his plane. Walter was very attached to his toys, and the only thing he loved more than his fishing yacht was his plane. The Boeing 737 had been stripped down and reappointed with luxurious hardwood tables, soft leather winged-back armchairs and at the rear was a circular bar made of Italian marble. There was even a Jacuzzi in the center of the plane that would comfortably hold ten people. For that reason, Walter's pilots were ordered to keep the rotation on take-off less than 25 degrees.

The waiter had just taken away the salad plates and topped off their wine glasses. As soon as he left the table, Walter asked the senator, "OK, John, spill it."

"Why the plane or why Egypt?"

"How about both."

"Fair enough. I needed the plane because time is of the essence to come to the aid of some very special people who may be trapped in what you might call a *cave-in*," said the senator stretching the truth a bit. "I had to get a rescue team to Egypt because that is where the *cave-in* occurred."

"What aren't you telling me, John?"

"You always were too smart to pull anything over on," said Poole. "OK, the people I'm helping are some very well-placed operatives in the congressional offices. Two are pages, and one is an administrative assistant." Now the senator was really being less than honest because the assistant he mentioned was Walter's own daughter, who had recently quit her job working for Senator Blake from Georgia. He continued, "You know that I'm drafting a proposal for a large troop reduction in the Middle East Theater, specifically Iraq and Afghanistan. These kids will be instrumental in getting me the votes I need. This is a big one, Walt. We're talking 40,000 troops back on U.S. soil."

"What's going to loosen the strangle hold from big oil, John?"

"We're counting on some changes of emphasis during tomorrow's conference." Senator Poole was referring to the Domestic Energy Commission's annual report before Congress. Both of them would be at the conference and needed each other's support.

"Well, you know you have my vote, John. I never saw much sense in all that *shock and awe* nonsense in the first place. The only *shock* was the price of gasoline and the only *awe* was *awe crap, why did we elect that guy*." They all got a good laugh at that one.

"I know that one hand washes the other, Walt. What's it going to cost me?"

"Oh, it's not too painful when the totality sinks in. I'm looking for a tax break for the entire Coal Consortium. Not just Virginia because that would be favoritism. I'm talking a unilateral tax cut of about twenty-five percent."

"Why on Earth would Congress grant that, Walt?"

"Because we're going to promise to produce less. Burn less and release less greenhouse gasses into the environment."

"Subsidies?"

"In a sense, yes. We're asking for a bribe to clean up the air. Power companies will burn less coal and supplement the loss with Blake's natural gas pipeline. That'll get me his vote. The members of the EPA have to get behind a reduction of coal emissions. That gets me their vote. The Coal Miner's Union has to agree to fewer man hours at a higher rate of pay. I think it's a win, win all the way around. And you want to hear the kicker? It wasn't even my idea. This friend of Durbah's came to me with the idea the other day and spelled it all out for me on my yacht."

"Is that a fact?" asked John Poole innocently. He and his wife Johanna were well aware of Shelly's plan. He wondered what Walter would think if he knew that his plane was being used to secure a *space/time exchange chamber* within the Great Pyramid of Egypt so his daughter could leave the Earth forever. It wasn't his place to break the news to him, and he hoped he would be forgiven once someone else did.

~

Sarah Poole and Brad Early purchased plane tickets online and decided to fly from Boston's Logan Airport to Frankfurt and then on to Cairo. The layover in Germany was two and a half hours, which made their total travel time just under fourteen hours. They checked into the Cairo Hilton Hotel, and the first thing they did when they got to their room was check Sarah's email. There were no messages. She sent a message to Jonah's email, hoping to get a connection to the other sirens who she knew had come to Egypt directly from the mountain retreat in West Virginia. They knew that the only hope they had of traveling together to the planet Siren hinged on meeting with a *sensor* connected with a *space/time exchange chamber* other than E.C.-2. The East Central U.S. mountain retreat might regain main power from the huge generators underground, but a power outage during a transfer would mean potential danger for the sirens in the chamber at the time. Therefore, they decided that the only safe way to travel to Siren was from another alpha omega retreat. Matthew told the sirens at E.C.-2 of the existence of Khufu and outlined the instructions for entering the tunnel from 1800 East Pyramid Road in the South section of Cairo. However, they knew that the particular time of transfer was to be determined by lottery by the Khufu *sensor*. Eventually, forty-eight E.C.-2 sirens would make the exchange at Khufu along with their human love interests once they were cleared by the *sensor* named Raphael. Sarah would have brought Brad Early back to E.C.-2, but there was no way of knowing if the power could be restored or not. They figured that the only thing they could do was contact Jonah through email and make arrangements for Raphael to give Brad the screening. They were confident that he would be accepted due to the fact that his nature was very serene and benevolent. Everyone loved Brad Early and was usually very vocal about it. Since there was nothing to do but wait for Jonah's reply to her email, that's what they did. Naturally, that's not all they did. They had a bit of catching up to do.

Chapter Fifty-seven

The Planet *Preculis*

There was an emergency meeting of the Department of Off-world Activities being held in the Great Hall of the *Preculis* Capital City called *Christos*. *Christos* was named after one of the original sirens who made the journey to Earth over 5,300 years earlier. A direct descendant of *Christos* just happened to bear the same name and was the sitting Grand Master Regent of the planet Siren.

Christos was a beautiful port city on *Preculis* and had great crystal spires atop huge buildings. It was situated on the leeward side of a large bay affording protection from the great waves generated by the swells in the Osiris Ocean. Although Siren had no moon, *Preculis* had two and the tides were much more turbulent as a result. For that reason, the only vessels that could cross the Osiris Ocean were very large hydrofoils or hovercrafts.

A three hundred meter hydrofoil had just arrived earlier in the day to deliver the Prime Minister of a country called Sentia Prime. As a highly ranked member, his attendance was required for an upcoming vote by the Supreme Council of *Preculis*. The Grand Master of the Council addressed the Prime Minister from Sentia, "Welcome Prime Minister *Shonguana* to the shores of *Christos*. I trust that your Osiris crossing was without incident?"

"Then you trust wrong, Grand Master *Phodan*. There were three nests of deep serpents that had designs on our vessel. Fortunately, our gunner is a thirty-year veteran from the *Xeries* conflict. He dispatched them in short measure."

"How very charmed you were. I'm told they are extremely fierce during this, the mating season."

"I will make my return journey from the air, *Phodan*."

"A wise move, my friend, *Shonguana*."

"Please, if there is no reason to delay, I am anxious to come to a decision regarding the situation on the planet Earth."

"Certainly. There has been a rather serious turn of events in two of the conference halls of the alpha omega. The one in the United States designated as E.C.-2 has had a massive power failure that we are attributing to a seismic anomaly."

"Is the structure still intact?"

"Yes, we believe so. However, our friends on Siren are unable to contact the communications center at E.C.-2. Their emergency power is not sufficient for that purpose. The alpha omega conference hall in Khufu has suffered a similar fate. It is a rather unfortunate coincidence, but should not pose a threat to their planned exodus. We believe that the sirens of E.C.-2 will be able to use the Khufu chamber for the *space/time* exchanges. A greater number of sirens will make the exodus from Egypt."

"History always seems to repeat itself," said Prime Minister *Shonguana*. "And now our responsibility is once again paramount. We have to intercede to expedite the safe exodus of the E.C.-2 sirens."

"How many are there?"

"Less than fifty."

"Well, at least that's something in our favor. Can we get a message to them to relocate to another *exchange chamber*?"

"That is the plan; however, that is also the reason for this meeting."

"So now the issue is whether or not we can accelerate the schedule of the exodus from Earth to free the sirens from Khufu, is that correct?"

"You are most wise, Minister."

"I shouldn't think a vote is required at all. We have forced this scenario upon the sirens of Earth. We are the reason they are there in the first place. They are the heroes of their planet and ours as well because they administered to our burden to protect their home world. I vote in favor of an accelerated schedule."

"Excellent. There are three more Council votes to be considered besides ours. As you can imagine, we were all in agreement for an accelerated timetable before your arrival."

"Due to the immediacy of the situation, I don't blame you for a moment. Let us divert power to the way station and extricate the sirens of Khufu at the earliest possible moment. They are probably getting rather thirsty by now."

"It shall be done. What of a message to the sirens of E.C.-2? Perhaps we can impose upon Siren to send one of their citizens to travel in the *space/time exchange* with the Khufu chamber."

"But would he not be trapped as well?"

"It seems that there is a force at work to gain entrance to the chamber as we speak. We estimate that they will complete their task in approximately two Earth days."

"Then the citizen from Siren will have to travel with provisions until the task force can free him."

"Precisely."

"It seems, Grand Master *Phodan*, that you have everything under control here in *Christos* and perhaps my journey was not necessary."

"On the contrary, Prime Minister *Shonguana.* Your council is always in great demand. We deeply apologize for your inconvenience and will report back to you with the news of our imminent success."

"Thank you for the kind words. Well, if there is nothing else to discuss, I think it's time for me to indulge in one of your local delicacies. I am aware that the oxala clams are in season, and as you know, the serpents spoil all of the shoals on our side of Osiris."

"I would be pleased to join you Prime Minister. The clams are some of my favorites as well."

Bill, Rudy and The Scot returned with Matthew to the basement of Mother Bakhawi's residence at 1800 East Pyramid Road. There they were welcomed by Durbah, Alex and Shelly and given a glass of some very fine red table wine. As a matter of coincidence, the vintner, Rothschild was a siren as well, but the full bodied luxury of the dry leggy treasure was an extreme pleasure no matter what the origin of its master. Durbah asked Bill, “So what are we dealing with?”

“We have to transport some very sensitive equipment through the tunnel to the opening of the chamber.”

“But it can be done, right?”

“Anything can be done, Durbah. It’s just a matter of when.”

“When do you estimate the job can be finished?”

“Two days,” said Bill. “The equipment we need is in Israel.”

“Would you like Alex and me to come along with you?”

“You, yes. Alex, no. I’d like him to go back to the Hilton and wait for our return. John Poole said that you are as influential as his wife Johanna. That skill may come in handy on the trip to Israel.”

“I think he wants you light on your feet, Durbah,” said Alex.

“You’re a smart man, Alex,” said Bill. “Don’t worry, I’ll take good care of her.”

“Oh, I’m not worried. Don’t be surprised if she ends up taking care of you.”

~

The Planet Siren

The Master Regent of the Grand Council on Siren greeted Grand Master *Phodan* of *Preculis*. "Master *Phodan*, we remain forever in your debt. What brings you to our humble planet this day?"

"I have need of one of your citizens as an emissary."

"Oh?"

"There has been a situation on Earth that requires our immediate intercession. A dozen of your future citizens are in a rather tight spot. It seems that a doorway has closed in the Great Pyramid of Khufu's Horizon, which, as you know, is the location of an alpha omega chamber. We intend to accelerate our schedule for the exodus in this one instance and exchange the Khufu chamber as soon as possible. We would like one of your citizens to make the exchange as well, and coordinate the exodus of forty-eight other sirens who have lost the operation of their exodus chamber located at E.C.-2."

"Certainly, Grand Master. You need a communications specialist, correct?"

"English is the spoken language. We will outline the message to be given to the sirens when they manage to gain entrance to the chamber."

"How many days' provisions should he take?"

"No more than two days. It would be helpful if he were able to remain among the population of Earth for another twenty days until the exodus proper will resume and continue the planned schedule."

"That shouldn't be a problem. I will screen our population for suitable candidates and have a volunteer for you within the next hour."

"Thank you, Master Regent *Christos*."

"No, Grand Master, it is I, who once again, must thank you."

~

Chapter Fifty-eight

Bill and Rudy were the only Scorpions to take Durbah to Israel to procure the EMR Sonic Pulse cannon. A little known fact among the general public is that *Star Wars*, an anti-ballistic missile program that the president of the United States used to bankrupt the Soviet Union, was largely based on Pulse Radiation. In the case of missiles, the pulse was one of light. It produced a concussion on the nosecone of incoming inter-continental ballistic missiles and destroyed them before they could reach their target. They were targeted with the use of a spinning mirror on a satellite hundreds of miles above the Earth. The Israelis took the technology one step further and produced concussive pulse values from sound as well.

The benefit was that light pulses were not as effective on stone as sound. It just so happened that the Israeli arsenal had exactly the right tool for the disintegration of the massive limestone blocks that made up the majority of Khufu's Horizon. Although Bill was aware of the existence of the pulse cannon, Israel was not in the habit of lending out their extremely expensive experimental weaponry. That's where he hoped Durbah would indeed come in handy. John Poole assured him that Durbah, Shelly, Charles and Matthew all could influence the minds of subjects as well as his wife, Johanna. There was a lot riding on whether or not he was right. A worst case scenario had them arrested in Israel for espionage and appealing to the

U.S. Embassy to negotiate for their release. Fortunately, that was not the case. Durbah immediately recognized a highly placed siren when they hit the ground in Israel and upon informing her of the situation, arrangements were quickly made to transfer the pulse cannon to their plane.

~

There was a knock at the door of Sarah Poole and Brad Early's room. They were lying in bed having just cooled down from their passionate lovemaking. It seemed that they had to remind themselves to eat because when they felt anything akin to hunger, they just assumed that it was a hunger for each other. They never tired of expressing their love in the physical sense as well as their spiritual connection. Brad got out of bed and slipped on his pants and shirt to answer the door. He found, standing in the hall, a short balding man with a slight mustache and very dark eyes. He said, "My name is Raphael. Are you Bradley?"

"Yes, I am," said Brad.

"I am pleased to meet you. If you would not mind, I need to ask you a few questions and perhaps make physical contact with you for a short while." Raphael looked over to the bed and saw Sarah smiling at him from under the sheets. He said to her, "Would you mind terribly giving us a little privacy, Sarah?"

"Not at all, Raphael. I'll go down to the restaurant and look at the menu. How much time do you need?"

"Perhaps, an hour. Maybe a little less."

"All right." She got out of the bed and crossed the room without a stitch of clothes on. Brad was surprised that there was no visible reaction by Raphael as though he saw a beautiful naked woman every day. She quickly put on her panties, jeans, bra and a tee shirt with the image of Khufu on the front that she had bought in the hotel gift shop. She kissed Brad Early on the lips and said to Raphael, "Nice to meet you," as she slipped on her shoes and left the two men alone. Raphael asked Brad, "Why do you want to go to the planet Siren, Bradley?"

"I want to be with Sarah."

"And what do you expect to find on the planet Siren?"

"A life with the woman I love."

"What if you find that you are not happy there? Are you aware of the fact that there is no coming back to Earth once you make the journey?"

"I am. I will always be happy as long as I have my love close to me. I am aware that I cannot return to Earth."

"Very well." Raphael walked up to Brad and placed his hand on his forehead. "Does this make you nervous, Bradley?"

"No, it doesn't."

"I'm going to try to read your emotions for a few minutes by way of a power with which the Creator has blessed me. Is that all right with you?"

"Yes, Raphael. I trust you implicitly. Do whatever you like to read my emotions. I have nothing to hide and everything to gain."

"You will feel some heat, but it is not overly uncomfortable."

"I understand," said Brad.

Raphael stood completely silent with his hand on Brad's forehead for a full twenty minutes. Brad was surprised to find that his legs did not tire, and he felt no fatigue standing in a still position for so long. There was a slight bit of heat that he felt, but it only made him feel a sense of serenity.

When Raphael was finished with his screening process, he said to Brad, "You are a very spiritual man, Bradley. I am sure you will make a valued addition to the planet Siren. Let me be the first to welcome you." With those words he reached out and hugged Brad in a very strong embrace. Without another word he left the room and softly closed the door behind him.

Alex returned to the Cairo Hilton and asked the front desk to deliver a written message to Sarah Poole as soon as she checked in. He was told that she was, in fact, already checked in and the message would be delivered to her room shortly. Alex simply gave Sarah his room number and expressed an interest in meeting Brad Early and joining them for dinner.

Chapter Fifty-nine

The Planet *Preculis*

Just as the Prime Minister of Sentia and the Grand Master *Phodan* were concluding their repast of oxala clams and fine wine, a messenger was admitted to their table with an urgent message. "The council must reconvene to address a matter of supreme importance."

"Something that can't wait until tomorrow?" asked *Phodan*.

"I'm afraid not, Sir. It seems the worst fears of Siren have been realized."

"Not here, if you please," said *Phodan*. "Take care of the bill, and we will meet you at the Supreme Council Chamber in the Great Hall." He turned to the Prime Minister of Sentia, "My apologies, *Shonguana*. It seems that I must impose upon your vote once again this evening."

"Public service is both a joy and a curse. It is a fact that settled early on in my career, and I have learned to live with it."

~

Alex got a call from Sarah Poole as soon as she returned to her room. Brad had given her the news that he was to be welcomed to Siren, and they both felt like celebrating. "Will you celebrate with us, Alex?"

"Most certainly. I can meet you in the restaurant in twenty minutes. Would that be OK?"

"Perfect," said Sarah. "I have a mental image of you from the way Durbah has talked about you, but just to be safe, what are you wearing?"

"I'll be in tan khakis and a blue shirt with a dark blue sports coat. Just look for a guy who looks like a basketball coach and lost his tie."

Sarah laughed and said, "OK, we'll find you.

~

Shelly Simon and Charles Donovan were soon to check in as well. They decided to have room service sent up instead of tracking down the other sirens in the hotel. They knew there would be plenty of time for that later. In fact, they might be staying at the Cairo Hilton for an indefinite period of time until their names appeared in the rotation for the exodus. They anxiously awaited the email from Jonah, which would explain the details of the departure schedule.

~

Bill, Rudy and Durbah touched down at Cairo International Airport, designation CAI, at 8:55 P.M. Their trip to Israel to procure the space age pulse cannon took a scant seven hours of total time. Bill was very impressed with the special skills that Durbah Purness possessed aside from her remarkable beauty. He wondered how his old friend, the senator, hooked up with these incredibly effective and influential people. He was having a difficult time keeping the Scorpions *on task* because without even a conscious effort, the female sirens were reducing them to nothing more than drooling schoolboys. Bill was affected by them as well, and cut the men some slack. Still, as enchanting as they were, Bill would breathe a sigh of relief when they could take their leave of the sirens.

They loaded the pulse cannon into a panel truck after, once again, being cleared through customs while still aboard Walter Purness' 737. When the D.I.C. addressed Durbah, he was beside himself with kind words and promises to do anything in his power to make her stay in Cairo more enjoyable. She assured him that he had done enough and greatly appreciated the special treatment they were afforded.

~

The following day, Walter Purness was successful during the annual presentation of the Domestic Energy Commission's report to Congress. He presented a written proposal for the reduction of coal production and utilization for the use in hydro-electric plants. It was welcomed in every quarter. Alyssa Grant immediately saw the benefit of natural gas supplementing coal as a more environmentally friendly combustible product. Big oil was oblivious, for all intents and purposes, because they would still enjoy the magnanimous profits from the refinery industry and the production of gasoline.

Senator Poole was also successful in getting some clearly honest commitments for votes regarding a proposal to Congress for the reduction of troops in the Middle East. In what was clearly an about-face move, Senator Williams, who was the darling of the armed services as evidenced by his Navy Cross prominently displayed in his office, decided to verbally commit to Senator Poole's proposal following a brief meeting with Poole's wife, Johanna, in the hallway. The aide who took Charles Donovan's position in Williams' office was clearly taken aback by the senator's abrupt change of position regarding troop deployment.

Senator Blake was successful in clearing the way for a natural gas pipeline coming ashore in the great state of Georgia from a drilling platform 12 miles off the coast. His stock in the company called Energix went up nearly 7 percent overnight.

~

The Planet *Preculis*

"This had better be a legitimate emergency, Mr. Undersecretary to call together the Supreme Council of *Preculis* at this ungodly hour," said Master Regent *Phodan*.

"I'm sure you will understand when you hear the particulars. I will now direct you to the monitor screen where you will see Dr. Hawkins from the planet Siren by way of a prerecorded pulse message to give you a complete rundown." The Undersecretary then started the playback, and the Council members watched the monitor.

Stephen J. Hawkins took the floor and addressed the Supreme Council of *Preculis*. "Distinguished Council members, I have urgent news regarding the deployment of a spacecraft from the planet Earth. We have just detected its presence approaching our planet, although it must have been launched from Earth nearly a year ago. We are not sure of the motive or mission of the spacecraft, but we have to be prepared for the worst. We are now in the unfortunate position to call upon your help once again regarding this potential threat. We believe that the craft will achieve an orbit around Siren in approximately two months. We are counting on the good will and protection from our good friends the *Preculians*. Any way that you can afford our planet some protection will be greatly appreciated and we will forever remain in your debt. Thank you very much, your faithful brothers of Siren.

Chapter Sixty

Alex walked into the bar at the restaurant within the Cairo Hilton and ordered a Becks beer. As he was standing at the bar, a woman came up behind him and asked, “Alex Jansen, I presume?”

“The very same,” he said. He was startled by the incredible beauty of the striking woman who stood before him. Her companion was a very handsome man in his own right. They struck him immediately as a remarkably beautiful couple and could be none other than Sarah Poole and Brad Early.

“I’m very pleased to meet you, Alex. I’m Sarah and this is Brad,” she said motioning to her handsome companion.

“Oh course, you are,” said Alex. “Durbah said you returned to Bar Harbor to tie up some loose ends, so to speak.”

“And to also retrieve one.” She leaned over and kissed Brad on the cheek.

“You’re a lucky man, Brad.”

“Well, although I haven’t met Durbah, I’m certain that you are a lucky man as well.”

“She’s remarkable, Brad. At this very moment, she’s on a mission to Israel to retrieve a top secret, cutting-edge weapon with which our friends the Scorpions hope to open the chamber in Khufu. Can you believe all this?”

“I told Sarah that I’m dreaming. I’m just being very careful not to wake up.” He laughed along with Alex.

“Yeah, I know how you feel.”

“Why don’t we get something to eat,” suggested Sarah. “I think we’ve had enough pecking at the airline food. We need something edible.”

“You guys must be beat. How long was your travel day?”

“About fourteen hours. It could have been worse. It took me twenty to get from Maine to Hawaii once,” said Sarah.

“Shall we get a table or eat at the bar?” asked Alex.

“Definitely a table,” said Sarah. “I’m pretty famished. We might be here for a while,” she said giggling.

The beautiful siren led her two human companions to the dining room. The Maître d asked for a name to put on the waiting list. Sarah held out her hand to shake his and caught his eye as well. “I’m Sarah,” she said simply. The man then said, “Yes, of course, Sarah, right this way,” leading the way to their table that was quickly being cleared and set up for them .

“Some service,” said Alex when the Maître d’ left their table.

“Get used to it, Alex. I’ll lay you odds that we don’t even get a bill.”

“Oh, nonsense,” said Sarah. “I’m going to insist on a bill and leave a very large tip. You know what they say about not being able to take it with you. Our money will be of no use on Siren.”

“We need to do some shopping tomorrow,” said Brad. “I hope that Cairo has a Cartier’s or Tiffany’s.”

“Oh, Brad, I’ll give you exactly two weeks to stop talking like that.” Her laughter was musical, and they laughed as well.

Alex then said, "I think I'd like to come along. I wish I could buy Durbah *The Star of India*."

"Uhh, I don't think it's for sale, Alex, but trust me, if Durbah really wanted it, it would be hanging around her neck."

~

Bill, Rudy and Durbah arrived back at 1800 East Pyramid Road at 9:40 P.M. The Scorpions were still *on site* and *on task* although any casual onlooker would be hard pressed to detect them. They seamlessly blended into the South Cairo scenery and sea of humanity. Matthew asked Bill if he could accompany the Scorpions during the operation to dissolve the limestone but was refused. He could, however, assist in the construction of the scaffolding equipment to build a platform eight feet above the floor in the anti-chamber just outside the pink granite door. He explained that, even with some very high-tech ear protection, the Scorpion who would fire the sonic pulses faced some permanent hearing loss. The Scot was the natural candidate for the job because he had previously suffered hearing loss in an explosion at a U.S. Embassy in Bahrain. Since the majority of the communication during a mission was silent hand signals from Bill, his ailment was not very consequential. He also explained to Matthew that one of the Scorpions, who was known as Perez, would soon scale the South face of the pyramid and lower down a message to the sirens trapped in the chamber below. He asked Matthew if he would like to include a note to his friend Alankha along with their instructions to assemble as far away from the doorway as possible and protect their ears. Matthew took him up on the offer and simply wrote, *"We will soon be together, my love, Matthew."*

~

Durbah realized that there was nothing she could do to assist the Scorpions with their appointed task of creating an opening in the chamber at Khufu. She wished them luck and then took a cab back to Alex at the Cairo Hilton Hotel.

~

When the Scorpion, Perez scaled the South face of Khufu, he was dressed entirely in flat black and had a flat black face as well, by using a burnt wine cork that he procured from Mother Bakhawi. He wanted to avoid grease paint because of the possible reflection of a flashlight from a curious guard or perhaps even a well equipped tourist viewing Khufu at night. At 10:05 P.M., he had made it to the air shaft opening in the South face and lowered a note along with a felt-tipped pen down on a two-hundred-foot nylon cord. When it reached the bottom, he felt a slight pull on the line as a confirmation from below that their communication was successful. His attempt to pull the cord back up was met with some resistance. He immediately understood that the captives below had not finished writing on the paper to return a message. The exposure to discovery was unnerving to Perez, but he waited patiently until he felt two short pulls on the line. He was then able to easily pull up the chord by wrapping it around his left wrist with his right hand. When he saw the note clear the opening, he silently made his way back down the South face of the pyramid. From there it was a simple matter to clean his face with a bottle of sanitizer and change into a white cotton shirt. He then joined a tour bus leaving the plateau at Giza and convinced the driver to let him off in South Cairo, telling him he had just realized he had gotten on the wrong bus.

~

Chapter Sixty-one

Durbah checked back into her room at the Hilton and called Alex on his cell phone. He answered, "I'm downstairs in the restaurant with a couple of friends of yours. Are you going to join us?"

"Not just yet, Alex. I'm kind of beat. We had to take the panel truck with the weapon to Mother Bakhawi's house, and I just got back. I'm going to lie down for a while."

"Would you like some company?"

"Of course."

"I'll be right there," said Alex smiling at Sarah and Brad. He said to them, "You'll excuse me, please?"

"Go," said Sarah waving her hand and giving him a knowing wink that ought to be illegal in any Muslim country like Egypt. "We've got the bill."

"Thanks, you two. It's been great meeting you."

"You, too, Alex. We'll see you later."

The last thing he said before he left them was, "Brad, give a shout when you're going to Cartier's."

"Will do," was Brad Early's reply.

~

The hike back to Mother Bakhawi's house was less than a mile from where Perez left the tour bus. He walked at a leisurely pace not wanting to draw attention to himself. His knowledge of Farsi was instrumental in Bill's decision to assign the task to him. He conversed very convincingly when approached by the local Egyptian population. He recognized the three Scorpions stationed outside on the street at 1800 East Pyramid Road, but he was surely the only one who did. He was impressed with their ability to blend in with an unfamiliar neighborhood. Without a word, he passed by them and went up to the door. He knocked once, and the door was immediately opened by a Scorpion dressed as an old man. Together they went to the basement room, and Perez placed the note on a table in front of Bill. Bill opened the note and said, "It says there are twelve of them in there. They are in good health and waiting patiently for their friends to affect a rescue. It's signed by Zaphi Hanass, who, if I'm not mistaken, is the Chairman of the SCA."

"That's right," said Matthew. Bill then handed the note to Matthew, who read a more personal message intended only for him. It read, "*My fire for you holds the chill of the night at bay. Love, Alankha*."

~

Alex fell into Durbah's arms and said, "God, I've missed you. What has it been, about a week?"

"It seems like it, Alex. Actually it's only been about eight hours."

"Did Bill say how long it will take to free the sirens from the chamber at Khufu."

"He said it should be sometime tonight. I'm sure they'll be fine."

"Were you serious when you said you wouldn't go to Siren without me?" asked Alex.

"Of course, I was serious," she said. "I belong with you no matter what planet we're on."

"But do you think I'll get through the screening?"

"I'm sure of it."

"What about your father?"

"He would if he wanted to, but I'm sure he won't be going to Siren. Naturally, my mother won't be going either."

"Did he try to talk you out of going?"

"He doesn't know that I am going."

"You're kidding me," he said.

"Believe me, Alex, that's not something I would kid about. There's something else he doesn't know also. He doesn't know that my mother and I are sirens."

"When are you going to tell him?"

"When the Scorpions return his plane, I plan to be on it."

"Would you like me to come with you?"

"Of course, I would, but it might be a difficult moment."

"I'm sure it will be."

"You're sure you don't mind coming with me?"

"My place is by your side, Durbah. Forever.

~

Matthew and the Scorpions all pitched in with the construction of the platform above the scaffolding. By 3:15 A.M., they had everything in place and decided this was the best time of day for The Scot to fire the sonic pulses into the limestone. They all patted him on the back on their way out of the anti-chamber and back to the basement of Mother Bakhawi's.

When they had retreated two hundred feet into the tunnel, they started the two huge generators to supply The Scot with enough power to fire the pulses. The Scot was confident that he could compromise the large limestone block they had mapped out to the left of the door in less than an hour. This was important because the generators created a carbon monoxide emission that would soon fill the tunnel. In the event that the operation took any longer, he was equipped with an S.C.O.T. Pack, which stood for Self Contained Oxygen Tank and was used by firemen to enter smoke filled buildings. If it took an hour or less, The Scot was confident that the air shaft within the chamber would clear out the emissions in the tunnel.

~

The Planet *Preculis*

The Grand Master *Phodan* was meeting with the Director of Off-world Operations named Dr. Zahn. Dr. Zahn informed the Grand Master that the *space/time exchange* from the chamber in Khufu could be completed at any time. Sufficient power had been diverted to the way station to complete one transfer prior to the planned exodus. Because they would only have the power for one transfer, the twelve sirens would have to remain on the way station instead of continuing on to Siren. Provisions have been assembled at the station to make them comfortable; however, the *sensor*, Zaphi Hanass would not be able to coordinate the transfers from Khufu for the sirens of E.C.-2. Therefore, a siren would have to make the journey to Earth to plan the schedule for their departure.

"Yes, Dr. Zahn. I have been informed of the situation and a replacement for the *sensor* has been chosen and is awaiting the transfer in the chamber at the way station."

"Then we are free to go ahead with the transfer?" asked Dr. Zahn.

"By all means, Doctor. The sirens in Khufu are currently without food or water, and we should make haste to retrieve them."

"Thank you, Master *Phodan*. It shall be done."

~

Zaphi Hanass was holding hands with his niece Alankha when he detected the pulse of soft blue light that he knew was the *space/time exchange* transfer taking place. He said to her, “Here we go, my dear. You will be glad to know that we have begun the journey to your new home, Siren.”

“But, Uncle Zaphi, what about Matthew?”

“Fear not, my child. I am certain he will make the journey from this very room. The *Preculians* are certainly aware of the situation here and will send a representative in the exchange to do what was to be my job as Khufu *sensor*.”

~

Chapter Sixty-two

Bill and three of the Scorpions were motioned forward by The Scot who had just come through the basement door from the tunnel to Mother Bakhawi's basement. They made their way back through the tunnel and were assaulted by the fumes from the generator's motors, but were well aware that the real danger was an odorless gas in the form of carbon monoxide. Bill's CO meter showed that the level was acceptable, and he knew that since The Scot had broken through the wall, the tunnel would be cleared of all fumes and harmful gasses in a short while.

The opening that The Scot had created was just large enough for a man to crawl through on his stomach. One by one they made their way into the chamber and were not at all prepared for what they found. Instead of the twelve people they expected to find trapped in the chamber, they found only one. He was dressed in a long white robe and had soft sandals on his feet. His hair and beard were long and brown, and his face had a peaceful expression accompanied by his soft blue eyes. "Greetings," he said.

"Matthew and the other four men were at a loss for words. Finally, Matthew uttered, "Who are you?"

The man held his open palms forward toward the men and said simply, "I am *Christos*."

~

Alankha and the eleven other sirens were warmly greeted by a man and a woman when the door to their chamber was opened. They found that they had not traveled to the planet Siren as expected. They found that they were actually aboard a space station and would be required to remain there for a brief stay before their journey could be completed.

"A space station?" asked Alankha.

"That's right," said the female station attendant. "We call it a way station. You are exactly half way home to the planet Siren. We are sorry that we couldn't store sufficient power to complete both legs of the journey at one time. This station would not even be necessary if there was a direct line of sight connection from Earth to Siren. The *Preculians,* who are lending us this technology, felt it would be dangerous to bend a beam of light around the sun, so they built a way station on *Preculis* and used the *space/time exchange* technology to relocate it here."

"Fascinating," said Zaphi. All the other sirens were impressed as well. They had never imagined, let alone experienced such advanced technology in all their years on Earth.

"How long until we can travel on to Siren?" asked Zaphi.

"Less than a week," said the male attendant. "Until then, you can relax and enjoy some good food and drink and take in some of the best scenery in all the cosmos. All the view screens have telescopic properties so you can effectively look backward in time. I recommend looking at the birth of the Crab Nebula. It's one of my all time favorite vistas."

~

"What the hell's going on here?" asked Bill angrily.

"Just a minute, Bill," said Matthew. He addressed the man named *Christos*, "Are you *Preculian?*"

"Siren."

"Zaphi's replacement?"

"That's right. I'll be here for the full twenty days it will take you for the exodus."

"I understand," said Matthew.

"Well, I'm glad somebody does," said Bill. "Where the hell are all the others?"

"I'll tell you, Bill, but you won't be able to retain the memory."

"More voodoo from Mrs. Poole?" asked Rudy.

"Or any one of us," explained Matthew. "We can all replace your memory of this day."

"And I suppose you will whether or not you tell us what's really going on."

"I'm afraid so, Bill."

"Are we still getting paid?" he asked knowing that they could even erase the fact that they ever hired the Scorpions.

"Of course, Bill. We're sirens, not pirates," he said chuckling.

"Sirens," said Bill laconically.

"That's right, Bill. *Christos* here is a siren, too. He just made the journey from Siren here to Earth to help us with what is called *The Exodus*. There are four hundred and eighty-six of us here on Earth, and we are all going back to Siren, along with a few select humans."

"And that's where the twelve people went from this room. Is that what you're telling me?"

"That's right, but that's not all," said Matthew. "There's something else missing from this room."

"What might that be?" asked Bill with a tired voice.

"The tomb of Alexander the Great."

"Sure, why not," said Bill resignedly.

~

Washington D.C.
The Oval Office of the White House

Bill Conlan was the acting Director of the Federal Bureau of Investigations based in Quantico, Virginia. The Director was attending a very sensitive meeting with President Amalah of the

United States of America and The Director of the National Aeronautics and Space Administration. The Director of NASA was named Sean O'Keefe. Conlan and O'Keefe were briefing President Amalah regarding a program called *Project Nautilus*.

"Tell me I'm not really hearing this, Mr. Conlan," said the President. "Tell me that I'm still upstairs in my bed asleep, and this is just a nightmare. Can you do that for me?"

"I wish I could, Sir."

"How did this happen?" asked Amalah.

"It was the previous administration's baby," said Conlan.

"And the baby was your monster, Bill," said O'Keefe.

"Now, hold on a minute . . ."

"STOP!" commanded President Amalah.

"Start at the beginning, gentlemen. Let's take this step by miserable step, shall we?"

"We have launched a weapon into deep space for the purposes of measuring the nuclear signature in a zero gravity environment."

"We what?" asked the president.

"We conducted a deep space test. At least the previous administration did."

"Now tell me the rest of it. Tell me why this country launched a nuclear weapon into space when doing so is strictly prohibited by the Nagasaki United Space Accord?"

"Sir, the Accord isn't worth the paper it's written on. Your predecessor began launching the 37-X B into space back in 2010."

"I'm familiar with that project, Mr. Conlan. When I was briefed, I was told that the crafts would orbit our planet for nine months at a time and then land at Andrews, correct?"

"Yes, Sir. That is what we were told as well."

"And is that the case?"

"We don't believe so, Sir."

"I was also briefed that they were not to carry any ordinance, nuclear or otherwise. Apparently, that was a lie also."

"Yes, Sir. The launch of the nuclear ordinance was ordered by the previous administration under the guidance of the Secretary of Defense. We just learned about it a short time ago when we were asked for the use of the Hubble telescope. It seems that the X-B 37 has veered off course and has disappeared on the other side of the sun."

"Jesus," said Amalah. "I knew I was going to inherit a budget deficit, but this is ridiculous. So the weapon is now in deep space, and we have no control over it?"

"Basically, yes, Sir. That is the case," said O'Keefe.

"Just what the hell does that mean? Now, tell me, gentlemen, just how do we put out this fire?" asked Amalah seriously.

"Well, we are not overly concerned, Sir," said O'Keefe.

"Oh, really, Sean? Tell me, just how exactly would you feel if your nuke turns around and bites us in the ass?"

"I don't think that's of any concern, Sir," said the NASA director.

"Oh you don't, don't you. Well you must realize that you've just bet your career on it, Sean."

"I'm confident that it will pose no threat to our planet."

"So we can't send an auto destruct signal? Is that what I'm hearing?"

"No, Sir. It was never designed for that. The weapon was never actually armed until it was very far out in space."

"And how long will the weapon's propulsion system last?"

"For a very long time, Sir. Unless something goes wrong. There's always the possibility that a meteor strike could change the trajectory or destroy the weapon entirely."

"Well, I would guess that is too much to hope for," said the president.

"The ordinance is designed to detonate at three thousand feet if it enters a planet's atmosphere," said Conlan.

"What is the size of the bomb?" asked Amalah.

"Roughly the same size as *"Fat Man,"* the weapon that was dropped on Nagasaki. Twenty kilotons, Sir."

"So it would wipe out an entire city if it happens to come back in our lap, is that what you are telling me?"

"That's right, Sir," said the NASA director. "At least a small city."

"Are you a religious man, Sean?" asked the president.

"Yes, Sir."

"Good thing. You now know what your next move should be, don't you?"

"Yes, Sir."

"Get out. Both of you, damn it. I'm not having a very good day." The president put his head down on his desk and never even saw the two men leave, but he heard the door close very softly.

~

Christos was the guest of the earthbound sirens and also checked into the Hilton Hotel. Matthew debriefed the Scorpions in Mother Bakhawi's basement along with Durbah, Shelly and Sarah. When the men loaded their equipment back into the panel truck, they were convinced that their mission was to deliver a very secret experimental weapon to Israel. Bill was given the name of a female contact within the Israeli military who would receive the shipment. They had the use of Walter Purness' Boeing 737, which was being fueled up at that very moment at CAI, the Cairo International Airport. Durbah and Alex would accompany the Scorpions and remain aboard her father's plane while the delivery was carried out. Upon completion of their mission, they were required to return the plane to an airfield in Alexandria, Virginia. Naturally, the mission would remain classified, and they could expect a payment of $473,000 in less than a week.

~

When Walter and Edith arrived at the Virginia airfield, Durbah and Alex left the plane and greeted them with warm embraces. When Durbah was introducing Alex to her parents, Walter noticed a tear in her eye and wiped it away with his finger.

"What's wrong with my little girl?" he asked. It broke his heart to see her sad for any reason. The reason this time would break his heart more thoroughly than ever before.

"Oh, daddy," she said and threw herself into his arms once again sobbing heavily.

"Hey, hey, what's all this?" he said and found himself crying as well.

"I'm going to miss you so much," she said through her tears.

"I know you will," said Edith through her own tears.

"What?" asked Walter. "What do you know, Edith?"

"We have a lot to talk about, Walt. Call your pilots and tell them to file a flight plan to Cairo."

"Egypt?" asked Walter. "Why do you want to go to Egypt?"

"It's not where I want to go, Walt, it's where we have to go."

"I love you, mom," said Durbah crying and wiping her nose with the back of her hand.

"Could somebody tell me what the hell is going on here?" said Walter.

"Your world is about to change, Walt. In a big way, but it's also a good way," said Edith.

"You know I'm not big on surprises," said Walter.

"Yeah, I know. And you're going to hate this one I'm afraid."

"I'm moving to another planet," said Durbah suddenly.

Durbah and Edith said nothing for a moment and just watched Walter for his reaction. He turned his head to the side and just looked at the floor blinking his eyes for a few seconds. He finally said, "Did you just say what I think you said?"

"I know it sounds unreal, Mr. Purness, but it's true. Durbah and I are leaving Earth to live on another world. It's a planet called Siren, and we are part of an exodus from Earth to go there to live."

Durbah finally found her voice, "I love you daddy and I'm going to miss you very much. But we can stay in touch with each other when you and mother go to the conference center."

"Edith, tell me that this is some kind of bad dream that I'm going to wake up from."

"I wish I could, Walt, but trust me, you'll get used to it."

"I don't think you know what you're saying."

"Yes, I do. The pain will pass and you will accept it in time. I can take away the pain if it comes to that."

"I'm a siren, daddy," said Durbah. "So is mom."

"A siren," said Walter rather deadpan.

"That's right. We are descendants of the people of Siren. They came to Egypt over four thousand years ago and lived among humans until now. Now we have been called home. To Siren. There is another planet called *Preculis* that has the technology to send us there in a very short time, but we can't ask them send us back here whenever we want. It's just a one-time transfer in a thing called a space/time exchange chamber."

"*Preculis,*" said Walter wrinkling his brow. Then he added, "And Siren."

"That's right," said Alex. "Believe it."

"So you are a siren, too, is that it?" he asked Alex.

"No, Mr. Purness, I'm just in love with one."

Chapter Sixty-three

When Durbah and Alex left Walter and Edith at the airport in Cairo, they checked into the Hilton and asked to see the guest registry to locate their fellow members of the exodus. Naturally, the poor man at the front desk could deny Durbah nothing. She had him connect her with Shelly Simon and Charles Donovan, who then met them in the restaurant for lunch.

"You two are getting to be globetrotters, Durbah," said Shelly. "Two bad you won't be able to cash in on your frequent flier miles."

"Daddy doesn't issue those, Shelly," she said with a slight giggle. Shelly could tell she wasn't feeling the smile that was on her pretty face. She sensed that her meeting with her parents was putting a heavy weight on her heart.

"Do you want to talk about it?" asked Charles knowingly.

"I'm not sure there is anything to say except that I broke my father's heart."

"He had a choice to join us, I'm sure," said Shelly. "He would be welcomed to Siren along with the rest of us."

"He told me he has a different mission and that his work is here. Of course, my mother would never leave him so she's staying behind as well."

"It just seems so final," said Alex. "I wish that the *Preculians* could give us the option of returning from time to time."

Durbah wiped a small tear from her eye and said, "They've already gone beyond the call of duty, Alex. We're just lucky that Siren has them as their benefactor. We don't have the right to ask any more of them."

"Of course, you're right, Durbah, but I'll miss them, too, and yet I've just met them."

Charles reached out and softly held Durbah's hand, "I know how it hurts you to leave them, Durbah, but I also know in my heart that this is what we are supposed to do. I feel more sure of it now than ever. This is our destiny. This is what our Creator has scripted for us. The whole concept is so fantastic that how could you ever doubt it for a minute. We never really had a choice in the matter. Who would ever say no?"

"*Christos* says there are nearly eighty of them, said Shelly."

Seriously?" asked Alex. "Eighty sirens are choosing to stay behind?"

"That's what he said. Some are too old, and some have a sense of purpose here on Earth that they can't turn away from."

"Sarah wasn't even sure her parents would go, remember?" said Shelly. "The senator will be sorely missed by his constituency."

"There are plenty of politicians to take his place. But there isn't anyone who can take the place of his son."

"What about his son?" asked Alex.

"You know about his gift."

"Of course," he said, "but you would think that must be fairly commonplace on Siren."

"Apparently not," said Shelly. "*Christos* said that there are no longer *seers* on Siren. It's like some kind of vestigial attribute that no longer is needed. Kind of like our appendix or something."

"I wonder how he will be received on Siren," said Charles.

"We'll soon find out," said Durbah. "I'll bet they won't let him buy any lottery tickets," she chuckled. The rest of them laughed as well. When they had finished their lunch, Durbah and Alex thanked Shelly and Charles for their company and excused themselves to go up to their room for a nap. Just as they had settled into bed there came a knock on the door of their room. Alex got out of bed and quickly put on his jeans. He crossed the room to the door and opened it to the hallway. A man stood before him with a pleasant smile and slightly balding pallet of dark brown hair. He had a thin mustache and peaceful blue eyes. "Alex?" asked the man.

"That's right," said Alex.

"I am Raphael."

"Oh, yes, please come in," said Alex. "We have been expecting you."

"And you are Durbah," he said motioning to her beneath the sheets of the bed.

"Yes," was all she said.

"Could you excuse Alex and me for a short while, please?" He made no attempt to leave the room.

"Certainly," said Durbah. She rose from the bed walked across the room to retrieve her clothing. "I guess our nap can wait. I'll be downstairs in the lobby, Alex."

Alex was surprised to see that Durbah's naked body had little effect on the small mysterious man. He acted as though he encountered beautiful naked women every day of the week.

"Sounds good, honey. I'll come right down and get you when we're finished up here."

"I promise that it will not take long," said Raphael.

Durbah slipped on her underwear and a pair of light cotton slacks. She slid some flats on her feet and a light blue cashmere sweater over her torso. She leaned over and kissed Alex on the lips and said, "I love you." With that she left the two men to complete the screening process necessary for Alex to make the exodus from Khufu.

With the help of Sarah Poole and Brad Early, *Christos* set up a base of operations within the Cairo Hilton Hotel. Sarah set up an alternate email address for him through her regular account. She gave him her laptop computer and went shopping the next day to replace hers. *Christos* was a fast learner. He had established contact with all of the sirens from E.C.-2 in under a day and quickly compiled a "contact category" that would send the same message to all forty-eight sirens.

He informed them that the exodus from Khufu would commence in seven days and be able to send twelve sirens at a time with a turnaround time of just under three days. If everything ran smoothly, the exodus from Khufu could be completed in less than three weeks. The larger alpha omega retreats would take much longer to transfer their personnel, but *Christos* planned to be on the last transfer in twenty days time. He knew from the logistics meeting on Siren that the exchange chambers would be filled with solid limestone during the last *space/time exchange* transfer. The two exceptions to this would be the facility at E.C.-2 and the chamber at Khufu. Khufu's chamber would remain intact because during the last *space/time* exchange, Alexander would be returned to his eternal resting place.

E.C.-2 would remain intact for the use of sirens who chose to remain on the planet Earth. The infrastructure and service personnel were self sustaining due to the large amount of seed money invested for its management and continuation. The mountain retreat in West Virginia would remain intact for hundreds of years with its uninterrupted operation. Walter and Edith Purness would use the retreat on a regular basis, along with nearly eighty other sirens who chose to remain on Earth instead of joining the exodus to Siren. There they could also maintain contact with Durbah and Alex Jansen on the planet Siren.

Christos entered the names of the sirens in groups of twelve and by random chance determined the schedule whereby each siren would report to 1800 East Pyramid Road and be ushered through the tunnel and into the exchange chamber. Matthew Winter pleaded with *Christos* to place him in the first group because he had become separated from his beloved Alankha. After a mild bit of encouragement from Alankha's uncle Zaphi on the way station, *Christos* agreed. Matthew Winter gave Joanne Riley the address at 1800 East Pyramid Road where she would find the basement tunnel to Khufu. He was sure that Mother Bakhawi would enjoy the celebrity along with sharing her fine wine with the archeologists and reporters. The mysterious disappearance of Zaphi Hanass was never fully explained, and some were led to the conclusion that he met with foul play. Durbah and Alex were among the last group to leave from Khufu along with *Christos, Brad Early* and the four members of the Poole family. During that last exchange, Alexander was, once again, back where he belonged in the hidden chamber at Khufu.

~

Chapter Sixty-four

The Planet Siren

The Heroes Welcomed Home

The city called *Christos* was chosen to enjoy the distinction of housing the *space/time exchange chamber* to be used in the extrication of the sirens born of Earth. It was located adjacent to the conference hall of The Grand Council of Regents within the capital building. The five members of the Grand Council were on hand to personally greet every one of the four hundred and six sirens who finally arrived from Earth. Eighty sirens stayed behind for various reasons, and it was a somber occasion for their relatives when they searched the monitors of the Conference Center's auditorium and leaned that the progeny of their common ancestry would forever remain apart from them. When they all were assembled for their first welcoming speech by the Grand Master Regent, *Christos,* he told them the specifics of how many of their direct relatives made the journey to the capital city to greet them. The Earth sirens were confused as to why *Christos* was standing at a podium behind a large glass wall that ran the whole length from side to side of the stage. He began, "Let me be the first to say welcome to your home. Your fellow sirens have grieved your absence for more than five thousand years and are anxious to embrace you, our heroes, who have suffered greatly at the hands of humanity. Your relatives here on Siren have enjoyed great celebrity and riches due to your sacrifice. They have collectively pledged to present you with the totality of their material possessions and do everything in their power to satisfy all of your needs and desires. You, my treasured sirens of Earth, are the closest thing that we have to a divine-right monarchy. Our government here consists of five Regents who are elected by the people of their respective territories to represent them here in the central seat of the Grand Council. Now, for the first time, we are pleased to serve the many Kings and Queens of our world. We, of the Grand Council, are now subservient to your collective will. We will not burden you with government responsibility; however, a majority vote within your ranks of two hundred and four can, and will, overturn any of our Council mandates. You have the power to shape the direction of your home world. We welcome the guidance you will bring to our society. Ours is a new hope for a fresh infusion of ideology as well as bloodline.

Your direct relatives are many. The four hundred and six of you who traveled here over the past few weeks have over seven hundred and forty-two thousand distant brothers, sisters and cousins. They all share your common ancestry and are anxious to meet you and pledge their allegiance to their brethren. You are about to experience a great wave of love and good will that you heretofore could never imagine. A receiving complex has been assembled for this purpose. Once you have determined the name of your collective family, each of you will be greeted by roughly eighteen thousand relatives. Welcome to the party, Earth sirens. Your subjects of the world kingdom of Siren await you. There will be a brief period of quarantine until it can be determined that no harmful organisms have been carried with you from Earth. We anticipate that this will take no longer than one week. In the mean time, you may explore your world of Siren through your personal monitors in your suites. Thank you for your patience in this matter, and let me conclude by voicing the collective declaration of the whole of Siren, which is, *Siren Brothers and Sisters of Earth, We Embrace You.*"

~

Alex Jansen and Durbah Purness were sitting in a tight group of seats occupied by the sirens of the E.C.-2 conference hall. Within earshot were, Matthew Winter, Alankha Hannas, Shelly Simon, Charles Donovan, Sarah Poole and Brad Early. The four couples were strangely quiet after the closing remarks by *Christos*. Matthew finally said, "So what's next? Surfing the internet of Siren? I find it kind of weird that we traveled one hundred and eighty million miles to play on computers."

"It is only for one week, Matthew," said Alankha.

"You *hope* it's only for one week."

"So what if it's two?" asked Durbah, "would you rather be back on Earth? You are a monarch of a wondrous new world, and yet you find a reason to complain."

"I'm not complaining, Durbah, it's just that I feel unsettled and I'm not used to it. I'm used to calling the shots."

"We all are," said Sarah. "We have to be flexible, Matthew. We are representatives now. We don't want to be seen as a bunch of whiners."

"Whiners?" asked Matthew. "That's a bit harsh, Sarah."

"I'm sorry, Matthew. Yes, it was, and it was unfair. Please forgive me."

"Done," said Matthew.

Charles Donovan addressed the group that was in earshot, which included Sarah's parents and Zaphi and Sophia Hanass, "Hey, has anybody noticed that we haven't seen any electrum in the eyes of the sirens here?"

"Now that you mention it," replied Shelly, "you're right. I wonder why that is?"

"Maybe they don't have any need to excite anyone. Maybe they are *purposely not* exciting anyone. These people are very sensitive. I sense only good will and protectiveness from them."

"I feel it too," said Durbah, "but I can't help wondering . . ."

"What? You mean you think that they can't trigger the electrum? Is that what you mean," asked Alex.

"Actually, yes. That's exactly what I was thinking."

"What does that mean, if it's true?" asked Brad. "Would that mean that you guys are more than monarchs and celebrities? Somehow I don't think that Godhead is a very prudent idea, on any planet."

"Absolute power corrupts absolutely," said Matthew.

"Speak for yourself, Matthew," said Sarah.

"I was."

Chapter Sixty-five

Two Months Later

The Master Regent, *Christos,* was approached by Dr. Hawkins with the news that an unfortunate collision with the space probe from Earth has begun to bring about decay in its orbit. The projected time frame for entry into the atmosphere of Siren was less than three days. The Grand Master of *Preculis* was again contacted and implored to intercede in the defense of Siren due to the possible damage that could occur when the probe crashed into the planet. The reply from *Preculis* was clear. The message was, *"Do nothing. We will return the probe to the planet from which it was launched. We will return it precisely to the location it was launched from on Earth when it enters the atmosphere of Siren. The space/time exchange will only take seventeen minutes, so there will be very little time to warn them. Therefore, we ask that you contact the remaining sirens on Earth and tell them to avoid the area known as Cape Canaveral for the near future.*

We believe that the area will sustain major damage when the probe is returned there. We recommend that the sirens seek shelter in the Alpha Omega complex known at E.C.-2 until further notice."

Trusting their benefactors of thousands of years, that is precisely what they did, nothing, except alert the Earth sirens and seek their council. When *Christos* made Durbah and Alex abreast of the fact that an earth vessel, containing a nuclear device, was imminently bound for detonation three thousand feet above Cape Canaveral, they asked for the Earth sirens to be assembled for their first vote as a governing body. The question was whether or not a message should be sent to warn the Earth sirens that Florida would ultimately become a target of their own madness. A unanimous vote led to the agreement to send a message to Walter and Edith Purness by way of their daughter Durbah from Siren to the conference hall at E.C.-2. When Durbah explained the situation to her father, he suggested that he should seek an audience with President Amalah, whom he knew personally, and alert him as well.

~

Chapter Sixty-six

Washington D.C.

The Situation Room of the White House

Walter and Edith Purness were sitting with Director O'Keefe and President Amalah in soft leather chairs across a huge mahogany table. They had just finished telling them that the space probe known as the X-B 37 would deliver its nuclear payload to the space center sometime in the near future.

"Do you know how fantastic that sounds, Walter?" asked the president.

"Yes, I do. Nevertheless, it is the truth. You remember my wife, Edith, don't you Mr. President?"

"Yes, Walter. It's a pleasure to see you again, Edith," he said.

"And it's a pleasure to meet you as well, Mrs. Purness," said O'Keefe. "But we don't have any evidence that the X-B 37 is anywhere near our planet. What you're telling us just doesn't make any sense at all. There's no possible way it could only be days away, and we wouldn't see it."

"There are some places where the impossible is a way of life," said Edith.

Walter addressed the two men, "I brought along my wife for a specific reason, gentlemen. She can explain the situation to you in a way that I cannot. You will soon know what we say is the truth and have no doubt about it whatsoever."

Edith held the two men in her gaze with the electrum clearly present in her eyes. She spoke in a soft voice and merely *told* them that they could be assured that the information they imparted was the truth and should have no doubts in their mind. Then they knew. They knew with certainty and realized the implications and the horrible but inevitable outcome.

"But can't they just destroy the weapon in their own atmosphere?" asked Amalah.

"I don't really know, and I have no way to ask them either, Mr. President," said Walter.

"Gentlemen," began Edith, "when the space craft is returned to Cape Canaveral by the *Preculians,* it will detonate at three thousand feet above the ground. It will be your duty to report to the American people and the United Nations that the explosion is the result of a launch pad accident. You will use this tragedy as an example of why weapons, especially nuclear weapons, should never be used in space. It will be a wake-up call to the entire planet. It should remain apparent that if something can go wrong, then it will. It's not a question of if, but rather, when will it go wrong. Hopefully this painful lesson to our planet will accomplish more than mindless destruction. With any luck, it may well serve to save future lives as well. You will retain the information that we have given you, but you will not retain the knowledge of where it came from. You will remember our visit with you today and that we discussed the proposed changes in the tax structure of the coal consortium and that is all. My husband Walter and I are not to be connected with this matter in any way. Do I make myself clear?"

Both the president and the NASA director were a bit shaken by her statement and merely nodded their heads in affirmation. Walter and Edith knew beyond a shadow of a doubt that their conversation would be erased from their memories.

~

The Planet *Preculis*

The Grand Master of the Supreme Council of *Preculis* was addressing the Director of Off-world Operations. The D.O.O. told him, "We have a projection of the orbit decay of the Earth vessel."

"Excellent, Mr. Director. Do we have a location of the launch site from Earth?"

"Yes, Sir. It is from the East Coast of their continent known as North America."

"Can we maintain a targeting beam to the area for the required duration of the exchange?"

"Yes, Sir. We have a direct visual targeting solution to an extremely large building at their space complex. It's called the Vehicle Assembly Building, or VAB.

"Is there sufficient power for the transfer beam?"

"Yes, Sir. We are awaiting the word from the Council."

"It is the position of the Council that our hands are tied. We cannot allow the probe to enter the atmosphere of Siren. We are therefore going to return to Earth the property that is rightfully theirs."

"Is that an order to power up the transfer chamber?"

"It is."

"It shall be done."

~

Chapter Sixty-seven

Washington D.C.

The Press Room at the White House

President Amalah entered the press room and quickly walked up to the podium, which had five microphones arranged in various angles to capture his address to the American public and a world network of journalists as well.

"I come to you tonight with the gravest of news. Our worst fears have been realized by a tragic accident at the space center at Cape Canaveral. The recent launch of a military space craft went horribly awry when it exploded much the same way that the space shuttle Challenger did in 1986. At three thousand feet, the craft's nuclear payload reached critical mass, resulting in a detonation equal to the force of 20 kilotons. The reason for the explosion is not known, and we are responding to the disaster in every possible way that we can. The Red Cross, FEMA, The National Guard and every branch of the armed services are responding to the area to treat the wounded and contain the nuclear fallout. We believe it has reached as far south as Palm Beach, as far north as Jacksonville, and as far west as Orlando. The blast radius has destroyed nearly ten thousand homes and businesses, and the area will remain with deadly radioactivity for close to five years.

It is the belief of this administration that this tragedy could have been avoided. We were remiss in our attempt to establish a weapon in space, which was clearly in violation of a world-wide agreement called the Nagasaki Accord. Some lessons are more painful than others, and it is our duty to make sure that this one does not fall on deaf ears. We don't have many chances to change our goals for the better, but this is surely one of them. We, as a people, can only survive this kind of disaster if we bring about a firm change in our agenda. We are called on today as a nation to stand together in the course of this tragedy and reach out to our fellow man in his hour of need. I'm confident that I can count on my fellow Americans to stand tall and remain a shining example for the entire world by the way we react to the greatest of misfortune. As you can well understand, my duty stands before me and much is asked of my service at this time of need, so I am forced to end this announcement and ask for the prayers and support of this great nation. Good night."

When the president left the room, he was accompanied by the director of the space center named Sean O'Keefe. He turned to him and said, "You picked a very good time to visit Washington, Sean."

"That I did, Mr. President. That I did."

The End

www.ingramcontent.com/pod-product-compliance
Lightning Source LLC
Chambersburg PA
CBHW070901260626
47162CB00007B/2520

* 9 7 8 0 9 8 3 3 1 4 4 0 0 *